# Fool's Mercy

# Fool's Mercy

Henry Allen

Houghton Mifflin Company
Boston 1982

*Library of Congress Cataloging in Publication Data*
Allen, Henry.
  Fool's mercy.
  I. Title.
PS3551.L3928F6    813'.54    81-13366
ISBN 0-395-32039-9          AACR2

*To, for, with, and because of Deborah*

# *Fool's Mercy*

## *Chapter 1*

*T*HEY WOULD HAVE SHOT HIM already from an upstairs window, Gordon decided. So the hell with it, they didn't exist, it was just paranoia talking.

If they did exist, they were listening to records in an old farmhouse, halfway down the pasture slope from the tree line where Gordon lay watching for them through binoculars. But since they didn't exist, he hadn't seen them. He'd merely lain in the underbrush—milkweed, ragweed, Queen Anne's lace, fox grape, poison ivy—and breathed the dry green smell of all this heat, the kind of sick, itchy heat you get every August around Washington when the sky turns grey-brown with smog and it won't rain. The pasture was dry as a skull. The farmhouse was redneck Maryland—gaunt windows, asphalt shingles and the rusty tin roof pounding a shaft of heat back up at the sky. Gordon was tired of looking at it, he was hot, he itched all over—three more good reasons to believe they didn't exist.

Plus the music, booming and spangling out the farmhouse windows. It was the Rolling Stones, just now, playing "Monkey Man" through speakers Gordon calculated to be the size of refrigerators. The music was that loud. If they were going to shoot you, they didn't sneak up on you with a two-hour prelude of rock and roll. That was part of the deal, life in America, keep the ironies to an absolute minimum. Then again, the music was so loud they could have been shooting at him for hours and he wouldn't have heard it. That was a thought—even if it was just paranoia talking.

" 'Cause I am just a monkey man..."

He looked fierce, sweet, tired and preoccupied.

He lowered the binoculars, which were John Cane's old yacht-racing glasses with the brass showing through the black. The farmhouse dwindled instantly by a factor of six, but the music played on, twisted up so high that between records he could hear not only a finger abrade the needle to dust it but the individual ridges of the fingerprint stuttering TUNKAHTUNKAHTUNK.

Whose? Most likely, or with luck—and Gordon had terrific luck—it would be Ellen Cane he'd spot down there through her daddy's binoculars. If his luck was bad, the possibilities were myriad to the point of zaniness: CIA, FBI, Palestinians, Israelis, the Irish Republican Army, the Japanese Red Army, the Italian Red Brigade, the Black Panthers, KGB, DINA, the Mafia, M.I. 6, the Baader-Meinhof gang, Muammar Qaddafi, Cubans either left or right, the Minutemen, George "Mad Bomber" Metesky, your local Ford dealer, the Mormon Tabernacle Choir...but they would have shot him already from an upstairs window, therefore they didn't exist. Not here, now. And if they did, they didn't play "Monkey Man" out farmhouse windows at Richter-scale volume.

"The hell with it," Gordon said. Go home and drink something cold.

He stood up, way too fast. He teetered against the no-color sky. He mulled the possibility that he was falling. Then his eyes cleared and he was merely staggering forward with his left foot asleep. Cane's binoculars arced back into his chest on their strap. An eyecup chopped him in the sternum.

"Wonderful," he said. He had a low, grating voice and big white teeth.

" 'Cause I am just a monkey man..."

He limped into the open. He swung each leg over a rusty barbed-wire fence; sweaty denim grabbed at his knees. He watched a hog snake taper away into a blackberry thicket, oozing and cruising. There was a daytime moon, serenely irrelevant. It was as if everything had a surly glow to it, even the air, like a phosphorescence, everything bright and dead and unreal. Someday Gordon—whose last name was Sault—wanted to know he'd never feel unreal again, wanted everything to be clear and perfect. That was his ambition.

He walked. He felt a rush of pins-and-needles nerve jive in his foot.

"Wonderful," he said again. He was big, almost lumbering, with tired, angry eyes and a fatigue jacket mapped with sweat.

If he found Ellen in the farmhouse, fine. He'd draw a map for Cane and watch the nightly news for what happened next. If he didn't, he was quitting anyway, maybe head down to the Smokies for some backpacking before the whole summer sifted away; unless, of course, someone behind one of the farmhouse windows was locking and loading preparatory to freckling him with a clipful of sucking chest wounds. (*They didn't exist, he'd always had luck.*)

He walked past the last available cover—a coil-top icebox rusting in a litter of oil cans and fractured headlight liners. They could shoot him with pistols, he was so close now. He remembered that it always came too fast, too loud, as if the air itself was screaming, you couldn't explain it to anybody who hadn't been there. Instead, Gordon preferred to boast that he'd never fired a weapon in Vietnam, as either Marine or journalist. It was true. It was also one of his major regrets, even after all these years.

He strode across the porch. He pounded on the frame of a

3

screen door. He felt the pounding in his knuckles but the music was so loud he couldn't hear it. He kicked the bottom of the door. It slapped and trembled, struggling against a hook and eye. The screen had been scrawled on with crayons. A faded decal on the door standing open behind the screen read: ASK ME ABOUT MASON SHOES. It was dark inside. He smelled old dust and grease, a bone-faced country poverty smell. He swung his toe against the door again.

The music dropped. It sucked back inside the house, weird and quick like a film run backward. It left Gordon alone with the cicadas winding up and up, and his pulse slugging away in his temples.

And then, she was there.

"You're Ellen Cane," he said.

She hovered toward the door like ectoplasm, a hip-shot, shoulder-hunched shadow, silver and black at the same time to his glare-blasted eyes. But he could smell her. She smelled like hair at the roots.

"Who else is in the house?" he said.

"Nobody," she said, a dactyl of indignation in a clear voice that rang through the vowels.

He could smell her and hear her but he couldn't see her. Why did he think she was beautiful?

"Where's Gerald Ravenel?"

"I don't know."

He squinted, trying to salvage more than a silver outline.

"He has the lease on this place, him and Gaia Stern," he said.

"Good."

"How about Eddie Conchis, he been here? You know who I mean, Eddie Conchis?"

"My father knows him."

"He was going around threatening your friends a few days ago. He said he was from the government and if they didn't tell him where you were hiding out, he'd get them busted for dealing."

4

"Some of my friends are dealers."

"They seemed to be scared of him," he said, as if she were to blame for Eddie Conchis.

"I'm not scared of you," she said.

"Seriously," Gordon said.

"Seriously."

"No, seriously."

"Sure," she said. "Seriously."

"You've got no reason at all to be scared of me."

"No, really," she said. "I recognize the binoculars. They're my father's."

His pupils struggled to dilate. He saw slivers of white on her thighs and realized they were the tips of her pockets peeking below the hems of Levi's cutoffs. She wore a T-shirt with a face decalled on it. She pulled her right hand from her pocket to dress back a floating hair. She was quick, a visceral spryness, her eyes pure Kentucky windage.

"Who are you?" she said.

"Gordon Sault. Your father called me after all this happened with you." He had a voice that detoured through the back of his throat. It was an East Coast noise that implied good breeding driven to the far edge of redeemability.

"Well, Gordon Sault, you can tell him I'll be back tonight. Seriously."

"Have you got any idea what kind of trouble you're in?"

"No."

"You read the papers, you watch the news?"

"Never."

"I can give you a ride. I'll take you to my place in Stuckey, you can call him from there, whatever you're comfortable with."

"Can't. There's a thing with some people later on. I should wait."

"One thing, I'm not the only person out looking for Ellen Cane. If I can find you, they can find you."

5

"Eddie Conchis," she said.

"Fuck Eddie Conchis. I'm talking about real crazies, the CIA, the Japanese Red Army, the next George Metesky..."

"Who's George Metesky?"

"The mad bomber? The guy in New York City with the pipe bombs in the movie theaters?"

"Sure," Ellen said. She'd never heard of George Metesky.

"Your daddy's been messing with a lot of weight. It has to come down somewhere."

"He didn't do anything wrong."

"It doesn't make any difference. Nobody believes him."

Insect noise spiraled up and up. It was like nature's own ears ringing, cicadas and crickets in the tulip poplars, the white oaks, the Queen Anne's lace frothing across the fields, a garden of untended zucchini, which grew so fast in this heat that if you got close enough, you'd hear them creaking.

"I understand all that," Ellen said.

"You understand how they'd tie your wrists to your ankles and pour water on you and hit you with a cattle prod till your spine snapped?"

"Absolutely." She looked away with the tired contempt women show when a man hits them one more time than they think they deserve.

"Don't forget to tell them that."

"Who? Who? Tell who?"

"Whoever," Gordon said. There was no point trying to set her straight.

"You want the ride or you want to stay out here by yourself?"

"It doesn't seem I have any choice," she said.

"Sure you do."

"Thank you." She had rich-girl eyes that looked huge and narrowed at the same time. She had hair that was blonde and thick, like you'd have a hard time getting down to scalp if you drove your fingers into it. She smelled like hair close to the roots but it was more than that. It was also vanilla, or almonds. He could feel the smell touching the insides of his nostrils. Or touching his whole body, in fact. It felt good. It felt as if he was turning more and more solid, pure muscle tone; as if even his stare had weight; as if, by her presence, she made him realer.

"It's up to you," he said.

"Don't do me any favors."

"I wouldn't think of it."

"Are you standing there waiting for me to say yes?"

"It beats lying up there in those weeds with a pair of binoculars."

"Okay, why not?" Ellen said.

With slow precision, he touched his forefinger to his own chest. "I'll go get my car," he said. He aimed the forefinger at Ellen. "You wait here."

"I'll be here," she said happily. "Dead or alive."

It was like seeing her behind something, a screen of her quickness, hands chasing stray hairs, her wise-guy shrugs, flinches of impatience...

"I'll be back." He felt good. He had his mojo working. He liked this girl.

"Listen," she said. "What do I do if George 'Mad Bomber' Metesky shows up while you're gone?"

"Easy," Gordon said. "Get his autograph."

*

Ellen stood inside the parched funk of the farmhouse and watched him stroll away. She noted the inertial heft of his chest, his head rising from his shoulders as if he were peering over a wall; a real Boy Scout, but with the glow of a mad metaphysician lurking in there somewhere; though now, leaning her forehead against the screen, she found herself oddly pleased to think of this. He would do, he was her ticket out of here. He came as no surprise at all. She'd already decided this morning that she was quitting the whole scam, bailing out. Therefore, the universe was obliged to fit her with a parachute. That was the way Ellen thought about things.

She watched as the terrible diffused brightness, like a dentist's lamp, began to claim him. She realized she couldn't call his face to mind. She could remember the conversation but not the face. She'd been very witty. She wondered if Gerald would have thought she was witty. She wondered what Gerald would say if she turned around and found him standing there in the farmhouse gloom. She decided he would hoist his most fatuous eyebrows and say: "Be *nice* to him, please."

Nice: she turned around. There was only the sorrowful grime of the front hall, and an old speckled mirror staring back at her like an acned conscience. She sauntered toward it. She observed her face to see what expression it might offer next. It offered the big eyes and small mouth of pity for her iniquity. Lately she'd been experimenting with the notion that she was a very wicked person indeed. She found this persona cozy. There was a kind of weight to it. It lent an instant nostalgia to the world. At least when she thought of herself as evil, she'd confessed to Gerald, she knew who she was. She'd said to him: "It makes me feel like the sorceress in that Walt Disney movie, the cartoon, the woman with her face, it's like, all triangles and jagged lines and she has this mouth shaped like a heart made out of lightning, with the edges all jagged. You know who."

Nice: no, not nice at all. She worried about this. Now, she closed on the mirror and saw her lips move soundless, creasing and gleaming around the words: *be nice.* Her lips were full enough that they always seemed to move slowly; not like the sorceress at all. Still... She braced the heels of her hands on the tabletop and leaned into the glass. Her breasts wandered beneath her T-shirt. Gerald and Gaia had bought the shirt for her yesterday in Georgetown. It bore an

8

iron-on likeness of F. Scott Fitzgerald, the photograph from the dust cover of *This Side of Paradise*. He floated away from her body, farseeing and dead. She leaned so close to the mirror that her elbows angled grasshopperwise and she had to choose an eye to focus on. She chose the right. She'd never looked at her eye so closely before. The inside corner was pink and wet and blind, like labia flesh. Veins clutched the ball. The iris fronds were blue, flecked with ocher and frosted with white where they tapered into the pupil. They floated like sea plants, lethargic.

"Evil eye," she said aloud. She glanced down over her cheekbones to see if her breath had lingered on the mirror. It had not. Vampire. No, that was when you couldn't *see* yourself.

Her head twitched back from the mirror, her eyes angular with alarm. "I'm sorry," she announced. "I can't believe this is happening."

It was like a prayer suggesting that God had not been entirely realistic in creating the last five days.

It was five days ago that her life had begun to confect itself into a great cotton-candy nimbus of panic. She had been sitting by her father's swimming pool with Gerald and a television. Her father's house was on Foxhall Road. From the pool, they could see an incendiary haze over the city. They were waiting to see her father on the television. Gerald had sat in the chaise next to hers, both of them staring through sunglasses at the television screen, and beyond it the pool, which didn't move. The water had just hung there in the dead-still August afternoon, a mammoth clear weight. They wouldn't have thought of swimming in it, even in all this heat. This was the summer when they were best friends, and they never once swam in her father's pool—they'd already decided that was how they'd remember it.

The first thing that had gone wrong, even before her father's testimony, was Gerald either asking her to marry him or telling her he didn't want to marry her, it was hard to tell which. What he'd said was: "Actually, if either one of us had any sense at all, we'd get married."

It was his presumption that she found so appalling.

She'd said: "What about sex? I don't want to have sex with you."

"We could have a *mariage blanc*. Wouldn't that be beautiful? People would tell us about their awful sex problems and we'd say, we don't have any sex problems because we don't have any sex."

"Poor Gaia," Ellen said, as if it were the eighth time that day she'd said it.

Gerald lived with Gaia in a house her mother owned in Georgetown. Gaia was a frazzled Bohemian who bought him all of his film equipment. Gerald made films, that summer, and the three of them rambled around Washington with a sporty, androgynous air about them, totally casual and exquisitely formal at the same time, such good friends. Ellen, for her part, told everyone that Gerald was a genius. Outdoors, by the swimming pool, he looked uncomfortable, she thought, like a man sitting on a horse for the first time. He had a huge head that pushed out the stems of his sunglasses. He had very red lips that never quite closed over his teeth.

"She could become my mistress, my long-suffering mistress," he said. "Then she could be a martyr full-time."

"You're so mean to her." Ellen and Gerald liked to scold each other for their cruelties.

They both sighed, sat slump-shouldered, and watched the television glow pale against the glare invading their shade under an awning. Her father was being called to testify again.

"The ghost," Gerald said.

"They're going to railroad him," Ellen said. She watched with acrid pensiveness as the figures on the screen went through the numb-fingered stage business of shuffling documents and adjusting microphones. "They've already charged him with perjury. You'd think that would be enough."

"They can't railroad the ghost."

"They can railroad anybody they want to. That's what he says."

The television breathed in and out with the murmur of the hearing room, which was a few miles away in a Senate office building.

"He says it's like being the last caribou in the herd, the one the wolves go after, and once they draw one single drop of blood they won't stop chasing you until they kill you," she said.

"I have a hard time imagining that," Gerald said. "Your father has always been so, you know, overwhelming."

On the television screen, Cane waited while a senator named Umstead asked a question. Cane appeared to watch the senator more than he listened to him. He watched him under slow eyelids which moved in a rectangular face he propped on long, long fingers. The last joint of his right little finger was missing. There was something coldly romantic and chronically skeptical about him. If midcentury America was full of leaders with ulterior motives, here was one with a whole ulterior being. He had hair that was no color at all, the color of smog, of August skies in Washington—"the ghost," Gerald called him.

"Would you repeat the question, Senator?" Cane said into the first available silence.

"I haven't finished the question, Mr. Cane." It was something about the "de-statusing of inventories," and the senator kept consulting papers that were being handed to him by aides who moved on and off the screen in perpetual crouches.

"This is such terrible video," Gerald said.

"He says they've already got the cell picked out for him at Allenwood."

"There's this one white-collar prison in Texas where they

have a golf course," Gerald said. "Only the prisoners aren't allowed to use their own clubs—they have to use government clubs. Isn't that wonderful?"

"No," Ellen said.

"I fail to follow your line of reasoning, Mr. Cane," said Senator Umstead, leaning forward on his elbows until his suit coat wrinkled up behind his neck like a mane.

Cane's brow puckered as if he were startled to find himself interested in something he was about to say. He and the senator squinted into the gritty wind of the television lights.

"Given this large a time lapse since the events under consideration," Cane said, "I have a hard time following it myself."

Gerald laughed, a little rolling groan through his nose. The television and the swimming pool jostled in his sunglasses. "So droll," he said. "The ghost."

"That's how you can tell he's scared," Ellen said.

"You're telling this committee that by 1963 you got as far as planning to subtract these two entries for the nuclear reprocessing facilities at both Spring Hill and Kankakee, is that correct?" asked Senator Umstead.

"No, sir. We added them to the inventories."

"Why was that?"

"So that they wouldn't be there when inventory was taken."

"You added them so that they wouldn't be there..." said the senator, his face going pudgily frantic with confusion, with classic twentieth-century mind-smog.

"We added the entries in the accounting, we didn't add the material. Even a president of the United States can't have a personal supply of weapons-grade nuclear material lying around to play with. The point was to have the material show up missing at the inventory."

"What material?"

"There wasn't any material, that was the whole point."

"Are you talking about actual weapons or components such as plutonium or what?"

"Whatever," Cane said, flaring his palms in an arrogance of helplessness. "Since they never existed, we can talk about them any way you want."

Gerald flinched his lips back in a sort of yawn. He showed small, wet teeth. He said: "I think I need to get stoned."

"It's all the Israelis' fault," Ellen said. She leaned toward the television.

"If I can't get married, I can at least get stoned," Gerald said.

"Sometimes, I could hate you."

"It's all so bureaucratic."

"Treason," Ellen said. "*Time* magazine actually used that word—*treason*. Can you believe that?"

"That the ghost did it, or *Time* magazine used it?"

"Don't they execute people for treason?"

"Only poor people, baby."

"If you hate rich people so much, why do you hang around us all the time?"

"It's where the money is. Can't we get stoned?"

"You have no self-respect."

"I have no money."

The sky shone, the pool lurked, the television glowed pale. Cane asked Senator Umstead to repeat the question.

Ellen said: "I don't like to be stoned when he gets home. I'm scared enough of him as it is."

"Paranoia," Gerald said. "Ghost paranoia."

"And how was this order routed, what was the chain of command?" Senator Umstead asked.

"It was routed across the desk from President Kennedy to me," Cane said in a voice that sagged with resentment. Ellen thought about John Kennedy. He was a girlhood memory, like her mother. She always thought of them together, both dead in the same autumn.

"It's *not* paranoia," Ellen said in an icy glissando of pique.

"You can't even imagine what he's like. And don't you ever tell anybody I said that, either."

"Why'd you tell me, then?"

"Because you're my best friend."

Now she was scared of Gerald too, she wasn't sure why. Sweat hung on her brow. The television rasped. It was all totally simple and totally confusing, a hideous funk of facts. It was worse than trying to read the newspapers. Her father was explaining it yet again on the television. His jaw chopped desultorily at the hearing-room air, and his eyes never seemed to blink. The ghost. Gerald was right. He haunted her, she'd been terrified of him ever since her mother died.

Kennedy's idea, he was explaining, was that "if we leaked word that some nuclear material was missing, actual weapons, it would turn into sort of a wild card. Everybody would be worried that everybody else had one, and they'd know they didn't have one themselves."

"At the time, did you find this idea to be a cynical one?"

"I believe, Senator, that President Kennedy said he'd like to have the rest of the world playing poker with our marked deck. Do I make myself clear?"

"All too clear," said the senator, desperately posturing for the television cameras.

"If I'm going to be asked to incriminate myself out of patriotism, I'd like the satisfaction of knowing for sure that the committee understands what I'm talking about."

"Go ahead, Mr. Cane," said Umstead. His voice was clogged with contempt for this ultraestablishmentarian, this relic of those shirt-sleeved afternoons of Camelot when everything was possible.

Gerald shook his big head at the television. "So clever. Pure John Kennedy all the way. How wonderfully *naive*."

"But it's all Israel's fault," Ellen said to the television. "Why pick on him?"

14

"Poor ghost."

"Stop calling him the ghost, please."

The Kennedy scheme had been dredged up in hearings to determine if, in fact, the CIA was right that it was the Israelis who had stolen 206 pounds of plutonium from a reprocessing plant in Spring Hill, Pennsylvania. Ellen had followed it all, her face full of the same sad fatigue when he denied it all, and then when he pointed out after his perjury citation that he'd been bound by a "higher oath." She watched the hearings as she might have watched a dam for cracks. It was just a matter of time. She had an instinct for these things.

"What if he did it all?" she said. "Really. All these other countries are saying he did." They were. Estimates of the membership in the nuclear club had risen radically, putting doomsday in the hands of everyone from the Libyans to the Irish Republican Army to Cane himself.

"Spare me the dramatics," Gerald said. "The ghost stories."

She stared at him, the black lenses of her sunglasses hard as carapace, her mouth pinched with the ruthlessness of the truly frightened.

"Just reach into your purse and hand me the dope and I'll roll one."

She tossed him a plastic bag with the same contempt of resignation that smoldered in her father on the television screen. Gerald shook a tiny heap of marijuana onto a slip of Bambu paper. He culled chunks of stem with a moistened finger. He licked the glue. He sealed the joint with opposing quarter-rotational twists of his hands, all the time softly singing "PAAA-ra-NOI-a" to the tune of the Hallelujah Chorus. He stopped when he saw her crying, the tears eking out under her sunglasses.

"Baby," he said, as if he were used to it. He paid no more attention.

They smoked, she got stoned, but she never really stopped crying that day. After an hour or so, she asked Gerald to leave, and, crying, watched him drive off in Gaia's old Mercedes convertible. She went inside the house and wandered barefoot through the archived air of the air conditioning, past the portraits, sideboards, tea sets, porringers, nested tables, and scroll-top cupboards with their beveled glass warping the circumference of a teacup inside. They seemed abandoned, or they seemed to belong to her father by some kind of default. She cried. Her throat ached and her face got tired with it. She took two Valiums. She drummed her fingernails on the dining-room table. She was waiting for her father to come home. She could feel her mind veering into little pockets of panic, psychic aneurisms. Her head ached. After an hour she took three aspirins and two more Valiums. The Valium promoted a dull alarm in her, a sensation that her flesh was dripping off her bones. She began to fear she was going crazy—crazy being when you couldn't announce to yourself what the world was, and make it stick by force of will.

A chandelier mourned in the oncoming twilight of the two-story center hall. She climbed the circular staircase, and even after she got to the top and was walking to her room her knees felt like they were lifting for another step, floating. She lay on her bed knowing it was only going to get worse. Her whole life was knotting into this one locus: here and now. Why was she so scared and miserable? She had no way of telling.

When she had finally heard the leathery, baritone clatter of the front door slamming, it came as relief—and then the sound of her father's feet coming up the stairs, or rather, the sound of no feet at all, just the stairs creaking.

Now, out at the farmhouse, watching the instant, impersonal twitch of her eyeballs in the hall mirror, she ran through it again, how he'd sat on her bed and never seen she was crying; how he'd said he wanted her to disappear, a week or two was all. His old pal Eddie Conchis would look out for her. He was worried, he'd said, that some madman Palestinian or Japanese Red Army type might try to assassinate either him or her. And: "If the rest of the world thought you were missing, fine. Maybe it would remind them that I'm more than some hit man in pinstripes, I'm a father too." He hadn't understood that none of it mattered to Ellen. Instead, she'd panicked, she'd backed away from him, hearing his feet creak behind her on the stairs as she edged down the stairs, telling him it was illegal, it was crazy and sleazy, it was *evil*.

Now, in the afternoon silence of the farmhouse, she could see that the plan had made sense, but she thought: *Is that my fault?* She liked to think of herself as having run, but in fact she had walked across her front lawn while he stared after her in amazement or disgust, she couldn't tell which. She had walked down Reservoir Road to Gerald and Gaia's. Gerald had given her more Valium. Gaia had made camomile tea. They had driven her out to the farmhouse, Gerald pointing out to her that if her father wanted her to disappear, she could bloody well do it on his money but her terms, the money being, say, $100,000. It was only fair.

The next day, Cane had reported it to the police. He'd said he was worried she might be kidnaped, that some fanatic looking for nuclear weapons would hold her hostage. Given the hysteria the hearings had already aroused, the media went berserk. And now she'd been out here for five days. If he gave her the money, Gerald had told Cane, she'd leave the country for a year; she'd hide, go along with the program.

Five days now of being scared, no letup. She resented it, the bad grainy feeling like a hangover, grief, Methedrine and having the wind knocked out of you, all at once. Everything scared her. She was sick of it. A raccoon would rummage through the garbage and she'd go nuts, panting so hard her lips would chap. It wasn't worth it. The hell with touring Mexico or Ireland or someplace with Gerald and Gaia. Go home.

The evil eye.

"Be nice," she said.

She backed away from the hall mirror feeling pleasantly chastened, as if she knew she were about to make some mammoth discovery about herself. Noting an infinite tolerance for human frailty, hers in particular, she popped a kitchen match into flame and lit a cigarette. She watched herself smoke for a while, in the mirror. In the next room, the amplifier was still on. With the gain turned up so high, it pushed an audible, booming hush through the speakers while it awaited another record. *'Cause I am just a monkey man*... She forsook the mirror and walked away to turn it off. In the ensuing silence the farmhouse seemed to shrink down to something hotter and drier. She sat down at the kitchen table and waited, fidgeting. Gordon would do. Had he really been watching all that time through the binoculars? She liked that and she didn't like that. She drew on the white enamel tabletop with the sweat of her forefinger. Depending on how she tilted her head, the colors shifted from dirty magenta to solarized blue. It all depended on how she tilted her head.

## Chapter 2

$E$DDIE CONCHIS'S Coupe de Ville, burgundy, seven years old, shuddered across the board bridge.

"What we need is a kitten," George Lally said, "like they gave Glazer, down in Nicaragua; he didn't know whether to shit or go blind."

Eddie was driving too fast. The Cadillac lifted for a moment when the dirt road sloped down from the bridge; then it sagged back into shock absorbers the size of golf bags. Two stomachs paused in minus-G quandary. Eddie figured driving a little too fast would burn the four-martini lunch out of Lally. Besides, he wanted an edge on things—at his age, you had to work to keep that. The Caddy cushioned through two dried-out mudholes, taking them easy as a snake. Eddie loved this car. Gravel stuttered and creaked under two tons of suspension. The rearview mirror billowed full of dust. There was dust on everything, the weeds and junk by the sides of the road, the old cars up on blocks in front of the shacks these people lived in out here. Pretty soon, the road would fork left up a hill, Gerald had said.

"Glazer, the guy who tried to fuck Bobby Diaz on that computer delivery down in Nicaragua," Lally said.

"Okay," Eddie said.

"You've seen him, he comes in The Company, always takes a back table and fucks around with a calculator."

"Okay," Eddie said. Listening to Lally was like reading a magazine in a dentist's office. It was hard to pay attention but sometimes you learned something. Like if the Earth was the size of a billiard ball, it would be smoother. Eddie had learned that right before root canal, one day.

"Never got the scam even close to Diaz, never got past the airport," Lally was saying.

"Glazer."

"Right. See, he figures he's going to jack them up for 10K good-faith money. He's got a Gulfstream II sitting there on the runway with IBM's pride and joy on board. He knows Diaz paid everybody off—customs, the freight foreman, everybody. They've even got an air-conditioned truck, IBM specs, they're backing it up to the plane when Glazer puts two guys with Uzi's at the door, and says unh-unh, he has to see 10K in good faith."

"Okay," Eddie said. He wondered how much Lally had heard firsthand from Glazer, and how much he'd picked up during those long afternoons at The Company, playing drums with a swizzle stick to the Frank Sinatra records.

"It all gets very dicey, lots of telephone calls, what-are-the-drums-saying. But very polite, very *por favor*. Glazer ends up in this colonel's office, inside the airport. Picture of his family on the desk, the girl friend sitting on a couch playing with this kitten, full-stocked bar, he's got it all. It turns out the colonel went to Penn. State so they talk football for a while."

"Okay."

"Then Glazer gets out the calculator and puts a lot of numbers on the screen, blah blah blah, all the money he's got up front on this thing. And he hits him for the 10K. All this time, the girl friend doesn't say anything, just sits there with her legs crossed, making noises at the kitten. The colonel gets up, walks over, and takes the kitten away from her. He sits back down and he covers its whole head with his hand. He starts twisting the head. He twists it all the way around. He keeps twisting it till Glazer said he didn't even have to pull the head off, it just came off, and then he throws it at fucking Glazer."

Lally flexed his fingers at the windshield, as if he were set-shooting a crumpled document into a wastebasket.

"The head," Eddie said.

"The head. Beautiful. Just like that. Glazer says he puked all the way back to Miami."

"He told you that, personally."

"He tells everybody," Lally said.

I thought so, Eddie said to himself.

"I'm not sure I believe the part about it being the girl friend's kitten," Eddie said. "I don't see her in the room, at all."

"She might of left, I don't know. But I believe the rest of it. Glazer'll tell you, he can't stop talking about it."

"So now you think we should run this thing on our friend up the road."

"The fuck, it beats an assault charge. Who they going to send after you, the ASPCA? A bunch of cat ladies waving their canes at you? Jesus, we had one of them in my building, she died and they found thirty-seven cats living in there. And half a million in her safe deposit box. You know who she leaves it all to?"

"The thirty-seven cats," Eddie said, thinking: the guy never shuts up.

"B'nai B'rith," Lally said. "Gotcha."

Eddie decided not to talk for a while. It wasn't Lally—it could have been anything. It had been happening for years, actually, and now he felt it ignite again in his back brain. It was a prickling of dirty light that rippled into a cloud of rage. Eddie got angry the way other people got migraines, days of it smogging his brain, flattening his whole face against his cheekbones until it ached, and he'd pinch the bridge of his nose between his forefinger and thumb and breathe out very slowly through his nostrils.

It was the price you paid in this world, Eddie figured, for being honest. Not legal, necessarily, or loving or wise. Eddie's specialty was honesty, of the negative-virtue sort: no bullshit. He suspected he had the field to himself. He knew that at best it was all he needed. At worst, it was all he had.

Lally, on the other hand, was a careful student of the spook mystique that floated like incense over the white tablecloths and the spider mums at The Company, the ambiance that suggested that everybody in there was only one Chivas away from explaining who really killed John Kennedy.

Eddie knew everybody in there: old CIA buddies, older ones from OSS days, new ones from the Drug Enforcement Administration; FBI and Treasury guys; lawyers who ran money laundries; guys who sold machine guns to Louisiana oilmen who thought the niggers were going to hold a revolution; plus the journalists with their six-second attention spans and scruffy shoes—one thing Eddie had to admit, the spook crowd might be long on bullshit and short on fingers but they dressed well.

The road forked left and climbed. The sky was a ragged little alley above the trees, a bright, dead color, like fish.

"We roust him, is all," Eddie said. "Open the glove compartment there and get me out that plastic bag."

"Marijuana, and, what, mushrooms," Lally said, handing it to him. He also noted a service .45. "Magic mushrooms."

"That's what he's got in his freezer, them and a quart of chocolate-chip ice cream, that's all there was room for with all the frost. Guy lives like a fucking pig. Grass up to your

22

ass in the front yard, mattress on the floor. I could've vacuumed an ounce of marijuana seeds out of the rug. I heard he was going around talking to all the daughter's friends, after she took off. I call Cane up to find out who's blowing smoke up whose ass, here. I say, 'Look, you hire me to straighten out your case. Then you go out and hire this pothead. Well, it turns out this Gordon Sault used to be a journalist, and he sent some nice things back on a swing Cane made through Vietnam. And Cane keeps telling me: 'He knows how these kids think.' "

"Think," Lally said.

"I said, 'That's all you need is the committee finds out you've got this hippie on your staff.' "

"The only thing I don't understand..."

"Don't understand. All you have to do is stand there and look bad. And tell him to shut the fuck up if he says anything to you. That's all."

"No, hey, slow down here. It's just, like, I figure it's something big going down, you aren't going to tell me everything, I understand that. But maybe you're gonna need people. I've got the training, the background, is all. The balls, frankly, you don't mind me saying so."

It could have been such a beautiful operation, when it started, Eddie knew. Cane had it all figured. It was worth $100,000, Cane said; Eddie would make sure Ellen stayed disappeared. The hearings would be called off; beautiful.

Everybody liked it but Ellen Cane, who went nuts. It took Eddie thirty-one hours, straight through with Dexamyl and cold showers, but he found Gerald Ravenel. It took him five minutes, once he got there, to make a deal. Ravenel's girl friend, Gaia, helped by screaming four of the five. All Eddie wanted was half. Gerald could have the rest. He'd said something about going to Mexico.

The way Eddie saw it, it was just a garnishee, collecting an old, bad debt. He and Cane went way back together.

"That's his car, gotta be," Lally said.

On their right, the hill fell away under a dank regiment of tulip poplars, clogged with vines. On the left, under a power line, was Gordon Sault's ancient Volkswagen Beetle—oxidized grey paint, snow tires, no back bumper, the exhaust-pipe liner mesh dangling out of one pipe, all of it moldering and pernicious, like some third-rate Teutonic omen.

"He walked in—he's probably scared," Eddie said, in the monotone of a coroner holding inventory on a corpse. He eased the Cadillac up behind it. They both got out. Immediately, Eddie felt the heat paste his pima shirt to the insides of his elbows beneath his eight-ounce glen plaid suit, "the uniform," they called it at The Company. They stalked forward, and stared down into the Volkswagen's windows. The back seat was littered with beer cans and books: *Black Elk Speaks*, *The Complete Poems of Sir Thomas Wyatt*, *Programming and Meta-Programming in the Human Bio-Computer*. There was a terry-cloth seat cover on the driver's side, and on the passenger's seat a paper tray bearing the last of what had been a dozen Sara Lee sticky buns.

"Maybe he's a junkie, they're always eating sweet stuff," Lally said.

"He's not a junkie," Eddie said.

"Washington fucking weather," Lally said.

Eddie didn't say anything. He slid a leather-bound note pad from his inside jacket pocket, and with a Mark Cross pen, he wrote down the license number of Gordon Sault's Volkswagen. He had thick, square fingers covered with little scars like leather, the outer split where the cow has rubbed up against the barbed-wire fences. It was skin that would look tan all the time. It vanished under his cuffs and it was still ruddy and thick when it rose out of his collar to his face. Eddie had a big block of a face covered with a craze of wrinkles, concentricities across his cheeks, deltas trickling into his eyes, frown lines, smile lines, and two clusters of vertical gouges beneath his eyes like the sad cheekbone marks on clowns. He looked like it had been too many years since the world had let him be the nice guy he'd tried to be, and now he'd lost the knack.

"We'll wait," Eddie said. He got back in the Cadillac. He hit two switches on the door and the windows sighed down. He turned off the ignition. The heat breathed in.

"I bet he loves that car," Eddie said, after a while.

"Oh, sure."

"I bet he's crazy about that car."

"I bet he is."

"Let's junk his car for him, scare the shit out of him."

"That's a felony, for what difference it makes."

"Not if he forgot to set his emergency brake," Eddie said.

Lally nudged open a monolith of Cadillac door. Eddie pointed to the downhill edge of the road.

"Find a place it'll fall for a ways."

Lally surveyed a bank of weeds, clay, and gravel. The air was freckled with butterflies. It was fifty feet before the first tree.

"Anywhere," Lally said.

He watched Eddie Conchis scramble into the front seat of the VW and coast it backward, with its last, low grumble of lopsided bearings. Eddie got out. Lally pushed. His tasseled loafers skidded in the gravel. It seemed like they watched it fall for a long time, slow and airy as a hat falling downstairs, before it wedged against a tulip poplar. They could hear the wheels spinning, down there in the shade.

## Chapter 3

GORDON STROLLED into the tunnel of shade over the road. Ellen lingered in his mind like a flavor, a slant— like that cushiony feeling you get when you walk out of a movie and everything's changed: something about her, as if her skin would be cool and warm at the same time; contradictions. He guessed at boarding school miseries, a bunch of colleges, and she'd needed a mother, he knew that—Carol Cane having been declared a suicide under the Calvert Street Bridge one Indian summer morning during the Kennedy administration.

Nice, he thought. I pull into Cane's driveway with the princess sitting in the passenger seat. I say: Need anything else? He says: No. I say: A check will do.

And she likes me.

Nice.

Way off in the woods a dirt bike stammered and howled. Pine trees sweated resin. The smallest of breezes patted leaves together as if they were tiny leather mittens, applauding. Gordon had a handle on the long view, now.

In this long view, Cane had called him because he'd already tried everyone else. Gordon had to admire him for persisting.

The list of phone numbers had started at the National Press Building, because Cane had known Gordon as a journalist in I Corps, South Vietnam. The secretary there told him to call Senator Moakley's office, which gave him the number of Gordon's ex-wife's father's law firm in Santa Barbara, which shunted him back to an environmental consulting firm where Gordon had worked for four months; then a commune in Virginia, where somebody thought he might be driving a cab for Barwood Taxi in Bethesda, where the dispatcher said he would be, he drove very well when he came to work, but he didn't come anymore, but Cane might try a number in Stuckey, Maryland, out toward Laurel racetrack.

"You know how these kids think," Cane had said when he found him. "Ask around for me, see if you can find her, talk to her friends." Cane hadn't been able to recall the full name of one of his daughter's friends, but his voice careened with bewilderment, and Gordon was, as he said to himself now, "a soft touch."

He rounded the last downhill curve. His soles slapped on the dirt. He wore no socks, Vietnam garrison style, and he skidded in his own sweat inside the boots. His left foot was just beginning to blister, a patch of heat on his heel. Call it maya, don't get attached. He might have gone on with a Buddhist rhapsody on the nature of pain—which was all life, in fact, the first of the Four Noble Truths—if the Coupe de Ville hadn't pre-empted it, swelling out of the cusp of the curve, a slab of burgundy weight.

Then he saw that his car was gone. He stopped. He felt his mind dither toward a still point of fear. There were two men inside the Cadillac. They got out, without talking to each other, and the road was filled with them.

The big one laid back, with his hands folded. The other one, who was Eddie Conchis, took a station in the middle of the road. He unbuttoned his suit jacket, spreading it with the backs of his thumbs till he could rest his hands on his hips. He was not carrying a gun.

"C'mere, Gordon," he said.

"I don't know who you are."

"You know who I am, all right."

"I parked my car here." Make flat, neutral statements. Don't give them anything to grab, any excuses.

Lally glanced over his shoulder, a gesture vacuous as a reflex.

Gordon walked to the lip of the ravine. He monitored each step. He didn't want to show fear. He stared down at the rusty gloaming of muffler, oil pan, worn snow tires cambered toward each other. He didn't understand. He wanted very badly to get things straight.

"You know who I am, all right." Eddie smiled an angry smile.

"I don't know. What can I tell you?"

Eddie slid his right hand into an inside coat pocket and retrieved a plastic bag that he held by one corner as if protecting important fingerprints. Gordon recognized his marijuana and his mushrooms. He was pierced with a sudden ruefulness that would have moved him to any atonement, if he could have thought of one. Instead, he fell back on the first rule of dope and women: never admit anything.

"You're the guy that goes around threatening to plant people with smack," Gordon said, regarding the plastic bag with a puzzled scorn.

"I don't have to," Eddie said. "Here's your dope back."

He walked up to Gordon, a tight low strut in Johnston & Murphy shoes. He tucked the bag into the breast pocket of Gordon's fatigue jacket. Gordon felt his fingers, strange and quick.

28

"It's not mine."

"You're being an asshole now."

"Not me," Gordon said.

It was an old man's punch, but it caught Gordon in the mouth and sat him down in the dirt, tasting blood. Tears choked the corners of his eyes.

"You're being an asshole," Eddie said. "Don't get up, just sit there till you can stop being an asshole. It's very important. My partner, here, he'd like nothing better than fucking you up. I told him no, the man doesn't understand the situation, is all."

Suddenly Lally was crouched in front of him. He reached out with one hand and flicked a forefinger into Gordon's upper lip.

"Got a fat lip there, asshole."

"Lay off him," Eddie said.

Rising, Lally cupped his hand and swung it, a roundhouse that slammed into Gordon's ear. It was a blow which, delivered properly, would have ruptured Gordon's eardrum. He felt pain leap at the center of his skull, then a loud, thin ringing. This guy was crazy. Gordon had every right and duty to be scared.

"You have no idea what you're up against," said Eddie. He had turned wistfully paternal. "You have no idea how it gets."

Gordon watched him with the leaden curiosity of the helpless. He realized they were running the good-guy/bad-guy routine on him.

"I'm sorry you had to go and piss me off, Gordon."

"I don't know what I did."

"Shut the fuck up," Lally said, swelling forward, frantic with power.

"Lay off," Eddie said. He hitched his pants legs and crouched, balancing himself with a left hand to the ground. Gordon saw his fatigue, the stale eyes he hadn't seen since Vietnam.

"Just one question is all. What I want to know is how the fuck you and Cane and Gerald Ravenel figured you were going to take this action away from me?"

"I don't know," Gordon said. He heard his voice through the ringing. He couldn't tell how loud he was talking.

"You don't know."

"I don't know. Cane asked me to see if I could find Ellen for him, that's all I know. I got the idea from talking to people she might be out here; the same people you talked to."

"You know who I am all right," Eddie said. "What made you think Cane wasn't bullshitting you, that he just wants you to find Ellen?"

"Nothing. I didn't think that."

"You didn't stop to wonder, either, if you could find this place, how come Eddie Conchis didn't find it?"

"I thought about it. I figured it was paranoia."

"Paranoia!" Eddie said. The word astonished him with rage. He said it to Lally, over his shoulder. "Paranoia!"

Gordon shrugged.

"No such thing as paranoia in this business. You know the score, you don't know the score, is all."

"I'm not in this business."

"That," said Eddie, "is where you're wrong." He licked his lips. Gordon saw a little white scar on the side of his tongue.

Eddie stood. He flicked his eyes at distance, at the flaccid sunlight through the trees.

"Cane and I go back a long way; I'll take care of Cane. What I'd advise is you be gone for about a week. You go someplace and smoke that dope and have a nice time. You forget all about this, and I'll forget all about this."

Gordon rose. He glanced again at his car.

"Why?" he said.

"Because I like you," Eddie said.

Strangely enough, and for all its irony, Gordon sensed that it was true. It was a sense of common enemies. He couldn't think who they might be.

He had to walk past Lally on his way down the hill.

"You know what they say," Lally murmured happily. "If you can't take the heat, stay out of Nagasaki."

It was at least a five-mile walk past cornfields, mailboxes and locked churches. After a while he stopped turning and looking for the Cadillac. The hell with it. The blister rose on his heel. Then it burst. The tissue beneath stung when sweat hit it.

Standing by the entrance ramp of Route 270, he flexed the heel free of the sole of his boot, to which it kept sticking. He was wounded, a state he equated with being free, released. He studied the sky hanging grey over silos and power lines. He didn't care if it rained. He didn't worry about life seeming real.

He hung out his thumb. Cars hissed past, swollen with speed, gorging on distance. He saw Gerald and Gaia's old Mercedes convertible slide down the exit ramp and dwindle toward the farmhouse. It didn't matter. He wondered if Ellen had waited for him, or if she'd known. He wondered if he should feel tricked, if he too should have known. It didn't matter. Gordon worked hard to avoid the attachments of pride and shame—they were the same when you came down to it, and they'd only complicate things. All he wanted was something in exchange for the car. The binoculars would do. They were Zeiss, 1927, good glass, easy to sell.

Two high-school girls in a Ford Ranger pickup slowed, then changed their minds and sped off, looking back at him and scolding each other. Seconds later, an old man braked a dirty vanilla Pontiac convertible to a hard stop. Gordon staggered up the ramp and got in. The old man did not seem to care where he was going.

"Bird watcher, is that it?" he asked. He accelerated with a

fussy intensity, gripping and regripping the wheel. He had ridgy fingernails and a faraway stare.

"How'd you guess?"

"Binoculars," the man snapped. He was not to be patronized.

Gordon got out where 270 joins the Washington Beltway. He watched the old man nearly collide with an eight-doored airport limousine. Then he sprinted in a crazy limp across six lanes of traffic, the dreamy tumult of rush hour.

His next ride was more unsettling, a jug-eared kid in a Dodge Charger who kept punching the tuning buttons on his radio. It was hard to tell what displeased him. The only time he spoke was when a deejay said: "Like to remind everybody that this is National Anti-Rape Week."

"Yeah, I get all choked up," the kid said, and snapped the radio off.

Gordon got out at an Exxon station. He spent several minutes sucking cool water out of his hands in the men's room, tossing it on his face, scrubbing his hands with gritty dispenser soap. Then he bought a can of Coca-Cola and carried it, frowning as if it were a talisman, into a phone booth.

# Chapter 4

STUCKEY, MARYLAND, was the "mean-dog and used-motorcycle capital of the world," as Gordon explained it to old friends when they asked. A lot of them weren't his friends anymore, but they all asked. Gordon was the only person they knew who had freely elected not only to live in Stuckey but to brag about it, too—mongrels, Harleys and all—a town that was also a contender in men who were proud to stand up when they worked and women who liked to turn the lights out when they made love. They painted their mailboxes red, white, and blue. They had a lot of handgun accidents. They went to church with hangovers and black eyes. Washington gleamed only twelve miles away, but they didn't know what this country was coming to, and still thought it was unfashionable to say "fuck" at the dinner table.

Gordon liked Stuckey, or he liked learning how to like it. He rented a two-bedroom 1938 Sears Roebuck prefabricated bungalow with fiberboard walls that beer bottles wouldn't break against no matter how hard he threw them.

He had neighbors who didn't care how late he tried. Televisions burned near dawn, and the strobe light never stopped twitching down at the highway intersection by the shopping mall. Stuckey was real America, which is to say a night place—night being the time people paid for all day at their keypunch consoles (minds full of sex and Jesus and state lottery) or walking dwarfed and silent under the blast furnaces at Sparrow's Point, or working for the government till they got a dead, dry civil-servant's con all over their faces and they sat up later and later in their kitchens plotting retirements.

Gordon had gravitated there after Everything Changed— after his marriage evaporated and he ran out of the kind of luck that only blind faith can bestow, and he realized he'd been in some sort of crisis for years and it was time he paid attention to it. He needed a rock, a lowest common denominator to start from. Stuckey would do. Where he'd come from, which was the country of the Bright Young Men in Washington, it was all talk, the half-world of media and politics. Ghostville, Air City, and Wordburg, Gordon had called it, terrorizing his wife of six months. He told her that his mind was starting to feel like your hand when you wake up in the morning and you can't make a fist. He said he was fogged in. The problem, he finally confessed, was that he'd known since Vietnam that It Wasn't Going to Work for Gordon Sault. He'd decided to Give It a Try (this included marriage), but it collapsed into an embarrassment for him, all of it—success, marriage, politics, journalism, name it. He couldn't explain it, even to himself, but he knew it was true. The day before his wife got on the plane back to Santa Barbara, her shrink assured her that Gordon was a paragon of self-destructiveness. Fine, Gordon said. Anything to make it easier for her to understand—he being prey, himself, to a craving for certainties, which also explained why he was spending so much time stoned.

By the following spring, he'd worried himself all the way

out to Stuckey, which was a certainty of sorts. Ur-America, he called it, with its chain link fences advertising PRIVATE PROPERTY with a penal vigor and its Saturday mornings bright with girls watching their boy friends writhe under old cars.

He'd have been saddened to know that the neighbors saw him as improving the block. While he liked to think of himself as a desperado, a moral sasquatch lumbering through the existential dilemma, the neighbors noted only that he kept odd hours. He didn't drive too fast past their kids, he didn't get drunk and pick fights. He didn't have a bunch of niggers coming around. He didn't collect unemployment, he was even said to work construction, part-time.

In fact, to the rest of the world, Gordon always looked like the all-American boy—a certain extravagance of heft, football shoulders he carried high as if to apologize for whatever exceptional gifts he possessed. He was brave. He was cheerful and reverent. For all his romance of failure, he had succeeded at everything he'd tried, from doing twenty pull-ups (overhand) to getting a 4.0 average in college to surviving Vietnam. He'd never been turned down for a job. His cohorts remembered him kindly, their only criticism being that he could be too hard on himself.

Sure enough, his features would tighten sometimes, anytime—nailing up drywall, watching a movie—with judgmental impatience, as if he couldn't forgive himself for something but couldn't quite remember what it was, either. Old business, worn-out karma; Gordon, being of a hopeful disposition, was convinced that a stay in Stuckey would render it moot.

Days—some days—he worked as a carpenter's helper, driving into Washington to renovate row houses on Capitol Hill. It was the only job he'd ever had where he could drink beer all day. Nights, he lay on the sun-bleached indigo ball-fringed Salvation Army couch he'd installed on his porch. He read books about death, revolution, Indians, porpoises, and The Void. He imagined a life that would match Minnesota Fats's poolroom heaven of "the dead stroke, the perfect stroke." He got bored a lot. He worried that he hated women, or that he liked them too much. He believed himself to be fundamentally lazy.

*

"You're not supposed to break them," said Dana Poynter.

"That's fine if you don't plan to walk for the next three days."

"They get infected."

"I don't get infections."

Gordon slouched cross-legged on one end of his couch, poring over the soles of his feet and nicking the blisters with a nail clipper. Droplets of salt serum soaked into the indigo cushion, which was shiny with old dirt. Dana couldn't stand it. She flicked her eyes out through the honeysuckle that curtained the porch off from the neighborhood. It was a cool, astringent look, focused but easy, like the face of somebody scaling cards into a hat. She had black hair, cut short and neat, and big brown eyes. She listened to Gordon breathe as he proceeded from blister to blister, the air patting through his nostrils. She wondered why she put up with it.

"Don't go," Gordon said, without looking up from his feet.

Dana lifted come-again eyebrows.

"You get that sad, tight look on your face, you're getting all practical, you could be home working on your dissertation, somebody decent might call, a doctor, the beautiful Mordecai..."

"He's married," Dana said in a voice cursive with big, round vowels.

"I thought you said he was gay."

"Who?"

36

"Mordecai. When he first took over the ward you said he was gay."

"I said maybe he was gay; maybe he *is* gay." Dana was a psychiatric social worker at St. Elizabeths, the District of Columbia mental hospital.

"And he's married, too."

"You keep fucking with it, you'll lose it."

"I know," Gordon said.

The trick was to see who could sidle closest to the edge of a dead, hard-eyed place where they wouldn't care about each other at all. The game was getting old. They'd been at it all summer.

Gordon braced himself on the couch, elbows flaring, then rocked forward onto his better foot, the right one. He limped to the porch door, stabbing his left big toe at the floor to balance.

"Another beer?" he said. He saw the piquance in her face, the adamant patience, her Jewishness. "Mushrooms? Do up a couple of mushrooms and drive down to the hospital and check out the roller skating?" Gordon liked to watch the crazy people roller skate; he liked it so much she wouldn't take him any more.

"It's bingo tonight. Sit down, you're hurting yourself, you do it to get attention, you do that, you do it all the time."

Gordon examined her with the glare of the merely curious.

"This craziness with Ellen Cane," she said. "And your foot and your car and all of it, your whole attitude."

"I'm not out to kill myself. Truly, I do not want to die."

They watched through the honeysuckle as a little girl staggered down the sidewalk behind a huge, tense German shepherd on a leash. Across the street, a man with a potbelly and drooping eyelids soaked a barbecue cooker with gasoline, then retreated to toss matches at it.

"We could roll a number," Gordon said.

He flattened against the jamb to look as she walked into his bedroom where the marijuana was, her poplin skirt glowing in the twilight, her white blouse purpling. She rooted through a bureau drawer with quick fingers. For an instant, he ached with a desire to marry her, but he knew from experience that all he had to do was wait it out, like an ice-cream headache.

A gasoline fireball thumped across the street.

Dana came back to the porch and sat next to him, thigh to thigh with him. He twisted up a marijuana cigarette with fingers just perceptibly atremble. They smoked it, listening to seeds explode inside the paper, both of them coolly, ritually voracious, canting their heads to pull at the roach. Then they were stoned. "Home again," Dana said. Everything was like a memory, it was all hypothetical, the smell of charred steak fat meandering through the honeysuckle, the lovely surprise of their two beer cans sweating on the old wooden packing crate—Schlitz and Ball Brand sweat socks.

"Relax," she said.

With exquisite lassitude, Gordon pivoted until he could lift his wounded foot to the arm of the couch. Dana dusted a fleck of marijuana ash off her skirt and he lowered the back of his head to her lap.

"The whole day was like Vietnam," he said. "Like this feeling that you don't belong, this dirty confused feeling."

"Sometimes you say you get nostalgic for Vietnam."

"That's another thing, another thing entirely."

"But did today satisfy that craving?" This was her official therapeutic voice—it was her way of showing affection.

"What craving?"

"The nostalgia."

"The nostalgia is just jerking off. Today really happened."

"Doesn't it bother you that you don't understand why it happened?"

"Vietnam or today?"

"Today."

"No."

"Why not?"

"Because there's a point where you have to take responsibility for being an asshole and leave it at that. I was an asshole to get involved with it, I knew that. Eddie Conchis just made sure I remembered it."

"What if he breaks in here again?"

"Wasn't that a bitch? I can't get over that." He arched his neck till his eyes met hers, which were huge with slow lids over her sweet worried mouth. "I warned him, though, when I saw he'd wrecked the car. I said: 'There's a copy of *The Complete Poems of Sir Thomas Wyatt* in that car. That's a library book, and you're gonna have to answer to Prince Georges County for it.' "

"No, you didn't, Gordon."

He'd brag to people: she doesn't buy any of my bullshit.

He rolled onto his side, holding his hurt foot aloft like a gimped dog. He pressed his face into her belly. He wanted to fuck her—the Orgasm Queen, he called her; helpless, lifting her head from the pillow, jaw working around some impossible word.

"Tell me about Ellen Cane," she said.

"No."

"Tell me all about Ellen Cane."

"No."

But she meant it.

"She's a rich-kid brat. When she gets scared she starts tucking her chin back into her neck."

"Was she scared of you?"

"No." He stared at the lath ceiling, white paint faded to a dingy cream that gave the porch a close feeling, like an old boat. Why did he lie?

"Was she beautiful?"

"No. It's all, the whole thing is over with. I'm gonna read about those people in the newspaper, like everybody else. Gonna wait for these feet to come back on line, buy some decent Eddie Bauer socks, spend a few extra bucks on freeze-dried chow and head down to the Smokies."

"How you going to get there now?"

"Hitchhike, take a bus, I don't know. I just want to get way up there above the tree line, sit there and watch the hawks spinning around. You know? And come back and be normal and ordinary. Go to work, come home, watch TV, be nobody. That's all. Everybody's pounding at you all the time you have to be somebody—your parents, your alumni review, your television. You read about the Vikings, the Greeks getting themselves greased for glory, so they could be legends. Two thousand years and we haven't learned a thing."

"Somebody has to be brave," she said, watching his flushed, tired face.

"Not anymore they don't. They've got it all figured out so anybody can be brave. All you have to do is get in line."

"You're talking stoned," she said.

"The hard thing for people is to be nobody."

"Sure," Dana said. "St. Elizabeths is full of them."

" 'Dust thou art, and unto dust shalt thou return.' "

"Very stoned."

"Eddie Conchis, he knows that. That's why I can respect him."

"You've got the tiniest crush on Ellen Cane."

"Stop it."

"That's your type, all the crazy ones."

"That's right." Gently he tugged a crescent of blouse out of her skirt. He kissed the skin beneath. It felt wildly personal and wildly strange at the same time, as if he'd just kissed, say, his own shoulder blade.

"Gordon," she pleaded.

40

"You're the craziest of them all," he said. She liked it when he said she was crazy. He lofted his hand beneath her blouse. He felt her sweet, frail nipple bend beneath his thumb. Her face went bleak with desire.

Across the street, the potbellied man yelled: "All right then, I'll eat the whole fucking thing myself."

"Barbecue Man," Dana whispered.

"The Briquet People," Gordon said.

It was a routine they did about Stuckey, like the anthropological documentaries you see in science class, *Australopithecus* and man-the-toolmaker. Here in Stuckey they had Chain-saw Man, Man the Motorcyclist, all denizens of the Television Age.

He blew the hair back from her ear to take the lobe between his teeth.

"*Homo erectus,*" he said.

"You take advantage of me."

"No," he said. "I think it comes out about even."

*

Later, when it was dark, half a mile from the Stuckey Shopping Mall and driving a stolen Mercedes-Benz 220S convertible, Ellen Cane ran out of gas. The Mercedes coughed, shuddered, bucked twice, and ran out of gas. It was that simple. Everything was wildly simple that night.

The Mercedes belonged to Gaia Stern. Ellen stole it because she needed it. It was old and heavy and as it slowed it got harder to steer, as if its tires had grown gigantic. She held firmly to the steering wheel, hands at ten and two o'clock. Her face bore the high, vexed, wide-eyed, aloof frown of a woman who had recently learned that her destiny was to accept life as a barrage of impossibilities. She heaved against the steering wheel twice, left and right, to rock the last gasoline out of the tank. The Mercedes snaked across two lanes. Horns howled, headlights lashed her mirrors, alien, impossible. Everything terrible was impossible; that was Ellen's creed. The creed made life simple—now, for instance, as the behemoth tires grumbled over the potholes and soda cans of the highway shoulder, and stopped.

She tugged Gaia's keys out of the dashboard. She studied her body, lifting her arms, turning her calves as if hunting for lice. All the way down from the farmhouse, Ellen had scrubbed at the little spots of blood. She had found one of Gaia's scarves in the glove compartment—Gaia's Gucci scarf, in fact; she recognized it as the one Gaia had shoplifted from Garfinckel's—and she'd spat on it and rubbed at the spots of blood.

She looked over her shoulder, and, as if her arm were pivoting off an eccentric cam, she flung the keys into the darkness. She climbed out of the car and started walking.

It was eighty-seven degrees, wind from the southeast at two miles an hour. Down the road, heat and exhaust fumes and insects hung under the light poles like riot gas; then the shopping mall, plate glass and pizza with the piny woods crouching behind it. Cars snapped past, clouting her with dirty wind. Passengers twisted to stare.

She was in a state beyond loneliness, a neon void. It was so crazy that she didn't know she was in any state at all. Images jostled against each other in her mind like grinding nightmare teeth. The images were of her best friends, which is to say her accomplices. She liked to think of herself as a gangster. Her friends had always been accomplices, like Gerald and Gaia the way it was before tonight. She remembered all her best friends. It was something to do, like tuneless whistling, while she walked. Her sandals slapped against her heels.

She thought about poor Pammy, who'd had a miscarriage in the room with her at boarding school and Ellen had walked with it down the empty dawn hall and flushed it away, a blastular clot inside toilet paper. She remembered her mother—her voice telling her, "You're too young, you can't understand." Her mother, though, had never been a best friend. After she'd died, Ellen decided she was wrong—you could understand anything, if you wanted to. All it took was will power.

She wandered into acres of parking lot in front of the Stuckey mall, walking slow and tiny and shadowed under the light poles. She wore the same cutoffs and F. Scott Fitzgerald T-shirt she'd worn at noon. She wanted a cigarette. In the muggy distance across the asphalt, kids lounged against cars and vans. She hoped nobody would cruise her, boys leaning out windows, trying to be tough and sweet at the same time, cute: "How come you treat me so *mean,*" they'd say if she ignored them. She wasn't scared of them, she just didn't want the hassle.

She didn't panic until she was in the phone booth in front of an all-night Dandee Donuts. She was dusting a dead moth off the metal tray beneath the phone when directory assistance said, yes, there was a listing for a G. Sault, on Patapsco Avenue, and she panicked. She wanted to back out of the booth and keep walking down the road. Her face winced into a tired, joyless flash of teeth as if she were driving a car on a too-bright day. Nothing panicked her like having to ask for someone else's benevolence, even when she knew it was her right, her privilege. Better for her to be the angel of mercy, shepherding the cruel and selfish and helpless of the world. It had been like that since her mother died; her panic and her secret pride.

She waited dry-mouthed in the phone booth till she could dial. Particles from the crushed moth glittered on her fingers. She hoped no one would answer, hoped as hard as she could. That way she wouldn't have to feel responsible for him if he did.

A deep voice said: "Hello."

"I'm terribly sorry," she said, embarrassed, suddenly, at

the shrill carillon of upper-class penitence in her voice. "I realize it's very late—are you still there?"

"Yes."

"This is Ellen Cane, from this afternoon."

"I recognized the voice."

"I think I'm in Stuckey."

"Then you probably are."

She thought of that acute presence which had shambled and sweated before her on the farmhouse porch. She couldn't reconcile it with this ease, this irony.

"I waited for you but something must have happened."

"Everything happened."

"They wouldn't tell me. I was afraid they'd killed you."

"It was just a bad day, was all."

"The reason I'm calling at this hour is that my car broke down."

"In Stuckey."

"I think so."

\*

Dana lay awake, and said nothing. She listened to Gordon hang up. Then the spastic syncopation of his limp through the clutter around the mattress: candles mounted in jar tops; a book of drawings by M. C. Escher; boots careened on piles of old dress shirts he wore unironed, right out of the Laundromat dryer; a carpenter's apron; two dishes where the last of their pint of Jamocha Almond Fudge ice cream had dried, gluing the spoons fast.

She heard a quick, sharp scratching.

A wooden match flared, a shaky blossom of light he sheltered behind his palm as he hunkered to rummage for jeans, wallet, sandals. She watched his eyes slide in the matchlight. He looked so distant, so zoological. When she'd met him in June, she'd thought he was naive. Dana tended to think men she liked were naive. With Gordon, it explained his intensity, his random relentlessness, the feeling that he was always gaining speed, with nothing to be late for. Now, watching him lean forward to gain enough clearance to zip his fly past his penis, she understood why she'd been wrong. She had confused naiveté with fatalism. Except that Gordon's fatalism was of the fey, knowing-better variety she saw in the faces of patients in their release interviews at St. Elizabeths, especially the alcoholics and the manics, the ones who lived as if they had to set themselves on fire to keep warm; the difference being that with Gordon, time and the right woman would change everything. She believed that.

She snapped on the photographer's flood lamp which was clamped to a wooden crate by her pillow.

"I didn't mean to wake you," he said.

"Who was it?"

"Ellen Cane. Her car broke down over at Stuckey mall."

"I'll drive you over."

"I can handle it. Just tell me where the keys are."

"It's not a jealousy thing. I had to get up and go home anyway."

"It'll be simpler if I do it."

"Really, I don't mind," she said.

"I don't want you getting involved with these people." In the glare from the floodlight he was all angles—joints, sockets, shadows twitching around.

"I'm not getting involved," she said, as if some professional ethic were being questioned. "But maybe I can help."

"You don't help these people, they help themselves," Gordon said. She felt a clutch of jealousy—not of Ellen, but of his fear.

"They're crazy," she said.

"It's the way they live. It works for them."

"I'll go along for the ride."

Gordon drove Dana's little blue Toyota Corolla past

bungalows and yards where big dogs sprinted after them behind wire fences, their eyes going red in the headlights. Dana knew what it was all about. She could feel him going away from her, his face preoccupied in the dashboard light. She wanted to see this Ellen.

She looked out the side window. Damp air hung under the trees, smelling of oil-soaked asphalt. She felt bad and good at the same time, as if she had a touch of fever or hangover. Ordinarily, she didn't think about herself much; it was against the social-consciousness code. Now it seemed right. She thought about love—how she dreaded it and Gordon despaired of ever having it again, how she wasn't jealous of Ellen, how she was never jealous, how she always understood.

He parked in the no-parking zone in front of the Dandee Donuts.

"That's her," Gordon said, setting the emergency brake with a tight little forearm move.

Ellen sat prim on a counter stool, studying a Coke. The fluorescent lights drew out a pale, subcutaneous scatter of freckles on her cheeks—the freckles looked too young for the rest of her face. She had thick hair that she'd finger-combed. She held her mouth small against her teeth as if she'd been waiting for somebody to hit her, and had long since given up thinking about whether she deserved it. She had long, tan legs and filthy feet.

"She's beautiful," Dana said.

## Chapter 5

GORDON LED ELLEN out to his porch, limping in front of her with two cans of Schlitz dangling from a plastic six-pack holder.

He held his palm toward the Salvation Army couch.

"Sit," he said. Instinct told him his job was to make everything as simple as possible.

She lowered herself to the couch with obedient precision.

Gordon sat in an aluminum deck chair with a buckled arm. He felt sweat on his temples and the back of his neck. He tugged a can of Schlitz out of the plastic.

"Please," she said.

He watched her take a long, long pull. She tilted her head back and poured half the can into her mouth. Her nostrils flared. There were little crumpled shadows on her T-shirt, between her breasts. Light strafed across her legs where muscles slid sleepily under the skin. Gordon remembered the words from a song:

> *Sail on, silver girl,*
> *Sail on by.*

"What happened to Dana?" she said.

"She's going to sleep."

"I like her."

"I'll tell her that."

She gave off both urgency and despair, as if she'd been shuttling between broken-down cars and dubious rescuers all her life.

"There was an accident with a gun," she said. She said it as if his accepting the fact were a precondition for any further discussion.

"Who got shot?"

"There were two men who showed up after you left, Eddie Conchis and a younger man. It was the younger one."

"Shot dead?"

"I don't know."

"Who shot him?"

"I don't know. The gun was in my hands just before it went off."

"Somebody pulls the trigger."

She drank more beer. She brushed her cheekbone with the back of her thumb and Gordon saw she was crying.

"Begin at the beginning," he said.

"I panicked," she said. "I completely lost it."

She stared at him. She frowned. Her mouth hung open as she studied him—she wanted to know if he *understood*, her eyes going narrow and her lips full; a brutal face that hovered for a moment.

She explained the whole thing, from her father's kidnaping scheme to finding refuge at Gerald's farm to her discovery that for her, Gerald, and Gaia to disappear in any style—Gaia wanted to rent a farm in Ireland and have horses—they needed money.

"So I thought to myself: I just solved all of Daddy's

problems for him. He wanted me to disappear, andI disappeared. He didn't even have to pay the guy to kidnap me. I'd done it myself. So why shouldn't I ask him for help?

"So Gerald called Daddy and said we needed a hundred thousand dollars. See, we didn't figúre he'd say no. And when he did, that's when I really got scared. I got scared that Daddy said no because he thought I was blackmailing him. I was scared he'd hunt me down and kill me out in that farmhouse. I was out there for five days alone. Gerald and Gaia drove out in the afternoons, but mostly I was alone. It was crazy. This morning I woke up and I knew it wasn't worth it. The hell with it. I'd rather be dead than scared like that."

"You do a lot of that? Just change your mind about things?"

"Do you think I was wrong?"

He let her question die there in the dark and the cricket noise and the whine of semis jamming up Stuckey Highway under the strobe light at the intersection. Dana slept in the bedroom. She talked once in her sleep, a thick, urgent sound that made Gordon's heart clench with sadness and guilt. She seemed hideously ordinary, mumbling in the bedroom while out on the porch Gordon was a-ring with a heightening of things, a foxfire illumination. This was the world the way he liked it, everything gone cool and deep, colors like wet paint, each breath a wind full of smells. It was his continuing faith that such a world was his due, the alpha and the omega. In fact, as either Dana or Ellen could have told him, he was only in love.

"Not that it made any difference," Ellen was saying, "because that's when you knocked on my door. I'd just decided to go home, and there you were, Daddy's special detective, offering me a lift."

49

"Amazing," he said.

"I waited for you."

"So did Eddie Conchis."

"And the other one? Lally?"

"Lally."

"I saw them get out of the car, that Cadillac. I thought: they just killed Gordon Sault and now they're going to kill me. I thought it in so many words. Then Gerald and Gaia showed up and I realized they were all in it together. They were extorting money from my father, that was all. Except the other one, Lally. He was just crazy."

She rolled her shoulders in a tremor of revulsion.

"He got a watermelon out of the garden and ate the whole thing. He wanted to tie me up. He killed a rat down cellar with a rock. He kept asking me if I thought I was going to like it in jail. He'd say: 'With all the bull daggers taking rides on your face.'

"After Gerald and Gaia got there, they all argued. They wanted the money from Daddy. They didn't know how to get it, unless they kidnaped me for real. I said: 'No way, I know my father, he's too tough. You might as well kill me right now.' "

"You said that," Gordon said.

"I said that. So then they figured maybe he'd pay them to keep their mouths shut about the original disappearance plan. Except they needed me to make it work. And I'd decided the hell with it, I was going home. Eddie warned me I was going out of the frying pan and into the fire; that you'd grab me before I ever got there."

Gordon laughed.

Ellen's hand stretched across the top of the couch with her fingers moving as if she were counting something.

"The shooting," Gordon said.

50

"I'm not saying none of it was my fault," she said. "I tried to sneak out, as soon as it got dark. Lally caught me on the back porch and dragged me back inside. He took off his belt. He wanted to tie me up with it. Gaia said she thought that wasn't necessary. Gerald told her to shut up. Eddie told us all to shut up. Lally let go of my arm and I ran upstairs. I was going to lock myself in the bathroom. Except he tackled me and carried me back. Gaia was screaming. Lally reached inside Eddie's coat and grabbed his gun and pressed it into my lip, right under my nose. Eddie told him to hand it back. Just when he started to, I grabbed it. Lally bent my arm up and back and then it went off. My God, the noise; the noise it made..."

"And it hit..."

"Lally. He fell down. He must have been bleeding because there was blood on me later, there still is, he was doubled up and his feet were kicking and everybody else was...I don't know. I got very cool. I panic when I shouldn't and then I'm ice when everybody else goes crazy. I just ran into the other room and grabbed Gaia's purse and ran out to her car and got away."

"So maybe there's a body still out there."

"Maybe there is."

"They could threaten you with a murder rap if you don't help them."

"Sure."

"We'll drive back out to the farm," Gordon said. "We'll see if anybody's dead."

"I can't. Really. I cannot go back out there."

"I'm not going to do it by myself."

"It's bad enough that I created this whole mess without you getting into it."

"Don't worry about me."

"I'm so tired of worrying about people."

She rose from the couch—through the spatter of streetlight and leaf shadows. It was a sudden movement; everything about her was sudden. She was surprising, like a new drug.

"What do you think about me now? Do you think I'm flaky?"

"A little."

"Everybody thinks I'm flaky. When it turns out they're wrong they always act like it's my fault that they're disappointed."

She was right out front, all right, pure Zen, the archetype of charm. He felt his whole body going quick, as if his skin were luminescently thin. There was little chance, he suspected, that he deserved her in any kind of basic animal sense, but he was lucky tonight, he knew it. Didn't the universe owe him some luck?

"I'll get the car keys," he said. He limped into the house.

He could smell Dana in the bedroom, the humid milkiness of her breath, a thin scent of marijuana. He squatted next to the mattress. She was sprawled on her stomach in a T-shirt, her breasts collapsed against the mattress. He saw her eyelids lift, puffed and wet.

"Did I wake you?"

"No."

"Yes, I did."

"Okay," she said.

It didn't matter. He was trying to forestall a lecture on her worries about his safety, a tirade of advertisements for her big heart.

"I need the car," he said. "I'll be back before morning."

"Oh, Gordon," she said. She snaked one hand out from the bed and rummaged in her purse.

"I could turn on the light." Her fumbling infuriated him.

She retrieved the keys and gave them to him with warm, soft fingers. She pulled the sheet over her shoulder and said into the pillow: "Should I worry about you?"

"No."

"Good."

When he stood up, he felt a wind of loneliness blow through his soul. It was a moment, and then it was gone.

## Chapter 6

*H*EADING SOUTH in his Coupe de Ville, Eddie Conchis mulled it all over with the perverse delight of a man who might respond to news of his bankruptcy by first of all tidying up his desk.

What a fuck-up. What a complete and total fucking fuck-up.

Gerald Ravenel and Gaia Stern sat next to him, licking their lips and blinking at the oncoming traffic, Gerald with his face the color of soap and Gaia pushing wisps of hair behind her ears. They were weird, all right, but at least they were in it for the money and they knew when to be scared. Gordon Sault, on the other hand, was in it for the adrenalin high. So was Ellen, but she didn't know it, and that was even more dangerous.

Eddie knew whose fault it was. It was his own fucking fault. His rage had refined itself, since its onset that afternoon, into a hard hiss of a breath in his back brain, all exhale, no inhale, like a welder's torch. He felt clean and clear with it. He knew whose fault it was.

Ahead of them, over pine trees, the damp air glowed with

a neon aura. Moths milled in it. Bats twitched through it. Beneath was a restaurant, a roadhouse of imitation logs.

"Why are we turning in here?" Gerald said.

"Because we are hungry," Eddie said.

He parked out of sight of the highway. He led Gerald and Gaia past garbage cans, propane tanks, and the fat, dead breath of a kitchen ventilator. His big shoulders didn't sway when he walked. His body seemed hung from them, with his feet gracing the gravel as an afterthought.

He held open a door pasted with credit-card decals.

"What kind of restaurant is this?" Gaia asked.

"It's a horseplayer's restaurant."

"If it's a horseplayer's restaurant, why are there all the stuffed fish on the walls?" Gaia asked. Lacquered swordfish, marlin, and tarpon arced against the pine paneling.

"What'd you expect, stuffed horses?" Eddie said. Gerald laughed, shaping his red lips around the sound as if he were pronouncing it. Gerald and Gaia: they were this year's cute couple; they worked together like the two halves of a yo-yo.

The hostess led them to a table under a wagon-wheel chandelier. The menu's highlight was called Surf 'n' Turf, which was a lobster tail and a filet mignon on the same plate.

"We're out of the lobster," the waitress said.

Gaia closed the menu and announced: "There's nothing on this menu that I'm not afraid of."

"Shuttup, Gaia," Gerald said with the amiability of a chronic taker of the long view.

"You people vegetarians?" the waitress asked.

"Not necessarily," Gerald said.

Gaia's face squinted itself toward a question. Her hand floated in front of her as if she were guessing something's weight. "What has your chicken been fed?"

"I just feed the people, honey."

"You want the chowder," Gerald told Gaia. "We'll both have chowder."

Eddie ordered two iced coffees and the prime rib, rare.

"With baked, mashed, or French?"

"Mashed."

"You're old-fashioned, like me," the waitress said.

"I don't eat them no matter how I order them," Eddie said. He watched the waitress walk away—the Dynel sheen to her hairpiece, the old woman's bow to her legs. He thought with sadness and frustration that he was even older than she was. He was older than almost everybody in this restaurant; in better shape but older.

For one fine, snug moment, a couple of weeks ago, Eddie had sat in John Cane's study on Foxhall Road, and they'd talked about one last run, enough money to put Eddie over the top, home free, the place in Sarasota, mondo condo. Get Janet out in the sun and the air, have dogs again and take them for walks on the beach. Eddie's wife was named Janet and she was a lush. Once upon a time, she'd raised and trained dogs—Scotties, which showed you how long it had been. Eddie hadn't seen a Scottie for fifteen years. But she could do Lhasas or Jack Russells, that was what the people were buying nowadays. She'd had the touch, she'd loved them, and now she wouldn't even go to the shows anymore.

One last run. What a fuck-up. If Eddie had stayed with the Bureau of Alcohol, Tobacco and Firearms in 1960 instead of going to work for Cane in the Kennedy campaign, he wouldn't have needed one last run. He'd have the pension now. You didn't get a pension for being Jack Kennedy's private wiretap man, but you expected other things. They hadn't happened. Eddie blamed himself for that—for trusting Cane. "I want to make it up to you," Cane had said two weeks ago. That was Cane: he had to make it sound like a favor.

It wasn't the pension that was important. Eddie had never been in this business to get fat and lazy off Uncle Sugar. It had been a calling; he'd been in it for when you could ride across the Triborough Bridge with some respectable mick

56

from Forest Hills, the gold pinky ring and the wing-tip shoes, and tell him he was selling machine guns to the Irish Republican Army, and you'd see his eyes go sad and slow because he knew that you knew he knew. For that one instant, there was less bullshit in the world. You couldn't expect to do more.

After he left BATF to work for Kennedy, and then all the others, the corporations and law firms, it wasn't so simple. Not that it bothered him to be on the other side of the law, the wiretapping and the microphones spiked in the walls and all; that was the game, everybody knew the rules. He expected hypocrisy. What had ground him down, all these years, was his discovery that out of decency and a sense of fair play, your average American who runs this country feels obliged to believe the same lies, himself. Friends of the workingman, fighters for peace, getting those boys killed in Vietnam, busing the black kids into the white schools—they were always sticking it up your ass for your own good.

Like Cane. Eddie couldn't even think about what Cane owed him because then the anger got so bad it worked against him. The trick was to make it work for you, and then it was the best shit cutter God ever made. You used it carefully like a tool, a gift you got once in a lifetime. You used it right and it kept you honest and gentle. Eddie worked at that. If he'd been gentler with Janet, it might have worked out better for her. He blamed himself for Janet. He blamed himself for Cane. Somebody had to take the responsibility. That's what freedom was all about, but how many Americans knew that anymore? Eddie admired freedom the way you admire a cattle stampede or a tornado—it was totally unforgiving, the great American bitch.

The food came.

"And some ketchup," Eddie said to the waitress.

They ate. Eddie sliced up his prime rib with fingers so thick that they made the knife and fork look like little surgical implements. The rare beef set the roof of his mouth aching. He sucked down iced coffee till the ice cubes jostled against his teeth and the musky coffee smell floated back up through his nose, cold and sharp. He mopped his upper lip with his napkin. He watched Gerald and Gaia. They ate their chowder as if they were negotiating with it.

Eddie liked them, the way an old cop can like losers.

Gaia had big breasts that lay beneath her black dress—she always wore black—as if they were sleeping, warm and heavy. Eddie wanted to scrub her face, then have her brush her hair, buy clothes that fit, and start getting some exercise. Gerald was a hustler, an intellectual con man. He looked like an overgrown child prodigy—the red lips and his jaw too big, a happy pout.

"How's the chowder?" Eddie said.

"Listen," Gerald said. "What are we going to do?"

This Gerald, Eddie thought: you couldn't give him an inch of slack.

"Won't his wife or somebody start asking questions?" Gaia said. She was all paranoia, stuttering her eyes around the room.

"There isn't any wife or somebody, I don't think. They'll ask about him maybe in a week at the bar I ran into him. But the only person they'll ask is me." His shopworn sun of a face beamed reassurance. "He's our ace in the hole."

"He was an asshole was what he was," Gaia said.

"Shuttup, Gaia," Gerald said.

"Just keep in mind we're not the ones who should worry," Eddie said.

"But Ellen will claim it was self-defense," Gerald said.

"That's because it *was* self-defense," Eddie said.

"I'm serious," Gerald said.

"So am I."

"Can you two keep your voices down?" Gaia said.

"Shuttup, Gaia."

"I...won't...shut up," Gaia said through locked jaws, her lips writhing around the words. "Why can't we just get rid of him and go home and forget that any of it ever happened?"

"We can't forget about it," Eddie said, "because Ellen might talk to the police."

Gaia shook her head at him. "She's terrified of the police. She thinks the police will give her back to her father, and then he'll kill her."

Eddie thought it over. He wasn't going to let them rush him. He thought about it and listened to the restaurant noises around them, the click and smack and clatter of people eating. Eddie had read once in a magazine how there were people in India who wouldn't let anybody watch them eat, the same way we don't let anybody watch us shit.

"He might," he said. "He killed his wife."

"He..."

"Killed his wife. She was dead before she ever got near the Calvert Street Bridge."

Gaia very slowly covered her open mouth with her hand. Then she said: "Ellen always thought so."

"You say it like you're surprised she could be right about something."

Gaia's whole body seemed to huddle around a sigh that said: include me out.

"You can prove it," Gerald said.

Eddie held up his thumb and forefinger, an inch apart. "Not quite. But I got everything else."

"Meaning..."

"I got everything," Eddie said with a sharp little swagger of a nod. "I got a tape of her doing a number on John F. Kennedy while he was shaving one morning in the Carlyle Hotel: everything."

"I believe you."

"*I* believe it," Gaia drawled, as if she'd known all along.

"Shuttup, Gaia," Gerald said. She looked sidelong at him with a bleak, smug smile Eddie wanted to hit with his fist; they were this year's cute couple, all right. Two halves of a yo-yo.

"The thing is," Eddie said, "this situation here, we got some time. We can think about it."

"We're holding all the cards," Gerald said. "The gun, the witnesses, and *habeas corpus,* so to speak."

"We're holding the cards," Eddie said.

"How much time do we have?"

"A day, maybe two, in this heat, before the smell gets bad."

"I'm sorry," Gaia said. "I don't believe I'm hearing this."

"The way I see it, John Cane asked me into this thing, I put out a lot of work, and I haven't seen jack shit for it," Eddie said. "I haven't done anything wrong."

"Ellen came to us, we didn't go to her," Gaia said.

"We've been carrying her for years, actually," Gerald said.

\*

In the parking lot, on the butt ends of all the air conditioners trembling on the windowsills of the restaurant, there were two men in a blue Chevy Malibu. One was fat, with the name of Farhad. He drove the Malibu, which had been stalling all night. Farhad had to start it two and three times at every stop light, sluggish clouds of exhaust jetting against the pavement while he curled his lip with helplessness. The other one, the passenger, was named Carlos.

"Park there," Carlos said, pointing to the Coupe de Ville. "Back it in."

He spoke English with metallic resignation, as if he had a

headache. He was lean but he seemed to possess terrific weight. He had a mustache. His body never moved, except for a tremor of gestures at its outskirts—his finger pointing, his eyes focusing as they estimated range.

"Leave it running."

He got out of the Malibu with a big screwdriver in his hand. He looked through the windows of the Coupe de Ville with tired eyes, then walked behind a Dempster-Dumpster and started kicking through the underbrush. He beckoned for Farhad to join him.

"A big stone, a piece of metal," he said.

"This?" Farhad said, holding up a cinder brick. He was panting lightly, a plaintive fat man.

Carlos nodded. He walked to the trunk of the Coupe and held one end of the screwdriver to the lock. He pointed at the cinder brick, then the plastic handle. "Hit as hard as you can," he said. Farhad spread a panicked glance around the parking lot. It was deserted. He rushed at the screwdriver, smashing at it with the brick until Carlos said: "I'll do it."

Carlos swung the cinder brick with a wristy coolness. On the third swing, it broke, half of it tumbling off the Cadillac's bumper to land on one of Farhad's square-toed cowboy boots.

"You are okay," Carlos said. It was not a question. It was at best a hypothesis.

There was a hole where the lock had been. Carlos angled the screwdriver inside it until he caught the latch and the trunk lid heaved loose. He looked around the parking lot before he lifted it; the point of no return, making your move—then you were free, every time.

"The car stalled," he said, shrugging at the Malibu as he nudged open the trunk. So Farhad, turning to restart it, saw it all in midturn, first the hair spiky with blood, sticking out from the head like cartoon astonishment, or like the hair in the strobe-lit knock-out-punch pictures on the *New York Daily News* sports pages. Except Lally was rolled from nose to knees in a Navajo rug. The eyeballs had dried tacky, but they still caught the light, staring with infinite preoccupation. He was the no-color of dead white people, the color of a newspaper. Farhad took it all in and never broke stride—three huge scuttling steps that landed him behind the wheel of the Malibu, which he'd started before his pants had hit the seat.

Carlos leaned into the trunk, over the body and through the smell of bile from inside the rug, the coppery tang of the blood. He dragged out a golf bag. He dumped the clubs onto the ground. He stabbed the spare tire with a curvilinear clasp knife whose shape looked like it had been generated by a computer. The air squealed out. He tore out the knife and shoved the heel of his hand into the tire, turning it to feel it all. He rolled the corpse over and patted it down. A nuclear device or a plutonium canister couldn't be much smaller than 155 millimeters in diameter, so he didn't have to unroll the blanket.

He shoved the trunk closed with the heel of his hand.

Farhad gunned the Malibu, spewing raw gas and hydrocarbons into the dusty grass at the edge of the parking lot.

"We should have followed the Mercedes," Carlos said.

Farhad coaxed the shift lever into drive. The Malibu stalled again. Farhad started it. He stood on the brake pedal and the accelerator at the same time, a fury of smog and frustration in the dank light in back of the restaurant, except for Carlos, who was so relaxed that when the Malibu hurtled forward toward the highway, his head sagged back. His lips were tight against his teeth. It was an old, sad look, a reflex.

In fact, his gut hurt. It was a pain that always caught him by surprise, for all the years he'd suffered with it. He had a very bad stomach. He drank Maalox till his shit turned beige. In the last year, his stomach lining had worn in spots to the thickness and strength of wet toilet paper.

He looked tired. He looked so tired that it gave him a moral lever, as if he had the right to make decisions faster than other people; which is to say he looked dangerous.

# Chapter 7

*H*EADING NORTH in Dana's Toyota, Ellen tore open two more beers and handed one to Gordon. He drank, watched the mirror, drove, and tuned the radio all at once with a brooding, reflective, big-fingered, white-toothed ease. She liked his style.

She nuzzled at her beer as if she'd just tapped into the river of life itself. Sometimes, she reflected, beer did it all. She unwrapped a fresh pack of Marlboros—her nerves were so close to the skin that she could hear the high, clean squeal of the cellophane tearing. She tapped out a cigarette. She lit it with a match, which she cupped inside her fist, the way her father had taught her on sailboats. She glanced at Gordon to make sure he wasn't looking, then she rounded her mouth on the smoke and floated a smoke ring into the wind past the window. She felt better now.

They were driving on I-270. They were tiny, nobody, fleeing across acres of concrete. It was dark. Every set of headlights coming the other way was a surprise, lighting the woods that stood by the highway like a wall—huge old tulip poplars, white oaks towering straight up and dangling vines, Confederate gothic. She laid her elbow on the windowsill and held her palm into the wind. Her fingers tugged back.

A sadness overcame her. She recognized it, a bouquet of pity and envy. She pitied Gordon for the power she had over him; she envied him for the power she didn't.

"You don't have to be here," she said.

"That's right."

"I just wanted to be sure you knew what you were doing, getting into this."

"I don't know what I'm doing." He looked at her: take it or leave it.

Terrific: she'd take it.

"You don't get along with your daddy," he said.

"We fight."

"What about?"

"Everything. We just fight."

"It must've been hard growing up without a mother and him gone all the time."

"All I remember about my mother, though, is them arguing. I think she was always sorry she had children. She didn't want to be a mother. She wanted to be beautiful and famous, but back then you had to have children."

She was tired of talking. She wanted to drink beer, blow smoke rings, and let her mind rest. Her mind touched on Lally for a second. That was painful. It veered back to her parents, and growing up. She could remember it all in an instant.

She had grown up in big, airy houses where everybody seemed to be on their way somewhere else—dinners, fund raisers, embassy receptions. Her parents called them "things," as in: "We have a thing at the Pan American Union tonight." They left lights on for her, one in every room, and hired housekeepers who told her about their tragic love lives, or the Bible, or their ancestors who were

Irish kings. Sometimes her father came home early by himself and fell asleep drinking a highball while he read newspapers. That was nice. Ellen would sit in her bathrobe and watch him. Once she crept up to his chair and studied the shiny purse of wrinkles where his right little finger had been shot off in Yugoslavia, during the war.

It was details like these that made your true life story, she said to herself. What you told other people was lies.

"What did you do on purpose to piss him off when you were a kid?" Gordon said. His voice hacked at the rush of air through his window.

"I didn't do anything to piss him off."

"Everybody does things to piss their parents off."

"Ah," she said. Now she knew what he meant. "Once I tried to prove to him that I was starving myself to death. After my mother died. I wanted him to think I was pining away with grief. Actually, I was scared he'd find out I'd never liked her very much."

"Why?"

"You're supposed to love your parents, aren't you? I was a crazy little girl. A crazy little anorectic. Except I cheated. I used to sneak down to the kitchen at night and eat."

"Did you piss off your shrinks, too?"

"I just lied to them. I was always afraid they'd tell on me. Every time Daddy sent me to a new one I figured it was because they weren't finding out what he wanted to know. It was all very paranoid. He sent me to the Menninger Foundation, and then this place up in the Berkshires where everybody was brilliant. They all became folk singers or committed suicide.

"None of it did any good—I just acted crazier. Finally one night I was staring at my food and then Daddy reached across the table and knocked it all against the wall—my plate, my glass, everything. I told him to go fuck himself. So he hit me. I deserved it."

66

"How old were you?"

"Fourteen."

She held her hand in the wind stream to shunt air at her face. She had said "fuck you" and her father had slapped her. That was the first time he slapped her. It always hurt and shamed her more than she could imagine, even at the instant the noise of it blew through her skull; and it disgusted her. She hated being hit with the hand that had the finger missing. It had a genital grisliness to it.

But it ended it—the anorexia, that whole craziness. She had learned then that he knew...that she knew...what? That if somehow the two of them together had killed her mother, it made no difference. It was a fact of life. All that knowing it meant was that ever after, in all the schools and camps she went to, the rest of the world would seem a little naive. Even now, riding up to the farmhouse, a ward of Gordon, she could feel pity and envy for him at the same time. It was like the way she felt looking at horses lathered up at the end of a fox hunt.

She watched him take the Toyota off the highway with a little dance of feet and hands shifting, braking, steering. He turned up a turtleback blacktop past shuttered churches and tin-roofed houses with lightning rods on the eaves. The road got smaller and rougher until there was no road at all.

Gordon drove the Toyota so far into a random-rutted cul-de-sac that the underbrush crushed against the windshield and they had to shove the doors into it to get out—a slow screaming against the oxidized paint. They struggled against the brush: briers and vines enough to drive them crazy, saplings whipping at them—they cowered along with hands covering faces.

"Where are we?" she said.

"We're where I should have parked this afternoon."

"Damn." The brush kept snagging in her sandals. She considered the possibility of a natural law stating that sooner or later men always took you someplace where you weren't wearing the right kind of shoes.

It was dark, which was what made it so bad, a smothering dark, like a window painted black. It was so dark that each footstep was an emergency, leg muscles scrambling for plumb with every pebble. On the other hand, it had an allure, as if whatever they were hunting—or being hunted by—were receding before them, a step at a time.

Their only hook in reality was the gauntlet of brush which eased as the road widened, the lop-sound of Gordon's limp, and a bird that sang and sang, raucous and cloying, singing till it sounded crazy. Ellen wondered if wild animals went crazy. She decided not to ask.

The road ran between the farmhouse and a country dump. The whole road was the dump, actually, with torn mattresses and piles of beer bottles and warped old laceless shoes peeking from the honeysuckle.

"Was Vietnam scary like this?"

"Yes."

"Are you scared now?"

"Yes."

"I think it's good that you don't mind admitting it."

"I'm proud to admit it," Gordon said. He took her hand. "I hope you're scared too."

She was—but it didn't matter so much anymore. Back on I-270, just north of Gaithersburg, she had made a decision—instantaneous and total, like a sacrament, a commitment she could feel in her whole body. She had examined the hungry ease in his face and decided she was absolutely sure she knew what he wanted, even if he didn't know it himself. He wanted her. So why not want him? It was a decision. To Ellen, love was a refuge, a choice she had no choice but to make. She'd been closing distance on him ever since she'd made it. Desire washed away all the anxiety, guilt, and scary stuff you had to live with. She held Gordon's hand, felt the syncopation of his limp, and knew desire would take care of it all; which was good—she'd never once understood why men were attracted to her.

"Less than half a day ago I swore it to Dana, I swore I was through with this job," he said.

"Dana's probably lying awake worrying about you right now. I feel sorry for her."

"You don't have to feel sorry for Dana."

They whispered as the road fell toward the farmhouse.

"Okay, I don't feel sorry for her, have it your way."

"I bet you don't lose many arguments."

"A girl has to pick and choose."

"Couple hours ago you weren't talking so smart. Couple hours ago you were walking wounded, my good deed for the day."

"I can hardly talk at all, my mouth's getting so dry."

They passed a row of white oaks with wisps of rusty barbed wire buried an inch beneath the bark from some improvement scheme that had failed decades ago—somebody's old hardscrabble daydream of a farm, the roof rusting, gates left open till the vines grew up through the slats, and held them there until they rotted; and dirt that after all these years had been proven by Gerald Ravenel to be good for growing only watermelons, zucchini, and marijuana, the bottom-feeders of the vegetable world.

"When Gerald first rented the place," Ellen hissed, "there was a redneck family living here, a nineteen-year-old woman with three kids. She used to throw their shitty Pampers off the back porch. A tree out there was covered with them. I found a letter the woman started to write. It began: 'Dear Mama, I had to sell your pistol.' I wondered a lot about that. I would've liked to have met her."

*

The farmhouse swarmed out of the darkness. It was unlit. They passed the truck tire where geraniums didn't grow anymore and Gordon remembered worrying that somebody would shoot him from the windows. After Eddie Conchis beating him up, and after the shooting, that kind of paranoia seemed like a luxury. This was a real death, even if he kept telling himself he was in it strictly for the high, the sport, the rush. The rush: actually the only reason to get it was to go beyond it. That was his ambition.

There had been days in Vietnam like that—where he'd be standing around listening to a fire fight in a village off across the paddies somewhere, and he'd be smoking a cigarette and everything would be fine—he could scale the dirt off his neck with his fingernails and his canteen water tasted like somebody else's spit, but somehow the world would be crisp as fresh linen, the whole world announcing itself to him with no ambiguities—white clouds and airplanes drifting beyond palm trees under a noon burning so hard that the top of the sky was black. Beyond the rush, riding the fear to the end of the line: there had been times like that in America, too—on an icy road in New Hampshire when a roommate's car broke loose, the wheel went limp in his hands, and there was nothing to do except to see if he got killed. Nothing to do! Gordon guessed that these moments were the closest he'd ever come to knowing the true fear of God. Things were so clear then, his mind floating like a hawk on a thermal updraft. Why couldn't it be like that all the time? If it couldn't, he wanted to know why.

This hypothesis had its problems. One of them was Vietnam when it was very bad, which Gordon preferred not to think about because it was persistently unclear. Another was Ellen. He hadn't counted on Ellen happening, figuring Dana would get him through. Now here she was: little Miss Adventure, a nun of the sacred hypothalamus.

They were edging toward the porch when her hand went

dead in his. He looked at her face. It was swollen with fear.

"The door's open," she said. Adrenalin rained through him. His eyes scrambled for a focal point till he found it, darker than dark behind the screen. He didn't like the door being open. It meant that whatever had happened here had happened in a hurry. Maybe it was still happening.

"Any advice?" he said into her ear.

"No."

He led her up the steps and past the rusty porch glider with its assortment of couch cushions. Their feet patted against the concrete. The door waited, an empty omen.

"How do we get into the room where the shooting happened?"

"Turn left in the front hall."

He gave up her hand, stepped over the threshold, then stopped. It was totally dark. It was The Void itself. Gordon tried shuffling. The darkness was like a medium that required a new means of locomotion. Everything was touch and smell. The house still held the day's heat, stale and dusty. Ellen's warmth was behind him. Her hand rested on his waist. He turned. He ran his hand up her arm to her head and gathered her ear to his mouth.

"Where are we?"

"About halfway into the room."

He smelled her: her thick hair, the comfortable tobacco of her breath. He liked the way she smelled.

"This is crazy."

"I know."

"If he's in here, the body, we'll have to crawl across the floor and feel for him."

"I don't want to do that."

"I don't blame you. But I don't want to show a light."

"But if we have to..."

What the hell.

"Where's the light switch?" Gordon said.

"It's a string that hangs down in the middle of the room."

"Have you got a match?"

"I left them in the car."

They shuffled through the room waving their arms like a ballet of dead people. Their hands floated goofy and private as thoughts. It was strangely exhausting. They listened to each other panting.

"I hit the bastard but now I can't find it again," Gordon said.

They both yelped when their hands touched in midair. Then: "Got it," Ellen said. "Let there be light."

The room leapt at them. One bare bulb glared needles down on no corpse, just the blood. Blood was everywhere. It was smeared, spattered, and puddled. There was a chaos of it.

"Jesus, I didn't do all that," Ellen said.

Gordon stared at the blood. There were hard round red drops where there was paint on the floor, and brown stains soaked into the wood where there wasn't; crusty maroon on the Indian bedspread that covered a mattress on the floor, sprayed across a 1950s blond-veneer-cabinet TV set with the knobs missing, a trail of smears where someone had wiped out footprints.

"If he's still alive he's in a hospital, and there'd be nothing for us to do," he said.

"Gaia's rug is gone. Gaia had her Navajo rug in here and they carried him out of here in it." Gordon realized he'd never seen an American woman in a choke situation. She handled it well. Sister Adrenalin.

"Anybody sees this mess, they'll call the police," Gordon said. "If he's alive, it doesn't make any difference."

"But if he's dead..."

"It's a question of how soon somebody finds out."

"The police."

"We just left about a thousand footprints in it."

"We'd have to burn the place down to get rid of it all." Gordon laughed.

"Sure," she said. "Why not burn the place down?"

Gordon mulled the problem that it would be a felony, but somehow, he was in too deep to mention it.

"Torch it," he said. She couldn't be serious. But then, did he have a better solution?

"Exactly."

She worked her jaw, she was so charged with the pleasure of devising such a scam. Overhead, the light bulb swung in diminishing arcs; shadows lapped at the walls.

"I don't want to be the one who pushes you into it," she said.

"We'd have to search the house to make sure there's nobody sleeping or passed out," he said. It was precisely the moral touch that was needed to take the edge off the fact of arson.

"What if there's somebody there?"

Was she daring him? Or was she scared—for either herself or him? There was an obdurate density to her, as if she, being perfectly clear about herself, were laying some burden of understanding on him.

"It's all right," he said. "I don't think there's anybody there."

"I don't think so either."

They started with the cellar. He told her to wait in the kitchen, by the trap door, while he clambered down the plank stairs by the light of a flyspecked forty-watt bulb. It was an old stone cellar with a dirt floor and a five-foot ceiling frosted with cobwebs. There were empty vegetable bins, an old car seat that looked like it had been torn apart by dogs, a bottle-capping machine, a blue block of salt, half licked and maybe bait for jacklighting deer, a large framed print of Jesus Christ with a crown of thorns and no worries at all,

73

and, crumpled against the wall in grey parenthesis, the rat Lally had killed. It all glowed with worthlessness and dank eternity.

"I was always scared to go down there," Ellen said when he came up the stairs.

"There's nothing there."

"Was there a rat? He said he killed one down there."

"I saw the rat."

They hurried through the house. It seemed to part before them like a tunnel.

"Somebody put some work into those," he said, nodding at a kitchen wall.

"Gerald's cabinets," she said. "He worked so hard on those."

Gerald had chosen to build oak cabinets whose posterity he had guaranteed with splined miters, mortise and tenon joints, woodworking's metaphysics.

"He'll be sorry to hear they had to go," he said. He slapped a counter top with affection.

"Gerald says art is not eternal."

"Well, he's right."

The prospect of the fire lent a nostalgia to everything: the tatters of screen in the open windows, the ancient heel marks on the stairway risers, closet doors that hung out into a hallway like rousted sleepers.

"Yoo hoo," he said, leaning into one. There was nothing inside except ancient wallpaper and a smell like tongue depressors. Windows shuddered the light back at them as they peeked in bedrooms. There were stems of burnt incense sticks angling out of the woodwork, an *I Ching* never looking more futile, lying by a mattress on the floor; there were crayon scrawls on busted walls beneath windowsills gnawed by dreaming baby teeth; Indian bedspreads over windows posted with American flag decals; a mélange of freak and redneck, the genetic sump of America, the skeleton in our closet, the dirty laundry, the huddled masses, the rancor and loss.

"Burn it down," Gordon said.

"Burn, burn, burn," Ellen said.

But the real talk was happening inside their heads.

He pointed to a trap door to the attic. "We don't need to look up there."

"No, we don't," she said, thinking that he was so fine and serious; that he looked like God had intended him to be small-boned but had given him more bulk by accident, muscle curving into his backbone, shifting under his T-shirt—he wouldn't know his own strength. A good man. Her sadness was coming back in the form of a proprietary feeling—knowing they were going to burn this house down made it seem like it belonged to them, their house. She could tell he felt that way too. He even killed a hornet with a rolled-up copy of Gerald's *Co-Evolution Quarterly*.

He turned at the top of the stairs and flashed one more hard look around.

"I have to get my stuff," she said.

"Bad idea. They see your stuff gone, they'll know you burned the place down."

"This is stuff I need—I need my wallet, it's got my driver's license. And I need my toothbrush. And my Valium."

"Okay, your Valium."

"My diaphragm."

"Okay, your diaphragm."

The strange thing to Gordon was that the argument was only incidental, verbal Muzak. The real business at hand was the fact that her lips never quite seemed to close as she talked, and he seemed to be looking through her eyes rather than at them. Her ribs rose and fell in slow sea rhythm. He wanted to press his hands to them, as if some estimating gesture were called for.

"I only meant that I don't care," she was saying.

"Right, right," he said. Why argue? He'd done his bit for common sense.

"Okay?" she said. She watched him as if he might be thinking about something else entirely. She looked puzzled and happy. Her face had the innocence of someone who is working very, very hard. She hurried into her room. Gordon heard drawers open and close. He heard her say "Nnnnnnn." She emerged to stride chin-up and blinking to the bathroom. When the bathroom door opened a couple of minutes later, with the noise of water flushing behind her, she had her wallet and her toothbrush in her hand, and she appeared to stare hard at him and not see him.

"Burn," he said. It was very exciting.

"Burn," she said.

Things were happening fast. They trotted downstairs, knees and elbows cutting at the air. They felt sly, happy, coiled, cranked—the mojo was with them.

"Nnnnnnnn," Ellen said, both of them realizing that it would take...whatever it took, it didn't matter. They smiled like people amazed by music. At the foot of the stairs he leaned behind her to punch the button on the old-fashioned light switch. Darkness closed on them with wild and terrific instantaneousness, like water when you dive at night and for a moment you're not sure which way the surface is.

"Ah," Gordon said, a laugh of satisfaction at the redeeming weirdness of the universe. He turned and bumped into her. She said "Excuse me" in the same way she'd said "Nnnnnnnn." And didn't move. So. In the dark it all had to be done in slow motion, make haste slowly. His hands found her ribs. She took a demure step forward, her wrists riding

76

back around his arms. She could smell him again, like a tent in the sunlight. He landed a kiss on her hairline, then her cheekbone, flying blind, then the rush of her mouth, hard, almost formal, tiny tooth click, sweet blitz of covenant, flash of tongue. He felt her hesitate, hovering over some thought as he nuzzled the warmth behind her ear. Desire was graining through him, he didn't want to fool around, he didn't want her going coy. She stepped away, holding his hand.

"Come on," she said. She was way, way ahead of him.

They floated to the door, which was a rectangle of the dimmest possible light. They pushed past the screen. South, toward Washington, the sky was a surly pink and the fields raged with crickets. Gordon brushed the rusty arm of the porch swing. Ellen pressed her forehead to his neck. It was an oddly formal gesture of regret. She could have been saying good-bye to him, except then she bit him with a wide, gentle mouth and they went down to the swing, halving distances and doubling speeds, denim and silk escaping down her thighs. He wasn't entirely hard, she wasn't quite easy, but it didn't matter, it was the meaning that counted, until they went into love's own back-brain lock-on and meaning didn't matter either—it felt as if they were cooling themselves with each other's heat, finding it and finding it. He didn't want to please her, he wanted to have her, she could feel that in the rolling shudder of the muscles in his back—that he was jealous of every cell in her body. She liked that. All she had to do was surrender. She could always surrender more than any man could possess, that was her pride.

When he came, Ellen closed her eyes and pressed her lips between her teeth as if his coming had revived an old memory. He lay on her. His panting eased. He rested his face in the hollow of her shoulder and addressed her skin with long, light kisses. She arched back into the cushions, looking for breathing room under his weight.

She dangled her hand from the swing till it touched concrete and she rocked them in the darkness and the heat. They sweated. Crickets and cicadas frothed against their eardrums; and the slow grinding of the swing chains.

"Oh my," Gordon whispered.

"I know," she said happily. She'd been afraid of his irony, his distance, and of Dana. Now she knew he could be had. She flexed on him and he shuddered into one last easy kneading against her. Sweet. She felt so good that she wished she could see her own face, heavy-lidded and happy.

For Gordon, just now, inhaling the delicate air that rose from her hair, the fear had softened to a glow of gratitude— she was such a prize, so fine. It was fear, nonetheless, and it was a question of riding it to the end of the line.

"Madness," he said. "We have to get out of here."

"I know."

It would be daylight soon, and people would see the smoke. He lifted back from her and stood, staring into the darkness. He buckled his pants.

"We need a match," he said.

"I saw some on the television."

He was running on pure instinct. He strode without a flinch through the darkness in the room with the blood. It stuck to his soles and hissed. He yanked the light string. This time the blood was merely terrible, old news. He spotted the box of wooden matches on the television. Behind it, the corner of the room had been rebuilt with drywall and patched with spackling. He turned and kicked it in with his good heel. He realized that since they'd made love, burning the house was nobody's business but theirs. That's what it was all about. They owned everything, a land-grant charter of the mind, as far as the mind's eye could see. The world had gone cozy on them, and there was plenty of time.

78

He tucked a sheet of newspaper inside the hole. On a windowsill he found a half a milk carton full of dirt and a dead baby tomato plant, which he dumped on the floor. Nice and waxy, good kindling. He stuffed the carton into the hole, behind the old dry lath. He rustled one match out of the box. He squatted and smeared it across the floor till it lit. With an innocent, speculative air, he touched it to the newspaper. A flame took up residence on a photograph of a man in a wheelchair holding a basketball and a trophy. Gordon hunkered and waited, man the fire builder. Inside the wall the fire fed itself.

The flame teased around the edge of the hole and caught a loose sheet of wallpaper. The paper blackened and reared back in sudden blaze. The fire builder pursed his lips and nodded. He could admire fire for hours, nuances like the newspaper shivering in a last skeleton of sparks. He waited till the heat hurt his forehead, knees, and knuckles; then he backed off a step. Slow, creamy smoke leaked out of the wall—wood smoke, the mother lode. The wall was blazing inside and out, he could hear it.

"You build a fine fire."

Ellen was standing on the far side of all the blood and she was wearing the smuggest something-for-nothing face he'd ever seen. She picked her way through streaks and smears, feet pivoting in their sandals till she was next to him, hanging her hand on his shoulder.

"It smells good," she said. "I hated the way this place smelled."

Flame flattened against the ceiling. Smoke scrolled back down toward them. It was a new smell, biting away at the woeful farmhouse funk of kerosene and underclothes; rotten teeth, gun solvent, hominy grits, diapers drying on stoves, hair oil, turnip greens, home canning, bad plumbing, wet boots and baby shit, all of it seasoned with an attar of Gerald and Gaia's Bohemia—marijuana, saffron, sandalwood incense, cat pee; and all of it transmogrified as the fire skirmished up the walls and Gordon and Ellen edged away with cheerful contempt. The light bulb paled in the smoke and the glow. They coughed. He took her hand and they promenaded out of the house.

There were pinheads of sweat on their cheeks.

"Feel the air," Gordon said.

"I feel it. It feels like fall."

"With the smell of the smoke."

"That must be it."

An orange haze frisked across the yard. It made everything into an artifact—an upended cinder brick, a gallon oil can torn by rusty bullet holes. He put his arm around her waist. She moved to him. She was all give and quickness.

"I think I feel guilty about setting it on fire," she said.

"No, you don't," he said.

"You shouldn't tell me how I feel."

"You're right."

She leaned her head to his shoulder. They walked up the pasture hill with arms around each other's backs. They took long, ground-gaining strides. She kept looking back over his shoulder. The fire heaved light after them, and their shadows floated in front.

"I know I feel guilty about something," she said.

"Maybe you feel guilty about feeling guilty," he said. "Like desiring desire."

"I do enough of that, all right."

One leg at a time, they performed a cautious vault of a barbed-wire fence.

"Look," he said.

The fire groaned away on the first floor. It rolled and moiled. Its light shone from the upstairs windows like a terrible suspicion. It sucked in wind to feed itself. Gerald's Tibetan prayer flags stirred on the wash line. A dingy rose nimbus swelled to reveal fence posts and honeysuckle and the dark tree line in a lurid, underbelly green. The heat pressed against their skin.

"We did that," she said.

"It's all ours."

It was burning so hot and fast there was hardly any smoke. Bats twitched around the edges of the glow.

When they neared the tree line, Gordon pointed and said: "That's where I lay and spied on you."

"Back when you were my enemy."

They were ancient, they were infinite. They sat cross-legged in the last stretch of the firelight. It was strange how bright it was, downhill, and yet so little light reached them, a red overlay that blanched their lips to the color of their faces. They listened to huge siftings and crashings as the house re-arranged itself earthward.

"Really," Ellen said in a cheerful, summing-up voice, "we've done a terrible thing."

"It doesn't make any difference, it's done."

"You're wrong, you're wrong."

"The house is on fire. That's the way it is. It's like the trees or the sky. It's all just there."

"You don't really believe that."

"I think it's true."

"But you don't believe it."

"I try to believe it. I try to believe in everything just being there, the trees and the sky, and now the house on fire. It's very hard."

"No. What's hard is believing in something that isn't there. Anybody can believe in something that's there."

"You say that because you never tried."

"I believe that things are what you think they are. There's nobody who can prove me wrong—my philosophy professor told me that."

"I wouldn't try to prove you wrong," Gordon said. "Not me."

He kissed her breast through her F. Scott Fitzgerald T-shirt. He pressed his cheek to it. He gathered her nipple and Fitzgerald's eyebrow with his lips, then assayed it with the tenderest of teeth. She smiled at him over her cheekbones. She was eternal nonchalance.

"You're beautiful," he said. He wanted to be the man who proved to her once and for all that it was true. "You know?"

"No." She'd never known why men fell in love with her; it always made her smile.

He pillowed his head in her lap. She watched the farmhouse. Heat rolled up the hill as flames covered the last of it. Rows of pale flames jetted from each rank of clapboard. Windows boiled with flames that were dark and full of falling timbers.

"Out, out, damned spot," she said.

The tin roof screamed and buckled and smashed a mass of sparks skyward. She watched the sparks out of sight. She wondered if they'd gotten too small to see or if they'd gone out. She became so lost in this question that she didn't see the lights until they were so close she panicked. She shoved Gordon's head off her lap. She was half-standing before she could even say it: "Headlights!"

"Get down!" Gordon said. The headlights jolted along the lane that led to the farmhouse, cones of light gouging through the dampness and smoke. Gordon scrambled to her. She'd frozen, half-standing. He tugged her to the ground. "Get down and don't move, and they won't be able to see us."

The car was coming too fast. Every time it hit a pothole the driver hit the brakes, and the car stalled. Clouds of exhaust flattened against the ground and it lurched forward again, walloped into another pothole, stalled, spewed, lurched...until a man got out of the passenger side and walked while the car—a Chevy Malibu—pitched along behind him. They watched him walk into the aureole of firelight: a wide face, mustache, dark hair, and precise steps full of fatigue.

"Anybody you know?" Gordon asked.

"No."

"The landlord?"

"There isn't any landlord. A bank owns it."

The man with the mustache marched around the house. He shielded his face with his forearm when he tried and failed to approach a window. He was all business. The driver, on the other hand, was unremitting panic, lurching and stalling as he turned the car around. He honked the horn as soon as the man with the mustache appeared on the other side of the house. He kept honking. The man ignored him, pausing to take a long sparkling piss in the firelight while he squinted at the windows. The driver stopped honking to leap from the car and shout. From the top of the hill they watched him wave his arms in frantic circles over his head.

"A fat, angry man," Ellen said.

"Not a happy couple."

The driver had the car in gear, straining against the brakes while exhaust smoke plumed over the taillights. The man with the mustache got back in. The car swerved across the yard hurling a wedge of rocks and dirt and dead grass back at the fire. This time it didn't brake for the potholes. The taillights stuttered out of sight into the woods.

"He'll break an axle," Gordon said.

"What's his hurry, I wonder."

"Maybe he thinks atom bombs were hidden in the house."

"I shouldn't laugh," Ellen said. "Me, of all people."

"Why not? Your daddy would have wanted it that way."

Ellen sighed a long, sweet, tired, martyred, sarcastic,

plaintive sigh. The fire ebbed. They could hear the noise of the insects again, see Washington glowing to the south, and feel the closeness of the darkness and the humidity. It felt like it might rain.

## Chapter 8

*A* WOMAN WITH SHORT, DARK HAIR sidled out
of the bedroom. She moved as if she didn't think she could
be seen in the half-light. She wore a skirt and a man's T-shirt
so big on her that Eddie could see her collarbone inside the
neck. He stopped knocking and stepped to the porch
window. He opened his wallet and slapped an ancient BATF
identification against the glass.

She shouted: "I can't let you in."

Eddie twisted the doorknob. He flipped the door back
with his elbow as he came through. He found a wall switch
and snapped on the light.

"You can't come in here," Dana said. She seemed to have
instantly shrunk, stricken with glare. Her mouth pursed in a
large, speculative O.

"I'm looking for Gordon Sault."

"He isn't here."

"That's all right. I'll just look around."

"I can't let you do that."

"I'm not going to hurt you."

"I know you're not going to hurt me," Dana said. It was her therapeutic voice from the hospital.

"No, you don't," Eddie said. "You only know it because I told you so. Otherwise, you don't know anything."

"Do you really feel you need to be threatening me?"

"Nobody threatened you, honey."

"Why are you so defensive?"

"Don't talk that shit," he said, patiently. "You don't have to be scared. I don't expect you to believe that, but I tell you so you won't do something stupid."

"I won't do anything stupid." Her eyes tensed into rectangles of fear.

"I'm a business associate of Gordon's, he tell you that?"

"He told me about you if you're the one. I think you should leave."

"You don't live here. You don't have anything to do with this except answer questions right now, is all."

She canted her head and sucked her teeth. It was a look that trembled between insolence and desperation.

"What's your name?" he said.

"It doesn't matter."

Eddie didn't shrug—it was more a reflex of have-it-your-way apathy. He wandered past her. He shoved the bedroom door back against the wall and toured the concatenation of bedclothes and boots; a beer can holding a dead tiger lily; binoculars; and her purse. He bent to grab the purse. With one shake he exhausted its contents onto her pillow. He picked up her wallet, which he opened with slow, impersonal cop fingers, as if he were wearing gloves.

"That wasn't entirely necessary," she said.

"You're Dana Poynter, you're a psychiatric social worker at St. Elizabeths Hospital and you live in Georgetown."

He chucked the wallet back on the pillow. He ambled out to search the rest of the house. His shoes ticked on the linoleum floors. He paused to look at Gordon's college diploma, framed on the wall. On the glass Gordon had scrawled in ironic red grease pencil: "I'M PROUD OF IT, TOO."

In the bathroom was a shower curtain that gave off the chemical stink of discount drugstores and Taiwan. Eddie pushed it back.

"Stay where I can see you," he said, without looking over his shoulder.

She followed him while he searched.

It was a tiny, shabby house. There were water stains on the walls, with brown edges like the spots on an old mattress. A coleus plant on a windowsill pressed red-and-green leaves against a torn screen. There were no curtains. The effect was a bleakness that verged on intensity.

In the kitchen an old round-shouldered refrigerator bore a reproduction of Hokusai's wave. Eddie leaned out the back door where grass tufted away into the darkness.

"He had a garden out there till the drought," she said.

"Where is he?"

"I don't know."

"Where do you think he is?"

"I don't know." She said it in a flat dead tone that meant she was going to keep on saying it. She kept her eyes on his hands.

"I tell you what I think. I think he's out someplace with a girl named Ellen Cane, and either they're in a cream-colored Mercedes convertible or they're in your car. I think he'll be back. When he gets back, I've got a message for him. Tell him he should get in touch with me. Tell him there's no reason we can't cooperate on this thing."

"I hear you."

"There's nothing stupid about you."

"No."

"When it comes down to it, there's nothing stupid about your boy friend, either. It's just ignorance. Maybe you know that already."

"Maybe."

"He's running on pure luck and he doesn't know it. When he runs out, it's toilet time. You met Ellen Cane yet? Right, you don't say yes or no, but I can look at your face. Sure, look at it. You met her, they were here and they borrowed your car and you're pissed off about it. What kind of car is it?"

"A blue Toyota," she said, blushing. "If you don't believe me you can go through my purse again."

"What reason would you have to lie to me?"

"I don't know."

"Sure," Eddie said. "That's just it. I'm the only friend everybody's got in this thing."

He considered the glassware in the sink. He chose a jelly jar from among the Ronald McDonald glasses and the plastic coffee cups. He washed and filled it. He carried it back into the living room. There were sweat stains under the armholes of his suit coat.

He spun around with lifted finger. "I tell you what else. I'd be very pissed off, myself, if I found out he's the one who punched my trunk."

"I don't understand what that means."

"Busted open my trunk, on my car, that Cadillac in the driveway." He indicated a window. Dana didn't look. She waited for him to drink the water.

"I don't hear from him, I'm going to think he did that. So he should call me before I have to call him. The other thing, if he didn't punch it, then the both of us got somebody else to worry about entirely."

He sipped at the water. He winced. "The water around here this time of year, you can't get it to run cold."

"There's no ice," she lied.

Eddie looked around the room. "I can't drink it."

"Pour it in that potted plant, then." She pointed to the coleus. He spread the water evenly over the dirt. He handed her the empty glass.

"Tell him to call me," he said. "I'm in the book."
She waited for him to go.

"He needs to talk to me. His luck's running out."

"You never know."

"Sure you do," he said with sudden heartiness.

He kept pausing on the way out, apopemptic flourishes.

"You need anything, there's anything you think I should know, you call me too," he said.

She found this solicitude terrifying. She wanted him gone.

"You Jewish?" he said from the porch.

"Yes." She guessed that he had meant the question to imply some variety of enlightenment on his part.

She listened to the click and sigh of the Cadillac starting. She saw the headlights jolt as it backed from the driveway. There were two other people inside it. She stood in the living room, bleary and outraged. She tried to tell herself it wasn't Gordon's fault until she had to admit that it was. It was all his fault. She had to stop absolving him. When was she going to realize that loving people and understanding them didn't give you the right to absolve them?

She'd been doing it for years, though. This thought made her angriest of all.

## Chapter 9

*I*T WAS JUST GETTING light, a dewless August dawn full of dust, cicadas, and mourning doves, when Gordon backed the car down the dump path and onto the dirt road.

"This is the day the Lord hath made, let us rejoice and be glad in it," he said.

"What's that?"

"It's what my father said at the breakfast table, every day of his life."

"Is he dead now?"

"He's dead."

They drove past dusty billows of honeysuckle, and syca-more trees peeling in the grey light. They were riding along the creek when Ellen said: "I hear something." She leaned to the window to listen. "You hear?"

"A siren," Gordon said. "They're playing our song."

It was a fire engine moving much slower than the siren implied. Gordon stopped the Toyota in the weeds to let it pass, doughty and howling. Little American flags flew from the fenders. A red light washed against the vines and lit the faces of the volunteer firemen riding on the sides.

"Poor things," Ellen said.

Their faces were puffy with sleep. They winced into the dust. They looked stunningly earnest.

"They make me feel like we should turn around and help them," Ellen said.

He watched them out of sight. He heard the engine straining uphill into the dust.

Halfway to Washington on Route 270 a second siren yelped once behind them. Gordon looked in the mirror. A state police cruiser was riding so close behind him he couldn't see its headlights. A carnival of strobes and flashers exploded on its roof, splintering light all over the vacant lot of his nervous system. He was tired, wasted, sore, jangled. His peripheral vision was alive with predation. He didn't need this shit. Fear leached his mouth dry when he glanced at the speedometer and learned he was not speeding. This meant he was being sirened—a clamor of pure ratcheting outrage now—to the roadside for something else, such as arson or harboring a fugitive or conspiracy to ensure the security of the People's Republic of Albania with stolen plutonium.

The trick was to keep playing the percentages. He pulled over. He dove across Ellen to tear open the glove compartment and shower her lap with a pocket pack of Kleenex, a spray of pop-top rings, brochures for Luray Caverns and the Divine Science of Eckankar, swizzle sticks, envelopes with maps penciled on the back...he wanted to find the registration before the trooper reached the window and got a good look at Ellen.

"You can break for the woods if you think it's you he's after."

"Why?" she snapped. She was full of an indignation Gordon found less than comforting.

He found the registration and turned to flash a smile and

a just-a-second wave back at the trooper. The trooper had a face Gordon had seen before—on a life-insurance brochure? A mail-order underwear ad? Ridges of mesomorphic cheekbone and brow surrounded sunglasses as black as telephones. A cop face. He looked like the ultimate ant in a fable in which Gordon was the ultimate grasshopper.

Gordon walked back to the cruiser. He decided to venture a gambit of misdirection.

"I didn't *think* I was speeding," he said, with a fretful brow that conceded that *thinking* was of course the least reliable of instruments.

"That's not the problem," said the trooper. He tucked Gordon's license and Dana's registration at the top of a clipboard.

"You've got a malfunctioning taillight," the trooper said.

"Got it," Gordon said. He felt fear turn to relief, then anger, then a high scorn that made his eyes go hard. "A busted taillight."

He waited, hands in back pockets. The passing cars slapped him with wind. *Rousted,* he thought. It isn't the taillight, I've been *rousted.* What's happened to me that cops are rousting me for the first time in my life?

The trooper droned syllables and numbers into a microphone. His radio coughed back. Traffic thickened toward morning rush hour. To the south a thunderhead rose, sheer and black. An early plane out of National Airport shone tiny against it. The trooper wrote on the clipboard, applying the letters with patient precision, like lipstick.

"Because of that taillight, Mr.... Sault is it? I might have spent my shift scraping your body off the concrete after a tractor-trailer drove right over you. I have done that job, Mr. Sault, but I just can't learn to like it." He was all wry paternity. He reminded Gordon of the big-jawed father figures who piloted rocket ships around the universe on

Saturday morning shows. No doubt he would have found the comparison flattering.

"Irregardless, I'm not going to cite you. I'm only going to issue this warning."

Gordon was willing to accept the cop as his penance for having laughed at the firemen, but this was unconscionable, all this hassle for a warning—the gratuitous mercy of it. He folded the warning around the license and registration.

"Fifty cents and a screwdriver, good buddy, and you won't have to talk to me again."

"I'm not your good buddy," Gordon said. "Don't call me your 'good buddy.'"

The trooper took it well. He was a regular human bomb of good will. The worst of it came when he laid his clipboard back on the seat and Gordon saw behind the sunglasses. He was shocked—the trooper had pale, unwrinkled eyes, he was younger than Gordon, a kid.

Gordon gave him the aviator's salute, thumb up, and said, "Keep 'em flying." He ambled back to the Toyota.

He slammed the door. "Preposterous little shit." He appeared to manipulate at least two dozen levers and switches in the process of starting the car.

"What," Ellen said sleepily, "did he want?"

"He issued me a warning for a broken taillight."

"It's not your fault the taillight was broken. It's not your car."

Gordon said nothing, just flogged the Toyota out to the passing lane and waited for Washington.

The thunderhead was either rising or moving closer, a great towering thing, dark, with little grey curtains in front of it, which were rain. Lightning lingered for delicate moments on the face of it. The light across the fields and trees was yellow. It gave the rush-hour traffic a furtive, scuttling quality. A flock of mourning doves lifted and settled and lifted again from a power line. Gordon steered against a gust of wind that shouldered the car toward the median. Cars coming the other way had their windshield wipers going. Thunder erupted, scouring through the quiet.

"It happens to me all the time," Ellen said. "They love me."

"It never happens to me."

"I bet it happens twice a month, they hassle me and hassle me."

"Why?"

"They're cops, I'm me. I don't know. Maybe they like my perfume. When I used to panhandle in Georgetown they'd walk past every dope dealer and scam artist in Washington to make sure they gave me my hard time for the day."

"You get busted a lot?"

"I talk my way out of it."

"You tell them who your daddy is?"

"Never. That just makes it worse."

Gordon thought about it. He never got hassled, rousted, sucker-punched, conned, double-crossed, two-timed, sand-bagged, fingered, Murphied, stiffed, badgered, flim-flammed, short-weighted, any of it. Life never canceled his stamp or punched his ticket. It let him pass, like a priest...

"Your money isn't good here, father"...

"I hate the police so much," Ellen said.

"It never happens to me."

"You're lucky," she said.

"I'm very lucky."

"I'm bad luck for people around me."

"So I can blame the cop on you?"

"Sure," she said. "Be my guest."

"What it is, though, I've always had the wrong kind of good luck. I had the kind of luck where you tell people you hate working for them, you tell women you don't love them, you tell the coach you don't give a fuck about football, and they never believe you. They don't even hear you. They start nodding at you and they say: 'Gordon, you can write your own ticket, you understand that, don't you, boy?' "

"Were you ever married?"

"Once. Once upon a time. We broke up last spring."

"That must have been hard."

"We're not enemies. I never hear from her. It was like an embarrassment she'd just as soon forget. I knew her for a year, it was like we were in a movie. We'd go down to Georgetown in our tennis whites and shop for copper crêpe pans. You know? I was lucky. Her daddy set me up in Senator Moakley's office; it turned out I was the only person on his staff who wasn't an alcoholic. Including him. It was like being in the Marines, except instead of having to stand formations we had to go to dinner parties. My wife was crazy about dinner parties. Everybody was very tough and crisp and they'd stare at you very hard when you talked, but you'd know all they were thinking about was what they were going to say next. They all wanted to be famous. They were all getting divorced and we couldn't figure out why till it was our turn, and then it just made sense. There was nothing to it."

"Maybe you didn't know how lucky you were."

"I knew. I've always known. I know exactly what it's worth, too. It's like being beautiful, right? You're beautiful, you know how it doesn't make life any easier. I had luck, charisma, some kind of light coming off me. I made the teams, I walked through Vietnam without a scratch, I always got the girl."

"Always?"

"The only women I ever wanted were women who picked me first. The same thing, I've never asked for a job I wanted. I always got offers. Life has been like endorsing checks."

"Why complain?"

"Because I don't feel real. I feel like I've been living in a fog. I wake up some mornings and the fog is in, I can't explain. I eat an orange for breakfast and the taste is like somebody's telling me about it over the phone. I go to the movies and all I see is colored light twitching around on a white screen. I say, now it's time to smile, now it's time to frown, but there's nothing happening inside. I feel like if somebody cut me open, there'd be nothing but dust, like an owl pellet."

"Are you in the fog now?"

"I'll say that much for this morning—I'm not in the fog."

"Good," she said modestly, bunching up her mouth and looking at the floor. Then: "I'm not sure I like you thinking that I picked you first."

It took Gordon a moment to retrieve the reference.

"I'm not sure you did."

"Sure, I did."

"What's the problem, then?"

"Most men never understand that's the way it works. They don't want to think it's true."

"You find me something true, I'll be more than glad to think it. That's what I figure my job is, nowadays."

"I wish that storm would hurry up and get here."

"They can hang for hours like that."

"It sets my teeth on edge."

Ellen appeared to examine the storm, then, with infinitely particulared fascination, as if she were thinking of buying it.

The light was the color of a bruise.

In the cars around them, commuters floated along with their thick morning faces, their coffee cups in the plastic holders on their dashboards, and the sweet dignity of animals all by themselves. Gordon envied them. He didn't want to be Somebody, he wanted to be Everyman. He wanted to be the commuters, the firemen, even the cop. But somehow he'd blown his chance. He didn't have the right. Was it because of Ellen? Craziness? Vietnam?

Living like a bum when he didn't have to?

When he looked back at Ellen her eyes were closed, and he was startled to see she was crying. Tears squeezed out from under her eyelids, slow and thick, like sap from a stump. She shook. Her face looked bloated and preposterous. He didn't understand. He disliked not understanding. It only lasted one blinding strobe of an instant, but Gordon hated her. Then he felt sorry for her because he'd hated her. He gripped her thigh. She pushed his hand away. He touched her neck, he stroked her hair. She flared both palms at him, a shoving gesture at the air—keep away from me.

"What can I do?" he said.

"It doesn't mean anything at all," she said. "I'm so sorry."

She held her eyes closed. She wiped the tears off her cheeks. She leaned her head against the headrest. After a while her breathing subsided to a slow rock. She was sleeping. She had cried herself to sleep. As suddenly as he'd hated her, Gordon saw she was beautiful, the real Ellen, Ur-Ellen. She had a wild, bony slant to her eyes. Her lips blossomed wide and pink—she poised them slightly, as if she were demonstrating some impossibly subtle vowel sound. She looked like a saint in midmiracle. She made Gordon feel ashamed of his finitude, and then of his lust, a damp pride swelling as he looked at her.

The wind jostled the Toyota. Raindrops slapped into the windshield. Then it was hailing, and traffic had to pull over to the shoulder, it was so heavy. Hailstones danced on the hood; they roared.

It was so violent it invoked claustrophobia, a distaste verging on panic. Ellen slept through it all.

*

The world, including Stuckey, Maryland, shivered green and tattered after the storm. Leaves littered Patapsco Avenue. Oily rainbows circled in puddles. There was a frantic quality to everything. A chain saw barked through fallen tree limbs. A little boy with hair cropped to the scalp, redneck style, clattered down the sidewalk, his feet cased in beer cans he'd stomped on till the ends curled around the soles of his sneakers.

The moment, the instant Gordon hustled the Toyota up the driveway, Dana stepped from the porch door. That was bad—she'd been waiting and watching. She stood in the grass—the hail had flattened it into cowlicks —and she smoked a cigarette with a jittery, lidless passivity.

"Your friend was here," she announced. She focused past Gordon to Ellen, who slept.

"What friend?"

"The one you told me about? Eddie?"

"I don't know," he said helplessly. "Older guy? Big shoulders?"

"He never said his name. He wants you to call him."

"Was it bad? You okay?"

He walked across the grass and kissed her. Her mouth felt hard. She was thoroughly preoccupied.

"He wants you to call him."

"But you're okay." He couldn't get her to look back at him.

"I'm just tired."

"How long ago was he here?"

"Hours. It was still dark."

"Was there anybody else with him?"

"Two people in his car. I couldn't see. That was the other thing—he said if you broke open the trunk of his car he wanted to know about it, if it was you."

"I didn't break open his trunk."

"He said if you didn't then somebody else did and you both have somebody else to worry about."

"I don't know what that means."

"You're supposed to call him."

"He didn't hurt you."

"He didn't have to hurt me. He waltzed in, he dumped everything out of my purse when I wouldn't tell him who I was, he searched the whole house."

"Did you think he was crazy? A psychopath?"

She glanced at him with eyes that suggested a permanent entry was being made in his karmic record. "Let's say he has an unusually clear set of priorities," she said.

"I'm supposed to call him."

"He said there was no reason you couldn't work together."

"Work together?"

"Why not? Nothing would've surprised me."

"I'm sorry. I'm truly sorry."

"I'm just tired," Dana said.

Dana looked at Ellen for a while, as if she were a painting from a period she'd never liked.

"She's just your type," she said.

"Fine, Dana. We're all tired."

Dana frowned sadly at the grass.

"Everything's royally fucked up," he said. He quailed with pity, he bristled with guilt. He felt dangerously exposed, standing in the middle of his front lawn on a Friday morning in August. Was it because of the thunder still slamming around behind them? Thoughts of Eddie? Ellen sitting ashen and oracular in the front seat of the Toyota? He decided they had to get out of there.

"Get your things. We can talk on the way into Georgetown."

"I've got my things," she said. She patted a cotton sack at her side. It was from India and it was covered with little mirrors that reflected nothing but the color of the August sky. They were like the glittery sensation Gordon got in the edges of his field of vision when he'd been this long without sleep.

He moved to the car. Dana waited while he opened Ellen's door.

Ellen was asleep with her head back, her long throat bare, her lips dried to a mat finish. He gripped the cage of her shoulder bones. She opened her eyes. They were a dense, pale blue, he discovered at this distance; they were opaque.

"Climb in back and sleep," he said.

"That's all right, I can ride back there," Dana said. Ellen flicked cool eyes to Dana, then back to Gordon. He realized he was supposed to decide. Women were at their worst when they wanted you to decide things, he thought. And now there were two of them.

"Get in back," he said. "Sleep."

Ellen got out of the car, pushed the front seat forward, and crouched into the back. She dusted the seat with her hand before she sat. She checked her face in the rearview mirror and shoved her fingers once through her hair. She ran the tip of her tongue over her lips with medicinal firmness.

"You must be tired," Dana said, buckling her seat belt.

"Well, yes," Ellen said. It meant nothing, it meant everything.

Gordon backed down the driveway. He had to brake to let the little kid with the beer cans on his sneakers clatter back the other way. Each step was a horrible baritone squeal. Then he turned the car onto Patapsco Avenue and accelerated for the strobe light that hung over Stuckey Highway. Once they were on the road, instinct told him, everything would work itself out, this being The American Truth: if it doesn't work, put it in a car and drive it somewhere else—a marriage, a kid with asthma, a memorized sales spiel for the *Encyclopaedia Britannica*.

"Get gone," Gordon said.

Rush hour on Stuckey Highway had thinned to midmorning lassitude: bulldozers chewed like old dogs at a field of red clay; a salesman walked tiny through a lot covered with mobile homes; a guy just off the graveyard shift at United Aero hacked away at a wire bucket of golf balls; there was an abandoned vegetable stand and an adult bookstore; pine trees shuddered in the monoxide wind of traffic; a woman in curlers shook her head no while she stood alone in a phone booth; there were empty-windowed morning houses with tents or badminton nets or birdbaths in their backyards...life went on and on. That's what was hard to take. Gordon had a taste for apocalypse and the long, slow mornings of America were always a disappointment.

He remembered the old Woody Guthrie song:

> *Take you riding in the car, car,*
> *Take you riding in the car.*

The heat was coming back. The first sweat droplet of the day completed the descent from his right armpit to his waistline.

"It's all my fault," Ellen said. "We took your car, we made you late to work..."

"No," Dana said. "That's the charm of Gordon. You never know what might happen next."

"Call in sick," Gordon said.

"I've got staff meeting."

"What if you were sick?"

"I'm not sick. I'm fine. I'm just tired. I'm not used to this."

"I'm sorry," Gordon said.

"I hope I never get used to it."

"I said I'm sorry."

"It's all my fault," Ellen said.

"Your friend Eddie is a very violent man, Gordon. It's

frightening to think that a man like that is a paradigm of sanity in this society."

"He's not my friend," Gordon said.

"No, she's right," Ellen said. "You're absolutely right, Dana. I couldn't agree more."

"You know him, too?" Dana said.

"He tried to kidnap me. He held me prisoner for five days."

"It sounds like he succeeded, then."

"I didn't know it was him, actually."

"It sounds complicated."

"Incredibly complicated," Ellen said. "I can't tell you how complicated. It's the worst thing that ever happened to me."

"It was in the news for a while," Dana said, "and then I lost track."

"I don't know what the news was saying. I never even thought to ask."

"You could read the back issues of the paper at the library. Your reputation has undergone some extraordinary manipulation by the media." This was Dana's social-science voice, her staff-meeting voice.

"Stop it, Dana," Gordon said.

"I want to hear," Ellen said.

"It's all overtones," Dana said. "Implications. They manage to give the impression that you're some kind of manipulative heiress type."

"That's not true," Ellen announced, three descending notes of integrity, disgust, and anger. She was all salt and starch now. Breeding would tell.

Dana turned to face her:

"I'm just the messenger bringing the bad news."

"I think," Gordon called back to Ellen, "that you'd do well both legally and emotionally not to talk about it."

"You're right," Ellen said.

"I'm not so sure," Dana said. "Really. I know what he's like when he gets like this."

"Oh shit," Gordon said.

"He tends to exaggerate. You do, Gordon, you spend your whole life reality testing."

The big-tired whine and clatter of a tow truck jostled past them on the right. Beyond it, the world looked like one huge gas station, a deserted continent of greasy asphalt, with a climate that was always August, dog days.

"I've always been a realist," Ellen said softly.

## Chapter 10

GEORGETOWN, TO ALL APPEARANCES, slept. Trees sagged in the heat, sunlight bounced off Volvo windshields in smeary glares that tracked them up P Street. It seemed like a memory. It seemed like something rendered useless by August, like a wool jacket with the pockets full of mothballs.

Georgetown: there was no one on the streets, not an undersecretary, a power broker, or a highly placed source; no wife with her face in subliminal panic beneath her perfect make-up, no seminarian in short-sleeved black shirt, no Central American press attaché with a briefcase full of cocaine. Georgetown was empty. On a porch, Gordon spotted a deeply tanned woman in a denim skirt sorting mail with scornful impatience—just back from the Vineyard for a funeral? Her husband's nervous breakdown?

Dana rode through it all with proprietary crankiness. She lived here. Ellen saw everything and nothing with her rich-girl's eyes. Gordon thought of it as a pornography of taste—it was too good, too real, too graphic.

"Perfectville," he said. It was all the reasons he lived in

Stuckey. There were bay windows, brick sidewalks, magnolia trees, and brass plaques, shined daily, reading TRADESMAN'S ENTRANCE. There were slate roofs, antique fire-company blazons over burglar-alarmed front doors, gas lamps lit all day, and serpentine walls, all of it looking a bit too precise, as if it were merely a scale model of a real Georgetown that was much larger, infinitely large, heaven itself.

Dana rented the attic apartment of a Victorian house otherwise given over to the offices of the Friends of the Environment. In election years it usually doubled as a campaign headquarters for one Kennedy or another. Gordon bounced the Toyota through an alley, and into a tiny, ailanthus-fringed parking lot in back. A Land Rover filled Dana's parking space. Inside the Rover, a college boy was licking envelopes. They were all college kids in August, they came to work here as summer interns. They held parties in the office every Friday night.

"Move it," Gordon yelled.

The kid waved cheerily. "Are you going out again soon?"

"It's a fucking private space."

The Rover started, after some application by the kid, who backed it up very slowly, like a trailer truck. Gordon sped into the space. He climbed out and stood squinting by a sapling that shook in the wind from an air conditioner. He squinted not so much at the glare of the morning but at the glare he felt inside his head, his disgust and anger at himself. All he was doing was making it easier for Ellen to rip people off, and harder for Dana not to. He was not being a good man.

Gordon and Ellen followed Dana up a back staircase. The top landing sported a potted Benjamin fig. Dana took a leaf between thumb and forefinger. "Poor thing," she said. The leaf was curled with thirst.

She held the door for them. She gave the impression they had to hurry inside; it was her hospital manner. They walked into a vista of sunlight and dead air, a gambrel ceiling, a color photograph of Dana in the sunlight, holding a white cat. The same cat watched them from a windowsill behind a couch. Dana turned on an air conditioner and vanished into the bathroom.

"This is a beautiful little apartment," Ellen whispered. "Are there a lot of apartments like this around here?"

"No," Gordon said.

Dana was the last of a serial coterie of bright young people to live here: Supreme Court clerks, White House Fellows, interns, public-interest types and journalists who handed the place down in a tangle of subleases, salad-days cachet, and locked suitcases stored in a crawl space. He might have described this to Ellen. Why did he think she wouldn't understand? And why, a moment later, when Ellen gathered the cat off the windowsill to hold it, was he alarmed that Dana would see her holding it? Ellen petted it and stooped to pour it to the floor. She rambled to a crayonned drawing framed over a bentwood rocker. It showed a pudgy little airplane pulling a banner which read, simply: THE SINGLE MOST IMPORTANT THING. It was signed "Mr. Wilgus."

"What's the single most important thing?" Ellen said.

"I don't know, it must be new," he said. "Her patients give her drawings."

"Why was she so mean to me in the car?" Ellen whispered.

"Because you piss her off."

"Why should I piss her off? What did I do to piss her off?"

"Think about it."

"It wasn't anything you didn't do, too."

"She was pissed off at me, too."

Dana came out of the bathroom.

"It's yours," she said to Ellen. "There's shampoo, conditioner..."

"Thank you."

Dana went into her bedroom and closed the door, after a flinty glance at Gordon. He heard Ellen throw the lock on the bathroom door. He'd made love to both women in less than eighteen hours and he wasn't allowed to see either of them naked. It just went to show you something. He couldn't think what.

He edged toward Dana's door. He waited for Ellen's shower to start.

"What's the single most important thing," he said, facing the door paneling as he talked.

"One of my clients gave it to me," her voice came back through the wood.

"That doesn't answer my question."

"I didn't think to ask."

"No, I did."

"I don't know, if that's what you mean."

"I was hoping to rouse a formerly playful spirit with a bit of facetiousness," he said. "But I see the error of my ways."

"Gordon, what have you gotten yourself into?"

He smelled his breath bouncing off the door stale and thick, like the ventilation from the back of a Chinese restaurant. "I'm tired of talking to the door."

"Well, come in."

He pushed her door back till it hit her bureau. He had always felt like an interloper in here. There was too much stuff—a brass bed crammed into a corner, an antique sewing machine, scientific papers and old Sunday newspaper sections piled on the floor, shoes lined up against the wall, pictures of her family—a busy, dusty, lonely place she liked so much it always made him jealous. He'd preferred making love on the living-room floor, on a pile of cushions and a sleeping bag, by the light of a television—*Saturday Night Live*—with the sound turned off, and Bobby Short singing Cole Porter on the underpowered stereo he'd always scorned as the phonographic equivalent of the classic too-small female ashtray. It had been lovely. Now he was losing it. He couldn't understand why.

She was standing before an oval mirror, brushing her black hair with defiant briskness.

"Close the door behind you," she said. He did. Quietly. He didn't want Ellen to hear. Realizing this, he was shamed by his gluttony. He wanted them both. He wanted them all. But he didn't want to lose Dana more than he wanted to win Ellen. When she turned from the mirror and she was smiling a tough, all-weather, long-range woman's smile at him, he knew it would be bad news.

"Face it. I tell my clients this. Need is a pretty poor basis for a relationship. If you need something, all it does is drive the price up. I don't *need* you, Gordon. If you vanished right now, I'd survive. But I care about you."

It was her therapeutic voice, but now it worked.

"I care about you but I don't think we should see each other for a while," she said. "For all I know, you've already decided to run off with Ellen, there, and I'm making a fool of myself saying it. But I don't care. I do care about you. I care enough that I almost got into a hair-pull with her in the car, I couldn't believe myself," she said, blushing. She tossed her hairbrush into her purse, then her keys. She mounted her sunglasses on top of her head, huge purposeful-looking lenses, as if she were bracing to do a spectroscopic analysis of the entire world. "But I do care about you and I want to say some things without you thinking that I'm only saying them out of jealousy or spite."

"You don't understand, Dana, I haven't even known her for one day..."

"Spare me, okay? There's something you have to get out of your system and I think..."

"What? What do you think is going on?"

"You and Ellen, for one," she said.

"What makes you think so?"

"She looks at me like she owns me."

"She looks at everything like she owns it."

"You wouldn't understand, it's a woman thing."

"Don't give me that woman-thing mumbo jumbo."

"Gordon, she's practically got come running down her leg."

Panicked that it might be true, he pictured it, a trail beneath her cutoffs. No, impossible.

"So let me finish," she was saying. "You're acting out, I don't know if it's Vietnam or you need a lot of intensive therapy or you want to break up with me. I don't know."

"Listen, one thing, Dana—Ellen is very young, she's a rich kid but I truly think that if you knew her you'd like her."

"Gordon, that's not worthy of you. I suppose you're going to tell me she really understands you, too."

"No," Gordon said. A gloom settled on his soul. She was right. There was no sense in arguing. She was on her turf. He didn't have any turf. That was the thing: when you went and pissed on your luck, threw away your breeding and otherwise tore up your own turf, you had to play on everybody else's.

"So what are these things you want to say to me, then?" he asked. His face tightened down to bone-bleak honesty.

"That. . .it will pass. If you let it." She tossed a comb into her purse. She lifted her wallet from inside it and dropped it back in.

"Maybe so," he said.

"How do you feel about this?"

"Helpless? Desolate?" he suggested. "I don't know whether I've been shot at and missed or shit at and hit."

She nodded. Her face bunched toward the puffy indignation that prefigures crying. She looked around the room as though she were leaving it for the last time.

"Everything in the room small enough to throw in that purse, you've already thrown in there," he said.

She brushed past him, tentative and determined. She

wore a brown cotton skirt, nubbly, like shantung, and a short-sleeved white blouse with little epaulets. Two gold bangles hung against a man's wrist watch. Outside, on the landing, she paused by the Benjamin fig. A pale, dead, late-morning light snagged in curls of peeling paint—the building was fashionably shabby.

"You can let yourself out."

"Thank you. Thank you for everything."

"Don't say that."

"I wanted to say it."

"Kiss goodbye."

It was a taut, foreign kiss, a kissing-game kiss. He watched her go downstairs until he could only hear her, a smug female tattoo of high heels, bracelets, stockings whistling together, car keys a-jingle, all business. Twelve hours ago she'd been arching her back, working her jaw, staring at him with glazed, frantic eyes, coming again and again.

What did she want, anyhow?

He heard Ellen's voice.

"She gone?"

Ellen stood before the bathroom door fully clothed—F. Scott Fitzgerald T-shirt and cutoffs. Her hair was wrapped in a towel, which made her face look blank, as if she wore glasses and had forgotten them.

"She is? Christ, I'm starved. You starved?"

"You can look in the refrigerator," he said. He was giving permission; it was a vestige of his rights here. Ellen did not seem to notice how depressed he was.

She bent inside the refrigerator door, hands braced on knees.

"Mangoes, papayas," she sang. She had a clear, sweet little voice.

"They wrote that song before you were born," Gordon said.

"That's all I know of it," she said. She tapped her toe as

the song went on in her head. She said: "Spinach greens, longhorn cheese, cottage cheese, cream cheese, OJ..."

He was wrong. She'd noticed. She was cheering him up, fluffing his psychic pillows.

"Eggs!" she said. "Watch this."

She carried an egg to the sink and cracked it at one end. She tossed back her head and poured it into her mouth. The yolk pulsed through the jagged hole. She swallowed.

"How about that?" she said. "I must've thrown up fifteen times one night in boarding school learning how to do that."

She bent into the refrigerator again and opened the vegetable drawers. "Wow, *more* mangoes. I *hate* mangoes. They're asymmetrical. I won't eat anything that's that asymmetrical."

"You must love pomegranates, then."

She looked at him with eyes that promised the real lowdown. "*Too* symmetrical," she said. "They're spooky."

She closed the refrigerator.

"I'm not hungry anymore. You going to take a shower?" she asked.

"I want to get out of here."

"Let's blow this pop stand," she said. "Wait while I dry my hair."

She went into the bathroom and reappeared in a cloud of hair and noise, rolling her head under dryer and hairbrush. He hoped it wouldn't take long. He felt exposed in this apartment, as he had on his lawn; a sense that Universal Superego was gnawing through the walls. And would devour them. It was all true, Gordon realized. It was terrifying. He had to get rid of Ellen, get back to work, make something of his life. He was driven by a sense that a clock had been started, that he only had so much time.

Then again, there was Ellen smiling and writhing in the bathroom door, the Dance of the Dryer. There was something so *clean* about Ellen. Her flesh had felt dry but oiled at the same time: rich. She let her leg loll and looked at her toes. She flexed them while she dried the hair at the back of her neck. Gordon watched her eyes go hard and soft while she wondered and made decisions and changed her mind, despair and appetite leaking out of her face like tatters of steam from a locomotive.

"You could borrow a change of underwear from Dana," he said.

She hooked the thumb of her hairbrush hand under her waistline and cocked her hip to reveal fawn-colored bikinis; plus her tidy navel and a meniscus of belly. "She left them hanging in there."

"They're your prize," he said. "For being so good."

"We could take a nap here."

"I want to get out of here."

"Did you have a fight?"

"None of your business."

"I tried my best to make friends with her. She gave me all that noise and I didn't say a thing. I thought Jewish people were supposed to be so warm and intimate and all."

"There's a distant thing that goes with it."

"You're not exactly Mr. Snuggle, yourself, you know."

"That's the nasty WASP in me. Inside every well-bred WASP is a redneck who wants to go crazy, stop brushing his teeth, and start shooting people."

"I did my best with her, really I did."

"No problem. We'd been trying to break up all summer."

When she'd combed out her brush, and sunk a slow-motion set shot of a puff of blonde hair in the bathroom wastebasket, and Gordon had eaten a mournful canister of blueberry yogurt, and washed the spoon, and put it away, he herded her toward the door.

"We have to go someplace," she said. "This city is alive with people looking for me."

"How could I forget?"

"It is."

"We'll figure it out."

She ran down the stairs ahead of him, quick hips loose inside her cutoffs.

On the next landing he heard a Xerox machine grunting out copies of something for the Friends of the Environment. It was just an ordinary Friday morning. All over Washington, secretaries watered plants, truck drivers humped weekend deliveries across sidewalks, clothing salesmen stared out windows at the heat. Life, ordinary life, was so beautiful. Why couldn't he have it? Ellen certainly did, it seemed. The world was hers, it was something she did what she wanted with. Merrily, merrily, I say unto you, life is but a dream.

The heat, humidity and glare caught them on the back steps. The Victorian brick of the house was radiant with it. Ailanthus leaves glittered. Parking lot pebbles glowed like gloomy jewels. The heat lifted them for a second, then seemed to physically slow them like the water trough the roller coaster hit in the amusement-park ride they advertised on television.

"LAMF," Ellen said.

"What?"

"Like a MotherFucker."

"Major heat."

"World class."

Their pupils pinned to a glaze. The sun on the backs of their necks had weight. They aimed for pools of shade, scuttling very slowly down the alley. At the end, Gordon looked at a cooked expanse of 31st Street. Cars hissed along the asphalt, which gave off a licorice smell.

"Where to?" Gordon asked. He didn't care. It was her problem. Let her solve it. Nothing he could do, except prove to her there was nothing he could do—he owed her that much; then twist away from the urge, the sweet, slow glandular surf that would tumble him into balling her a million more times. No. And leave. Head down to Sunny's

Surplus, pick up some freeze-dried chow, hitchhike back to Stuckey for his backpack, then out to the Shenandoah, be out there by twilight, easy. Quiet dusty light of the woods, the leaf-mold smell...and when he came back, he would know what he was going to do next, for the rest of his life.

"We can hide out in Montrose Park," she said.

"Sleep. Got to get some sleep."

They walked up brick-sidewalk slopes. Perfection reigned around them. Rained. Reined. Doors sealed against the heat. Chandeliers in empty dining rooms.

"I've lived in Washington all my life," Ellen said, "and now there's no one, absolutely no one, I could call."

"No," Gordon said, of himself. "Nobody comes to mind."

It was a frightening thought.

"Dana."

"Especially not Dana."

"Well..." Ellen said.

"We're outlaws. That doesn't go down well in this town."

"Desperadoes," Ellen said, floating each syllable into the air, *des-per-a-does*. She stopped. She composed her face. She looked at him with warning eyes: promise not to make fun of me. She sang as they walked, then; she sang just loudly enough to sustain the notes.

"Desperado, why don't you come to your senses, you been out riding fences for so long, now."

She sang it lick for lick like Linda Ronstadt, each requisite vibrato, fade, lag: "Desperado, you know you ain't gettin' younger. Your pain and your hunger are driving you home."

Everything seemed to ring with it, the magnolia leaves, the colonial yellow of a clapboard wall. She stared at him with happy eyes—she knew she was astonishing him.

"And freedom, oh freedom, that's just some people talkin'. Your prison is walkin' through this world all alone."

He imagined her sitting alone by the hour, listening to the

record, lifting the needle back to study each fillip. It was the measure of her loneliness and intensity that she'd learned the song that well.

"Better let somebody love you," she sang. She mouthed the line again in silence, because that was where the back-up chorus would have sung it on the record. Then she sang it aloud, paying out the last line: "Before...it's...too... late."

"Wow," he said.

She was so high with the triumph of it she couldn't look at him.

"Yeah," she said.

Her face was clear all the way down, like a stream.

"Let's get married," she said.

## Chapter 11

*J*OHN CANE WAVED his right hand in front of him like a blind man. He kicked one last time, and the hand found the pool gutter. The hand had big veins snaking around under wet black hair. It had beautiful rectangular nails, except for the little finger, which was a stump ending just below the knuckle in a shiny little purse of scar tissue.

He stood. Water fell away from him to the pool.

"We could find a suit to fit you, Eddie," he said. "We used to keep them in the pool house for guests, but then Ellen's crowd stopped wearing them entirely."

"Thanks," Eddie said. He shook his head no. The sun jittered on the water. Points of light stuck up all over the place like periscopes. The humidity made his suit feel tight. Sweat stung a cut he'd gotten shaving at Gerald and Gaia's.

"You swim, don't you? You know how."

"I never liked it."

"You know how many times I've used this pool this year?"

"I don't," Eddie said.

"Twice. Yesterday and today. I haven't got anything to do

but swim in it. I can't even get my own lawyers to have lunch with me. Everyone else is out of town."

The glare hurt Eddie's eyes. It used to be you wore a hat, keep the sun out of your eyes, buy a new Palm Beach coconut straw every May. Now you looked like an old-timer, wearing a hat.

"I drove over to Baltimore by myself to see the O's play the other night," Cane said. "When's the last time you saw a ball game?"

"Years."

"It still looks great—you walk in, it's all bright and green."

"The players look like kids to me now," Eddie said.

"I caught a foul ball. Belanger fouled one off and I caught it. Do you know anyone who wants a baseball? It's sitting on the hall table on your way out if you want it. I can't seem to give it away."

Eddie suspected Cane took some kind of pride in offering the baseball to people and being turned down. Rich guys.

Cane braced his hands in the gutter and hoisted himself to a seat on the side of the pool. A scatter of hair across the shoulders. Dago in the wood pile, thought Eddie. None of these rich guys know who their real father is. Cane gathered his feet under him. He touched his right hand to the ground, rocked forward, and stood. You wouldn't see many guys his age try that.

Water soaked into the flagstones and evaporated.

"I've talked to some people," Cane said. "This whole business is turning into a Chinese fire drill. Word is that every spook in the world is taking the first plane to Washington to check this thing out. The Pakistanis have supposedly got half their UN delegation on it, so naturally the Indians are in a tizzy. It's very big with the Libyans, the South Africans...DGI's in a swivet that the Miami right-wingers are going to turn into a nuclear power, the Israelis have the Mossad boys chasing a PLO contingent, and of course the last thing the Russians want is Yassir Arafat with a nuclear strike capability, so the KGB is supposed to be running around, looking for somebody to blackmail. I hear they're canceling vacations at the FBI, and naturally the CIA has to keep an eye on *them*..."

Cane sighed. It sounded like he was watching a movie of a favorite sunset from a vacation a long time ago.

"It's the most successful plan I ever came up with, absolutely textbook. Planting a rumor, good old basics. None of this business of trying to make Castro's beard fall out. It's the one thing that's worked since the U2 went down, and I'm being attacked for it. Isn't it wonderful?"

"Wonderful," Eddie said. You never knew what Cane was getting at.

"You sure you wouldn't like to take a dip?"

"I never liked it, John."

"We've got to get you out of the sun, then."

"Suit yourself." Heat clouded up from the flagstones like a gas. Eddie felt his hair lying hot on his scalp. He followed Cane under a green-and-white-striped awning. There was a power mower parked under there, a wrought-iron glass-topped table with no glass in it, and a stack of folded director's chairs. Cane unfolded two chairs with busy bewilderment, as if they were gadgets he'd just received in the mail. He seemed not to touch anything with more than his fingertips, even when he dusted off the seats of the chairs and set them perpendicular to each other.

"How about something cold to drink?" Cane said.

"I'm not thirsty," Eddie said, thinking: the bastard, he's treating me like an old man.

They sat.

"You look tired, Eddie."

"I work hard for a living. It's the only way I know how to do it."

"The last five days must have been tough."

"I've been chasing your daughter around the landscape. It's turning into a career."

"She's been trying to extort money from me. Is that any of your handiwork?" Cane's mouth hovered open, a hard smile like somebody snapping a towel in a locker room.

"Extort, I don't know. She's asking you for 100K, I know that much. It's the same 100K you were going to pay me if we'd done that thing last week. So extort, I don't know, it's a family matter what you call it."

"Would some of that money be yours if I gave it to her?"

"Let's say I've acted consistently in your interests."

Cane laughed. He had the sun behind him. He was a mass of shadows with drops of water catching the light around the edges.

"John, for one thing, for openers, your daughter blew the back of a guy's head off with a pistol last night."

Cane glanced poolward, at nothing. He gathered his lips and straightened them again, as if he were moving a toothpick an eighth of an inch to the left. Then he turned back into the shadows. He seemed to be waiting for Eddie to change his mind, or apologize. He seemed like he could wait all day.

"I can take care of it, John. That's what I came to tell you."

"What guy?"

"A guy. Nobody. You don't need to know."

"Gordon Sault?"

"Not Gordon Sault."

The big silence set in again. Behind Cane the pool settled into a calm that brimmed like a puddle of mercury.

"Given what I know of my daughter, this all seems unlikely in the extreme."

"There were three witnesses, John. There's a body. There's a room covered with blood, there's a pistol with her fingerprints on it."

"Where's Ellen?"

"She's out running around with your number-one boy, Gordon Sault."

Cane folded his hands behind his head. His arms framed two triangles of light from the pool. His biceps floated tense beneath the skin, which was just starting to turn satiny, toward an old man's skin.

"But her life's not in danger," he said.

"Not unless they bring back the death penalty in Maryland."

"What I need to do is talk to her."

"Another thing you should know, maybe you already know, she's convinced you want her dead, and also, she thinks you killed her mother. All right? That's what you're up against, you try talking to her."

Cane looked annoyed.

"Assuming everything is as you say it is, you're telling me that you can take care of it?"

"I can take care of it."

"What happens if we don't take care of it?"

"She's looking at a murder beef. You're looking at the whole can of worms, the whole last two weeks if she takes the stand."

"I expect this is going to cost me some money."

"Sure it is. This isn't some intelligence stunt with phony atom bombs, this is a hundred eighty pounds of guy starting to smell bad in this heat, blood all over the place."

"What place?"

Eddie pinched the bridge of his nose and felt the anger, a hurting behind his eyes like a rope burn or a paper cut, all the worse for being so petty.

"A place. A farmhouse out in the country where she was hiding out. Where she shot the guy."

"The police don't know about it yet."

"Not yet."

"How much money?"

"Think about it, John: what difference does it make, a guy with your kind of money and your daughter in the trouble she's in. If it makes a difference, I'd like to know about it, just personally, so I know what I'm sticking my neck out for, here. Because I don't have to. You should realize that."

Eddie's voice ricocheted off the flagstones, and died in the canvas awning. Beyond Cane the pool twinkled like the only living thing in view. The money: Eddie had known he'd be a prick on the money. Rich guys.

"Eddie, all I hear about from you is what's good for me. Tell me this: what's in it for you?"

"The money."

"What concerns me is that you're trying to settle some kind of score."

"The money, is all. I could tell you it was the principle of the thing but I decided, I made up my mind that on this one I was going strictly for the money."

"I can't help thinking there's something you aren't telling me."

"When did I ever bullshit you or anybody else, John? Pushing thirty years we've known each other, I can look back and I can say that anybody ever did business with me, he never came away saying he got screwed. That's one thing I've got at my age."

"Everything's okay at home—your wife."

"Janet," Eddie said. "She says to me sometimes, 'Give John Cane a call, he might have something for you again.' I say, 'I never asked anybody for a favor, I earned everything I got.' "

"She's still got the dogs? Didn't she raise Scotties?"

"You've got a memory."

"We go back a long way together, don't we?"

"Long way," Eddie said. He felt expansive. Cane could bullshit all he wanted, but Eddie knew he had the body, the farmhouse, the witnesses. It was just a matter of money.

"Well, we're alive and well, you and I," Cane said.

"We should count our blessings?"

"I think so. Why not?"

"I don't know why not, I never thought about it."

"Tell me this, is it some kind of money problem you're having right now?"

"Listen to that," Eddie said. "Me, I fucking work for a living. You get old in this line of work, you don't get a money problem, you get a work problem. You understand? You don't understand."

Cane waited.

"I've been working, I do shit for these religious cults and the Arabs, but lately, I'll be frank with you, I'm just as happy spending a day at The Company talking to the barmaid. She thinks I'm cute, I've got a twinkle in my eye. Fucking twinkle. I want a rest. But I'm broke. What have I got? I'm looking at some trailer park in Florida, spending my golden age counting up how many cigarettes I got left before the Social Security check comes every month. What the fuck, I deserve it, I voted for Franklin D. Roosevelt. But I'd like to finish up with more than that."

Eddie laughed. It was a dry, throat-clearing noise, the kind of laugh he might have laughed at something he thought of while he was riding alone in his car.

"Used to be, I would've been too embarrassed to talk all this shit, but when you get old you don't get embarrassed anymore, that's one thing I'll say for it. What I'm saying is, when you got nothing, you got nothing to lose. So you can take it or leave it, as far as I'm concerned. It's a job to me. I'd like the money, I wouldn't kid you about that, but it's your daughter, your life."

Cane looked at him for a long time. It was a trick he had, Eddie remembered.

"Exactly what are you proposing to do for this money?"

"There's a body, a murder weapon, witnesses."

"I'm not asking you to pull any rough stuff."

"I don't need to pull any rough stuff, I'll leave that to your daughter. She's mean as a fucking snake, John. You must be proud."

"Eddie, how much money are you talking about?"

"I'm talking 250K, a hundred in front by tonight."

Cane sprawled back and flung open his arms with amazement, almost relief. "Eddie, Eddie, Eddie. That's impossible."

"Fine, it's impossible," Eddie said. "Like I said, I'm only in it for the money."

Cane clapped his palms against his knees.

"Look at it from my point of view, Eddie. All you'll see is that same old extortion scheme, but for more money. I wasn't about to be muscled before, so why would you think I'd do it now?"

"You're sitting there and telling me you got too much honor, you're too decent a human being."

Cane gathered his mouth. Age lines exploded away from his lips. "Sure," he said.

"You can think anything you want, John, it's a free country."

Eddie saw that what seemed so tough about Cane was just stingy. What seemed boyish was actually a lethal indifference.

Cane had transparent brown eyes that appeared to squint and scrutinize even when they were wide open. All around them were bags and folds a sculptor might have smeared in clay with his thumbs. He would smile with his eyes or with his mouth but never both at the same time. He had a wide, snug mouth that never moved when he listened. He had hair that was no color at all, like the August sky over his swimming pool. He was an overgrown prep-school bully, Eddie saw, and he had fun at it. His eye whites and his fingernails glowed in the shadows. Cane was death itself. You could slow him down but you couldn't stop him.

"One thing, John. I know the difference between being a winner and being a decent human being."

"We'd all like to be both, wouldn't we?" Cane said instantly.

Eddie stood. Sweat collapsed down his chest. His damp shirt battened against his belly and the air was cool on it.

"I love my daughter," Cane said.

"I wish her all the luck in the world, myself. She's always had everything else."

"You don't understand," Cane said. "It's not like I have a choice."

Then Eddie understood that he had no choice either.

All Cane was scrambling for was an excuse for surrendering to his side of the inevitable. Wasn't everybody?

"You come back at nine tonight," Cane said. "I'll have the money."

"The hundred K," Eddie said.

"That's what you asked for."

"Cash."

"Nine o'clock."

Eddie walked across the terrace. The heat and humidity flattened everything out so he felt like he was walking into an overexposed photograph. He listened to his own footsteps. He tasted the foulness of his Dexedrined mouth. His hands shook. The swimming pool was still.

I should have taken the baseball, he said to himself. Maybe I could have found some kid to give it to.

# Chapter 12

BECAUSE THE NEW YORK mission had been nagging to know what they'd gotten for all the time and money Carlos had spent; because Carlos hated Farhad for being a coward; because it would be only an unlawful entry charge if they were caught; and because the high and manic note of boredom was whining like a frequency check in Carlos's back brain, he and Farhad broke in the door from Gerald and Gaia's garage.

Actually, it was Gaia's mother's garage, but Gaia's mother lived in Paris now.

The cellar was jammed to the ceiling with her belongings, which Gerald and Gaia had stored: bags, boxes, old furniture with the legs sticking in the air. There was a dank, dark summer smell.

Upstairs, a dog barked.

Carlos unfolded his knife. It was a quick movement, like somebody breaking the spine of a paperback book.

"Stay here," he told Farhad.

Farhad held Carlos's pistol, a Walther. He looked uncomfortable with it—he kept glancing at it.

Carlos said: "You search down here." There were clothing bags and sagging shelves, a whole midden heap of gentility—a bunch of model ships piled together like firewood; furs, a croquet set, a stack of dirty aquariums; luggage and linens bearing monograms from a couple of Gaia's mother's marriages.

"Look for documents, propaganda, journals..." Carlos said. "Look for any record of nuclear material—it is possible."

It wasn't possible, Farhad knew. There was no material, but believing in it made people happy: the politicians, the press, the mission in New York, the left, the right, Carlos. It was like a throwaway religion, use it once and by autumn there'd be something else to panic about. It was all-American. Farhad, in the wisdom of his corruption, understood this.

"We'll be here too long, it's dangerous," he complained. His face hung between eagerness and frustration, a fat man's sadness.

"Yes," Carlos said. Carlos didn't worry whether the material existed. His job was to look for it. Doubt was useless.

The dog barked again, overhead.

Carlos, with knife, walked to the stairs. Even as he climbed, dodging a stalled avalanche of dirty laundry, newspapers, tools, and a rusty hibachi, Carlos moved in a flat-footed, deliberate glide, as if seen moving from a huge distance, a grainy telescopic photograph, nobody, minding his own business.

Knife first, he pushed through the door at the top. It opened onto a hallway, which was shiny and empty, white walls and oak floor. There was nothing in it except the dog.

The dog stopped barking. It was Gerald and Gaia's Irish setter. It danced in place on the floor. Its toenails clicked. It watched Carlos shut the door behind him, and yawned. It bowed its spine and farted. It groveled toward him. It shuddered with delight. It loved him.

The setter ran ahead of him through the house, barking at nothing. The house was a perfection of near-emptiness, it was great and wooden oceans of floor bearing archipelagos of furniture, a button-tucked leather couch here, a café table and two Breuer chairs there, a coffee cup on the table, a cigarette butt in the saucer, even the butt burgeoning with simplicity.

It would always be midsomething here—morning, afternoon, passage—the lyrical austerity of a lull, as if somewhere there should be a ballet dancer massaging her calves.

The setter barked. The noise clattered off the walls.

Carlos paused to study huge photographs of Gerald and Gaia, big as windows, so big that their faces resolved out of the clouds of black-and-white grain only when he backed to the middle of the room. Gerald was pale, as white as the paper the photograph was printed on. He had colorless eyes and dark lips. Gaia was dark. Her mouth verged on a cringe of puzzlement. She peered through stray, kinky strands of hair.

Carlos turned away. The setter barked.

Room after empty room, the house was like this. It was supposed to represent an idea, he saw. This was the capitalist decadence, turning something as practical as a house into an idea. Mao had said: there are no ideal houses, only concrete houses. Carlos had read that in English before he knew English well, and he had pictured Mao's new China dotted with concrete—as in cement—houses.

He climbed to the second floor with a look of styptic distraction on his face. Each room was like a shrine to nothing in particular—Tibetan thangkas, beautiful reed baskets, Palestrina on a turntable, and Gaia's loom with a basket of rags by the stool in front. A half-woven rug trailed out the back. Perfect. It was a perfection which was the essence of fascism, he said to himself—a place that looked best with no people in it at all, an idea.

He followed the dog. The dog was his tour guide. It skidded around a corner and into a bedroom. A brass bed stood in the exact center of the room, like an altar. Overhead, a parachute hung from the ceiling to form a canopy. The dog leapt on the bed. It trembled and barked. Carlos lifted his knife. The knife looked like it had been streamlined for use at Mach 2 and above, all knurls and bevels with the blade raking up and out. He climbed on the bed with the dog. He reached up and sliced a foot-long hole in the parachute.

He poked his head through the hole. He looked up at a skylight, which showed part of a chimney and the August sky, scalding and dingy. There was nothing else there. The dog jammed its head between Carlos's legs and whined for attention.

Very slowly, the thought came to Carlos that with his head hidden in a parachute and an Irish setter writhing between his legs while he stood on a bed, he looked ridiculous. He climbed down. He grabbed the dog's collar and looked at the tags.

Its name was Savonarola. Carlos scratched Savonarola behind the ears. He closed his knife.

Meanwhile, and by contrast, Farhad was miserable in the cellar.

He pried through the gloom, looking for some order to things, but there wasn't any. There were upturned lampshades filled with galoshes, suitcases full of underwear, a clothing bag bulging with women's shoes, a deep sink stacked with photograph albums, all of it smelling of book dust, mothballs, and mucilage.

The only way to find anything in here would be to blow it all up.

Carlos would be angry at this attitude. But then, Carlos

was insane. Farhad was scared of him. Carlos never ate anything but Maalox. He sat absolutely still for hours in the car, never even stretched. But when you touched him he was hard as the side of a tire. He had once killed four policemen with five bullets in Amsterdam. Farhad knew that for a fact.

So what could Farhad do?

He did what every case-hardened fat man does when faced with the existential dilemma: he sat down, and he tried to think of what he'd like to eat.

It came to him that not only had Carlos refused to stop at, consecutively, the Mighty Midget Kitchen, a Ponderosa steak house, a McDonald's, a Bob's Big Boy, and even a 7-Eleven for coffee to go and a Moon Pie, but that he, Farhad, had neglected to search as likely a place as any in this cellar to hide things—the refrigerator. He arose with a sly sprightliness. He scuttled through a sway of silk dresses. The refrigerator stood next to an old sheet-metal stall shower. Farhad laid the pistol in the dust on top.

He had only to touch the door and it opened, way too fast, pushing against his hand. It had a sickening animation. Farhad flinched as the door swung wide; a foot extended past the jamb. The foot, or rather the shoe, which was spattered with something dull and sticky, like chocolate syrup, floated into the cellar air. Then it subsided to the floor, as if the man inside with his neck braced against the light bulb were going to stand up.

Farhad skittered backward, his fingers flared in a protest of innocence and amiability. He stared with woeful, wincing oh-no-not-again eyes. He saw the hair, the horny spikes of blood, and he recognized the man from the trunk of the Cadillac.

Lally was compressed into a position somewhere between fetal and ritual-burial. His eyes were nearly closed. His mouth hung open. Blood had dried on his teeth. His skin was the color of a sidewalk. A cold, fatty, not so much rancid as overripe smell caught Farhad in the back of the throat.

He stared and waited for the return of his courage, or appetite—they were the same. He stepped forward. He looked at the door to the garage, then the stairs Carlos would come back down. He steeled himself. He leaned into the refrigerator and with a squeamish deftness he ransacked Lally's pockets. He found: a swizzle stick reading, "The Company"; a Zippo lighter embossed with the seal of the Eighty-second Airborne Division; a pair of aviator sunglasses; and a wallet containing eleven dollars and a badge reading "Special Investigator."

He tried on the sunglasses. They were cold against his nose and the sides of his head. The lenses fogged. He decided to keep only the eleven dollars. As an afterthought he peeked in the freezer. It was stocked with nothing but color film and frozen yogurt. He hated yogurt. Looking at it made him hate being hungry, too. With Carlos he was always hungry and afraid. This was no way to live.

He squatted to lift the foot back into the refrigerator. It was cold, heavy, and stiff. It was the leg of a big, dead animal. He heaved against it, and listened for Carlos's footsteps overhead. Carlos would be angry if he couldn't get the foot back. Carlos was always angry, full of a kind of tired contempt that only served to enhance Farhad's self-pity when Carlos was right, and his gloating when he was wrong.

Farhad hated Carlos. He also hated Marxism, the Iranian Communists called Tudeh, plus Fatah and the Popular Front, the American Immigration and Naturalization Service, and the Iranian secret police, called SAVAK. He hated being at the mercy of all of them.

Once, years ago in a golden age, he'd had a valid visa as a predental major at Michigan State University. Then an oral-hygiene student named Eunice Brown had charged him with attempted rape. She was a Negro and he didn't think she'd mind, but she did, and he'd had to run away. He'd gone back to Iran, then Lebanon for training. But now he knew he hated Iran and world struggle and he loved America. He loved Las Vegas, each and every International House of Pancakes, pornography arcades, Qiana shirts, toilet seats sanitized for your protection, Baskin-Robbins' flavor of the month, Chinese restaurants where you could order drinks with little paper parasols stuck in them, and both sex and television of any description, from bondage to sermonette. He was supposed to hate America, its oppression and decadence, but he loved it with the desperation of the true gourmand. His only hope was in knowing that his mission was futile: which was to say bringing America, the imperialist bully, to its knees. Meanwhile, Carlos and the rest of the underground would keep him here.

He shoved Lally's shoe against the refrigerator wall and slammed the door. He heard the knee bump, inside. The door swung open. The foot floated out, riding on the wedge of light cast by the light bulb inside. He horsed the foot back up again. He slammed the door. It bounced. Farhad saw he was slamming it on a hand. The door left dents in the hand. He jammed the hand back in Lally's lap. The foot floated out. Farhad lunged for it. He was wrestling with a dead man, he couldn't believe it. His lips cringed back till the teeth were bare to the gums. He jammed the foot inside and leaned against the door, panting. Maybe if he waited long enough it would get stiff. He hated it, all of it, even the eleven dollars he'd stolen.

He heard a noise in the garage. An engine sighed. The windows in the door from the garage darkened. The three-pointed star of a cream-colored Mercedes eased into view, gentle as the foot.

Farhad's face writhed with anguish. He panted so hard he was almost yelping. His eyes twitched through the gloom, looking for a hiding place.

The stall shower: he tore back the curtain. Inside was a thigh-high slope of old linen napkins, sheets and tablecloths. The engine died. Two doors chunked shut.

He scrambled up the avalanche of linen until he could pull the curtain shut. He braced against the sheet-metal walls with his palms. The walls clattered. They sounded like the old-time radio sound effect for a thunderstorm. He had to balloon them out rigid to keep them still. He couldn't last very long like this.

The door from the garage opened. He heard the kiss of footsteps on the cement floor. They moved toward the stairs. Then, through the curtains, Farhad saw the light go on. The refrigerator had opened, the foot was taking another stroll.

A man's voice asked: "What in God's name?"

Farhad remembered the pistol—he'd left it on top of the refrigerator.

A woman gasped, a shrill sucking sound.

Not only were Farhad's arm muscles shuddering as he braced himself against the shower walls, but the hill of linens was giving way beneath him, a monogrammed landslide.

The man said again: "What in God's name?" He walked toward the refrigerator. The woman whispered, "Oh my God, Gerald," over and over, but Gerald didn't answer.

Farhad's arms were bonfires of lactic acid. The muscles were going spastic. He realized that if Gerald found the pistol, then himself, he was apt to get shot, an order of things he decided to pre-empt. He would attack. He would hunker down on his big thighs, then explode through the shower curtain. He hunkered down. The sheet-metal walls boomed and then the pile of linens skidded out from under him. Instead of exploding through the curtain he tripped on the sill and careened onto the floor.

Gaia screamed. Gerald flattened white-faced against the refrigerator door. Farhad scrambled into an alcove by the deep sink. He groped for some kind of weapon but there were only the photograph albums stacked in the sink. Gerald stared at him—his mouth was wrinkled into a tiny but wildly thoughtful O, a man he could deal with, Farhad saw.

Gaia screamed.

"No," Farhad pleaded. "I don't hurt anybody."

Gaia crouched and screamed as if she were screaming while she was giving birth to something: "Do something, Gerald, he'll kill us both."

"No, no, no," Farhad said.

"He'll kill us."

"I don't hurt anybody, everybody's okay, don't worry."

"Gerald," she screamed.

"Shuttup, Gaia," Gerald said. He floated pale eyes over Farhad.

"Gerald..."

"I don't hurt..."

"Shuttup, Gaia."

She was screaming at both of them now. Farhad's mistake was in watching Gerald, because by the time he realized she was rushing him, she was on him, a pudgy, birdlike, hairy blur that was all teeth and fingernails. Farhad cowered behind his forearms. "No, no," he said, still trying to coax Gerald into believing it was a terrible misunderstanding.

A fingernail tore the flesh all the way down the side of his nose, ripping it like the paper zipper on the top of a cereal box. He twitched away as the fingernail dug for his eyeball. He dove under her. He struggled for footing. She laced him across the back of the head with something that turned his mind into a flash of blackness, and then he was crawling while a set of hedge clippers spun away from him on the floor. He crawled. She bounced a tennis racket off his back, then a peach basket full of neckties, then caught him in the kidneys with a stack of nested flowerpots that smashed. She screamed for Gerald. Farhad rolled and scuttled for shelter under the clothing bags. He saw Gerald standing by the

**133**

refrigerator and shouting something to Gaia about a gun. Then Farhad saw Carlos, holding the pistol. He had both Gerald and Gaia in his field of fire.

"He's got a gun," Gerald shouted at her.

But Gaia was berserk. She flailed and thrashed. A shelf collapsed. Mason jars spun and smashed across the floor. Clothing bags fell in clouds of dust like bombed buildings. Farhad ran for the haven of Carlos and she attacked both of them. Cool as machinery, Carlos cracked Gaia across the cheekbone with the pistol. It made a wet, snapping sound.

She wailed with astonishment, shoved past Farhad and broke for the door to the garage. Farhad tackled her. He was amazed at how light she was when she fell, and how quick and strong when she leapt to her feet. He grabbed her dress. She kicked him in the face.

"She's crazy, crazy, crazy," Gerald said.

Carlos watched from behind his gun and said: "She has to stop."

Gaia lunged for a workbench and appeared to be trying to climb on top of it when Farhad threw himself on her. His lungs burned, his chest spasmed. It felt like he was breathing some inert gas, no oxygen at all. He couldn't imagine that anyone, much less Gaia, a woman, could fight this long. She twisted around beneath him and bit him in the chest, bit him deep. It terrified Farhad, like a snake bite.

Then Carlos was over her, his hands flying as he pinned her left arm with his gun hand. In the other, raised over his shoulder, the knife appeared as if it had been handed to him. Carlos's arm coiled. Gaia screamed and closed her eyes. He drove the knife into her throat, until it grated against her spine. He stepped away, one gentle step, like a matador. Gaia's hand reached for the handle of the knife, but she was dead before it got there. She slid to the floor and fell onto her side with a luggagey thump. Her eyes opened, wet and dead.

Carlos's body heaved. His face didn't move except for his

nostrils flaring. He stared at Gerald with tired curiosity. "I had to stop her," he said. "People would hear."

"Right," Gerald said. He spread his hands, like the baseball umpire's "safe" signal. "Right, right, right."

Blood streamed out of Farhad's hairline and down his face. He was still wincing. He was frantic with amazement.

There was a moment of silence, an audible truce among the three men, then they all looked at a noise on the stairs. The Irish setter, Savonarola, whined and wagged his tail.

"Right," Gerald said again. "I told her to cool it but everything's cool now, we can talk about this."

Savonarola barked. It was a ratchety scolding that meant he wasn't getting enough attention.

"No problem, nothing that we can't straighten out," Gerald said.

Carlos tore the cord out of the bottom of a Dresden lamp.

"I have to tie your hands," he explained.

Gerald's eyes racketed around like roulette balls when they first hit the wheel. "I can dig it, I know where you're coming from, I'd do the same myself. But you don't need to. You heard me tell her to stop it, you saw how I stayed cool, calm and collected, how I was on *your side*, man. And I'm still on your side. None of this shit belongs to me. This isn't my house. I can show you three sets of sterling silver flatware. You can back a truck up and take the Steinway, I'll help you..."

He was crying. Carlos stood behind him and tugged the lamp cord into knots in back of his crossed wrists.

"We're looking for Ellen Cane," Carlos said. He had an odd, quick accent, as if he pronounced all his consonants with the sides of his tongue.

"Oh my God, it's a political thing," Gerald said.

"Yes," Carlos said.

Sweat fell on the floor in front of Gerald's feet. He wore espadrilles. "It's a political thing, a fucking political thing. It had to happen, right? How could I be so stupid I didn't know that?" He sighed, a long, mournful watery noise of resignation. He looked up after a while, nodding at Carlos.

"You guys are pros, right? And we're amateurs. We've been acting like idiots from day one, you had us scoped all the way. You must've been laughing."

Carlos brushed the tears off Gerald's cheeks. Then he wiped his fingers on Gerald's shirt.

"Thank you, man. I get very emotional, you can understand it."

Carlos took the upper of two nested Hitchcock chairs, set it upright and motioned for Gerald to sit in it. With his hands tied behind him Gerald had to sit on the edge, leaning forward. He had pale blue eyes, almost water clear, and skin the color of poached fish. His heavy lips moved in a sleep-talk algebra as he calculated his situation.

"Don't lie to him," Farhad said.

"I wasn't lying, man."

"Just don't lie to him," Farhad said. It was a request, not advice. He devoutly wanted to see no more killing. Gaia had given them no choice but he felt bloated by it. It was a heinous alchemy and he understood now what it had worked in Carlos over the years—that surly charisma that suggested that the joke was constantly on the entire rest of the world.

"Lie? I'm the only guy who can help you guys. I know what you need to know and you're welcome to it," he said with a laugh that didn't quite make it out of his throat.

"Don't lie," Farhad said again. He sounded impassioned.

"I hear you."

Carlos squatted in front of him. The whole time he questioned him about Cane, Ellen, the farmhouse, Gordon Sault, Dana Poynter, Eddie Conchis, the blackmail scam, plutonium, gossip, addresses, all of it, Carlos stared at the fingertips of his right hand, which he worked together, rubbing, sifting, assaying. He looked like a farmer squatting to feel the soil, except that he was squatting in the bloody, broken-glass wreckage of the cellar, next to a woman crumpled up tiny with unshaven legs and a slot in her neck.

Savonarola whimpered on the stairs and whacked his tail against a riser.

Farhad leaned over the sink and patted his wounded scalp with cold water.

Gerald told Carlos everything, starting with Cane's reputation as John Kennedy's in-house privateer. He licked his lips and rocked back and forth. He recited names, dates, and addresses with plaintive fervor. He told the truth, only lying at the end, when he told Carlos what he wanted to hear.

"I think she knows where there's a stash of plutonium."

"Where do we find her?"

"With Gordon Sault, maybe. But I'll guarantee you she calls here before the day is out, looking for me, we wait long enough. I can set it all up for you, I'm the man you need."

Carlos arose. He looked at his watch. He looked at Farhad.

Suddenly his face was all diagonals—cheekbones, the corners of his mouth pulled tight, mustache, eyebrows, jaw flexing.

"I was telling you the truth," Gerald said, "and there's all kinds of shit I can do for you guys. I used to be very tight with the movement, I mean the people talking revolution, violent overthrow. I'm with you people."

Carlos blinked.

Farhad walked to the stairs and held Savonarola's collar, a gesture that seemed appropriate for reasons he didn't bother to analyze.

Carlos seized Gerald's hair and sliced his throat with one move. It made a kind of a munching sound.

Farhad didn't watch. Savonarola did. He barked.

## Chapter 13

*I*N MONTROSE PARK, on a grassy slope deserted in all this heat, beneath a mammoth tulip tree that shrouded him from the sky with a levee of branches thick as thighs—the sort of tree beneath which you'd expect to see Robin Hood and his Merry Men disporting themselves with quarterstaves, or people signing treaties or plighting troths—beneath this tree, in the thin, dry grass of August, Gordon awoke.

"You were having a nightmare," Ellen said.

"I know," he said. The dream was all-pervasive, like a quality of light between him and the tree overhead. But he couldn't remember it. When he moved, his body was stiff, rheumatic and disjointed. He'd slept for hours.

"You were groaning and shaking your head," she said. She sat next to him on the slope, hands clasped around knees, feet pigeon-toed in her sandals.

"Did you get any sleep?" Gordon said.

"I dozed a little. And I watched you. Like the song: someone to watch over you."

"Someone to watch over me." Gordon rolled onto his side and propped himself upright.

"It was the longest nightmare. You'd groan and shake your head and then you'd give out the saddest sigh, over and over." She seemed proud and pleased that he'd survived it and awakened.

He flicked sleep grit out of the corners of his eyes and ran his fingers through his hair. Down the hill, in the woods, cicadas worked in chronic crescendo. It was hot; hotter than noon; a sick brutal naptime of a Washington midafternoon.

It came back to him that she'd asked him to marry her, and he'd laughed and comforted her, as if she'd been trying to signal some woe through a figure of speech, as if saying "marry me" was like saying "back to the old drawing board," or "caught between the rock and the hard place." Or "Nagasaki," Gordon thought. That's what Lally had said after they worked him over: "If you can't take the heat, stay out of Nagasaki."

He touched her knee. It surprised him with warmth and give—its reality.

"I watched you sleep this morning during the hailstorm."

"Don't tell me," Ellen said. "I can just imagine."

"You looked beautiful."

"No. I can imagine what I looked like."

"You looked like you were about to say something incredibly beautiful, your lips were so nice and full with just the faintest pucker, as if any second you'd think of the word you were trying to say."

She shook her head. Her hair was so thick it hung in place while her face moved inside it.

"Beautiful," he said.

"Don't say that."

"Why not?"

"It's weird. Somebody tells you you're beautiful when you sleep, it's like being beautiful when you're dead. There's something evil about it."

"Don't worry. Evil's out of style. Nobody believes in evil anymore."

"What do you believe in?"

"Ignorance."

"No, evil is real, believe me. I had a roommate in boarding school who was a witch. She used to keep a cat under her bed and feed it nothing but onions. She called it the neon void."

"The cat?"

"The evil. Why would anybody name a cat 'The Neon Void'?"

"I knew a woman with a cat named 'W,'" Gordon said, watching the woods downhill. "She named it 'W' because it was so easy to spell."

A woman and a golden retriever floated behind the tree trunks.

"Pammy would say, 'I was thinking about the neon void,' and then it would be so weird in the room the hairs would lift off your arms, like when you wash paint off them with turpentine."

"This girl was your roommate?"

"She was my best friend. Poor Pammy. She had a miscarriage right there in the room and I was the only one there to help her. Then she went off to Stanford and her English professor killed himself and named her in the suicide note. So she quit and went to Morocco and ended up being married to a fisherman for a year. She used to write me letters about how he'd just beaten her."

Gordon pulled a blade of grass out of the ground, tore it lengthwise, and let the halves float to the ground. Sweat gathered in the pillows of his collarbones, and ran down his ribs from his armpits. He looked at her face and saw the sweat clustered behind her nostril wings and standing out on her brow like seed pearls. Her cheeks were red from her talking. Blonde down showed on them when the afternoon light came across her face.

"Maybe poor Pammy was just a masochist," he said. He noticed a sleep hard-on lingering, nothing to do with the conversation, but rather with the lethargic edge to things, a tone that suggested some exotic deal was being struck.

"She wasn't a masochist, she just kept meeting men who were sweet but they were so crazy. The English professor used to have her tie him up with *dental floss*. She'd wrap it all around his legs and chest and everything, and then he'd flex his muscles and try to break it. She said there'd be little cuts all over him."

"Poor Pammy," Gordon said. "Poor professor."

"That's what he wanted her to do, she didn't think it up."

"Imagine what she could have come up with if he'd asked her, though."

Downhill, the woman paced with acolyte slowness behind her golden retriever.

"Look," Ellen said. "They're wearing matching scarves."

Dog and woman alike, they each had red bandannas tied around their necks, like old-time railroad engineers. The woman also wore gloves, which were unbuttoned at the wrists, for a sporty effect, as if at any moment she might throw a stick for the dog or break into a little prize-winning gardening.

She looked very rich and very hot.

"I know her," Ellen said. "That's Claire Umstead."

Senator Umstead sat on the Intelligence Committee, Gordon recalled. "Maybe we'd better go somewhere else."

Ellen rolled onto her stomach, facing away from Claire Umstead and her dog.

"Where are we going to go?" she said.

"I don't know yet."

"We could always go get married," she said.

"You can't just go get married, you have to have a license."

"Gerald marries people without licenses. He just marries them."

141

"Then they aren't really married."

"They're really married if they believe they're really married," she said.

"Fine. You want to walk down to Gerald and Gaia's house and get married by him? Have Eddie Conchis as the best man and Gaia for the maid of honor?"

"We could drive to Las Vegas and get married in a wedding chapel. They're open twenty-four hours a day and they even rent wedding gowns. I went out there with Daddy one time when he was giving a speech, and I spent the whole time going to weddings. They're the only weddings I've ever seen where ministers wear sunglasses."

"We could resurrect my car from the woods and drive across the country."

"Or steal one!" she said. "I'm serious."

"How? How do you steal a car?"

"I don't know but it can't be very hard—people do it all the time. Don't you know how to steal cars?"

"I don't have any idea how to steal a car."

"I know how, I just don't know what you do."

"How."

"You hot-wire it," she said.

"Great, how do you hot-wire it?"

"That's what I mean, I don't know."

"She's looking at us," he said. He saw Claire Umstead bend from the waist to pick up a stick for the golden retriever. She rendered the bend genteel by lifting one foot rearward, toe out. She threw the stick. The retriever watched its flight and didn't move.

"She doesn't know me well enough to recognize me from the back," Ellen said.

"Good." He didn't really care. He was finding himself increasingly preoccupied. Ellen was like a whole new taste, or like a language in which he'd just been granted instant fluency. He was focused so hard on her that the rest of the world boomed uncensored through the peripheral vision of his psyche: the glitter of the heat, a fever spot on Ellen's right eyetooth, the echo of a motorcycle down on Rock Creek Parkway, the colorless sky, flakes of red polish on her big toenail, Claire Umstead strolling out of view with hands on hips, thumbs forward. There was a sense of caesura.

"We could rent a car," Ellen said. "A big air-conditioned one, and drive straight through."

"No credit card." he said. He scratched her back. His fingernails crawled down her vertebrae.

"That feels wonderful," she said. "We could rob a bank!"

"No getaway car."

"Take the bus. Those little black kids do it all the time."

"No gun."

"Right there, that's a mosquito bite. Gerald's got a gun. We could steal it. Higher."

"A good mosquito bite can be good for days of fun," Gordon said.

"I used to make *X*s in mine with my thumbnail. It's even better than taking off shoes that hurt."

"It's too late, the banks are closed. And tomorrow's Saturday."

"We'll stick up one of the drive-through tellers out in the 'burbs."

"No car."

Her head lay canted over her shoulder at him. Her eyes were a hard, empty blue, pure thought.

"We've got to do *something*."

"We don't have to commit a major felony."

"What difference does it make? We're in it this deep already."

"No, we're not," he said. "You can go home, I can go home, Gerald and Gaia and Eddie Conchis can go home, we can all go home and forget all about this."

"Oh sure," she said. She was angry. "We might get gunned down any minute by some crazy private eye, and every cop in Washington is looking for us, and every spook and Arab in the world thinks I know where atom bombs are, and I've got a father who'd feed me to the sharks. Sure. We can all just forget about this. What about George Metesky, and your boys with the electric cattle prods? All that stuff you told me yesterday—that's why I'm here."

"I wasn't lying to you."

"Why not? Everybody else does."

"I wasn't lying to you," he said. "I wanted you to come with me, but I wasn't lying to you."

"And here I am."

"Listen, I went home last night. I quit. I was heading down to the mountains with a backpack. Then you call me on the telephone."

"You're right," she said. "What can I say?"

"Don't say I was lying to you, is all."

"I didn't say that."

"You want to have a fight?"

"We do seem to argue a lot," she said. She stared at the grass, he stared at her: caesura. Through the woods came the sound of rush hour breathing down Rock Creek Parkway. The afternoon was dying; foul air, the sun burning like napalm over Rosslyn, the whole city defeated by it, an embarrassed, funereal hush.

"We've got to do something," he said. He stood. He stretched and held a roll call of his musculature.

She pouted at distance.

"Nobody's making you do anything," he said.

"I don't need any favors."

"Sure you do."

"You just told me yourself, we could all go home and forget about this."

He walked up the hill, wary with disgust. Her world was

144

all words, a story she told herself, and he hated her for believing she could afford to live like that. Fucking rich kids.

"Go," he said. "Help yourself."

She moved to him with shoulders hiked in contrition.

"Sorry," she said. "I've got a terrible temper."

"So do I," he said.

It was too hot to talk about it, to analyze and explain, the metaphysics of apology that pass for conversation when you're in love.

He touched her neck and kissed her mouth. She kissed him back. It was a long, careful, tender kiss. They swayed together in the sunshine. They hugged in the heat. The world was their oyster, they were the world's.

"You realize," he said, "I've never seen your breasts?"

"Yeah," she said.

They wandered toward R Street; past an American Holly, *Hex opaca* NATIVE, as the plaque said, and an Eastern White Pine, *Pinus strubus* INTRODUCED. Both trees were taking the heat badly. Leaves curled. Needles fell. The tennis courts were deserted. Across R Street, the shades in the Henry and Annie Hurt Home for the Blind were half-pulled.

"I don't know where we're going," he said, as they headed toward the middle of Georgetown. "But I know I don't have enough money if it's very far."

"I've got some stuff at Gerald and Gaia's."

"I could pawn my Rolex."

"I've got a Hasselblad with two lenses I bought for Gerald. And I know where they keep the key."

"Hasselblad. We could fly to Katmandu with a Hasselblad, we get any kind of price for it."

"I hate Katmandu. It's all dogs running around with sores on them."

"I didn't mean it literally."

"I'm sorry."

"Right now," Gordon said after a pedagogical pause,

"let's think about a motel with a pool and perfect air conditioning."

"And a shower. I would kill for a shower right now."

"Scalding hot, with the needle spray so hard that it makes your skin numb. Then you put the air conditioner on supercool and stand in front of it to dry off."

Ellen shuddered to think of it.

"Do the motel tonight," he said. "Feed up on prime ribs and all that good American chow, and tomorrow we duck down to Sunny's Surplus, put together some camping gear, and head out to the Blue Ridge. Picture this: a rock-lined mountain pool with water the color of an emerald and trout so tame they just hang there and look at you. The sunlight comes down through the trees and you can just sit there all day. Or get stoned. Cut out to my place and pick up my mushrooms before we go. You ever do mushrooms?"

"No."

"Everything gets clear. You know, *clear.*"

"That's what I want, all right."

"After I do mushrooms I feel like a Finnish scrubwoman has gone through my brain on her hands and knees with a brush and a pail of cold salt water."

Ellen pretended to be writing on a note pad.

"Don't...forget...mushrooms," she said.

On Q and P streets, it was rush hour. Traffic hissed and stalled. Men in horn-rimmed glasses and summer suits paced down the brick sidewalks in the pristine gait of the ruling class, as if their shoes were too small.

Outside a corner grocery on P Street, Ellen dialed Gerald and Gaia's number on a pay phone. She handed the receiver to Gordon. He stood in the dying sun and listened.

"Hi," Gerald's voice said, from an answering machine. "This is Kermit the Frog. If you'll leave your name and number..."

Ellen watched him hang up.

"Who was it?" she said.

"Kermit the Frog."

"He used to do: 'Hi, this is Godot. Hope I didn't keep you waiting.' "

"Any chance they're home and just not answering?"

"Gerald? The original hustler? Are you kidding? He spends all day on the phone with his rich old ladies, looking for dinner invitations."

"Let's reconnoiter."

An alley ran in back of Gerald and Gaia's house. It was an arroyo of chain link fence, empty garbage cans, and ailanthus and mulberry trees. A row of central-air-conditioning motors breathed emptily like a ward of life-support systems from which all the patients had been removed.

Gerald and Gaia's house was in the middle of the block. Gordon resisted a temptation to have them patrol opposite sides of the alley.

Ellen seized his arm. She stood on tiptoe.

"They got the car back!" she said. "That's what I drove to Stuckey in last night till I ran out of gas."

*

A cream-colored Mercedes convertible—solid, old-fashioned Nazi heft—was parked in a garage under the house, actually a kind of alcove under a sun porch with a trellis on one side.

"Maybe they came home since we called," Gordon said.

Ellen edged past the Mercedes, toward the cellar door. She reached into a hole where an I-beam entered the brick foundation. She braced with her other hand against the wall while she searched. The muscles in her calves danced.

"Key's gone," she said. "That would make sense. I threw their keys away last night so they used this one to get in."

147

"They could be in there right now."

"I don't know."

"How about I walk around front and ring the bell while you wait here?"

"How'll I know if you get in trouble?"

"What could you do if I did?"

"Run?"

"Sure," he said. "Anything bigger than small-arms fire, you run."

He was walking down the alley.

"I'll wait here," she said. "I wouldn't run."

As soon as he was out of sight she opened the door on the passenger side of the Mercedes. She looked in the glove compartment, ran her fingers along the juncture of the windshield and the dashboard, and checked under the seats in front, then in back, where she finally found a stray cigarette. She spotted a tear in the paper, by the filter. She ripped the filter off. She got out of the car, boosted herself onto the front fender, and set fire to the bushy end of the cigarette. She inhaled, and flinched at its strength. It was like in school: Pammy's cigarettes had always been torn, she recalled. It came from carrying them in her pants pocket, which was one of Pammy's mannish affectations.

The smoke hung in the humid air. She watched a smoke ring expand till it vanished. The nicotine tightened her corpuscles, raced her heart, and made her gut feel hollow, sensations that were indistinguishable from those induced by fear, heat exhaustion, or falling in love.

She pressed her lips together, then opened her mouth to make a popping noise. She swung a bare heel against the right front tire. She wondered if the rivets on the pockets of her cutoffs were scratching the paint. She decided she didn't care.

She wasn't scared of Gerald anymore. Or Gaia. Just like she wasn't scared of teachers, cops, next-door neighbors, or psychiatrists anymore. She wasn't scared that she'd killed

Lally, either—she was glad he was dead. She was scared of Eddie Conchis only when she thought of him as working for her father. She wasn't scared of Gordon, except when she thought he might leave her. In fact, she wanted, she needed to be more scared of him than she was.

She knew that from experience.

Pammy would tell her: "You're not selfish enough. You always make yourself the victim." Pammy didn't understand that she made herself the victim *because* she was selfish. And deeper than that, in her most private ego of all, Ellen knew it wasn't self-victimization at all, it was noblesse oblige. She patronized the universe. She fell in love with everything: taxi drivers, Vermont, her friends' parents, blind newspaper vendors, Elvis Presley, *Saturday Night Live,* Austin-Healeys, kids playing on a lawn after a wedding. They were all her children, her subjects. Especially men.

That way, she didn't have to trust men to love her back. Why bother? She charmed them. She made surrender an art. She gave them presents, stuff with an edge of fantasy to it: reflecting sunglasses, a white silk fighter pilot's scarf, cocaine. She proved to them that they were exactly who they wanted to be, and that it was good.

She had never let herself have an orgasm.

Pammy told her she hated men, but Ellen didn't notice Pammy had any kind of model love life. Pammy, Ellen had noticed, fell in love with men she felt sorry for, and when she left them, they were basket cases.

Pammy scared her, sometimes. Sometimes she hated Pammy.

It was all very complicated, the kind of thing you thought about while you smoked a cigarette and waited for a man to come back.

The tobacco was stale. It left a bitter spot on the back of her throat she couldn't wash away no matter how much she swallowed. Why did she smoke? She always felt worse afterward.

She thought about her father. He scared her. He scared her so much she was afraid to hate him.

Gordon reminded her of her father, a little. If she thought about it enough, it would be a lot: the way his eyes could go quick and flat, and a way of tensing his upper lip while he listened.

She dropped her cigarette onto the greasy concrete. She watched it burn for a while, then climbed down from the fender to step on it. Through the trellis on the side of the garage she saw a string of mourning doves settle on a phone wire. They came every August, like the fireflies came in June.

She wondered what was taking Gordon so long. She realized, suddenly, that there was no point in Gordon going around to the front door anyway, because without the key, they wouldn't be able to get in, front or back. So why had he gone, then? Had he left her? Quietly, leaning against the Mercedes, staring through the trellis, she panicked. It was the heat, it was fear, it was being in love, it didn't matter. She pictured him hiking toward Dupont Circle or hailing a cab, running after the first bus he saw. Why shouldn't he? He'd said as much himself, and she'd felt him wanting to leave her all day, ever since they got in Dana's car at the farm, after the fire.

She wanted to run down the alley and find him. Or walk away herself, leave him before she could know he'd left her. It had been too long. What if Gerald had opened the door, and now they were coming down through the cellar to get her, tie her up, give her back to her father, kill her?

By the time Gordon appeared she was angry at him. Then she was so relieved she felt sad.

"Nobody's home," he said. "I'm not even sure they've *been* home. I looked through their mail slot and there was mail on the floor. Also, no furniture. I couldn't see any furniture."

"That's Gerald's style," she said.

"No furniture."

"He calls it Zen Baroque."

"And a dog. An Irish setter."

"That's Savonarola."

"You okay? You stay cool back here while I was gone?" He joined her by the side of the Mercedes. He leaned against it and braced one foot on the trellis.

"You look like you had something you wanted to say to me," he said. "Or you look like you just got stoned, maybe."

"I was worried about you."

"I was worried about myself," he said. He gave the trellis a shake with his foot. It was woven with a couple of vines, a failed grape arbor. The grape leaves rattled. "I'm walking down the street out there, and I'm getting this feeling where everything is too clear, like the air is full of fog or smoke, but it's absolutely clear smoke, transparent. I'm checking out the parked cars, I'm eyeballing the people coming past, I'm freaking out on the reflections sliding along in the windows, and then I realize what I'm doing. I'm doing Vietnam. It's rush hour on an August afternoon in Georgetown...you know? And I'm doing Vietnam. It made me feel like an old man, like a dinosaur. I have this adaptive mechanism that's totally out of place. It made me feel like I was my father saying he wouldn't buy a Japanese TV set because they tried to kill him at Leyte Gulf."

He shook the trellis and brought his foot down.

"Once I got over that, I realized there was no point in me ringing the bell anyway, because we didn't have the keys, we can't get in."

"I thought of that after you left," she said.

"So what the hell, I rang it anyway." He looked proud of himself.

"Let's see if we can start the car," she said.

"The old hot-wiring fantasy."

"It's not my fault they didn't leave the keys where they're supposed to."

"But it's not your car."

"It's not their Hasselblad, either," she said.

"I understand now," he said. "You don't get mad, you get even."

"Listen, I put my life into their hands, and they almost got me killed. I respected Gerald as an artist and a teacher for the longest time, and now look. I got him that Hasselblad, I paid his fare to the Venice Biennale, round trip. I believed in him. He had me eating nothing but brown rice for three whole days once, so I'd be 'macrobiotically clear.' He used to make me read these books, *The Principles of Form* by G. Spencer Brown, and *Cosmic Consciousness* about how Balzac and all these people were really saints."

She pressed her lips together and popped them again. "See?" she said happily. "Then you came along and saved me from him."

He had the powerful feeling she was testing him. It was a cool burn in his gut. She was daring him, was what it was. In her presence, the simplest of gestures—walking, sleeping, a kiss—became acts of courage. She kept him racketing between paralysis and inspiration. He felt like a character in a movie. He felt very much in love.

"We could try," she was saying, her brow sweetly knit, as though she were worried about him.

"Try," he said.

"Hot-wiring it. It wouldn't hurt."

"You have to have wire to do the hot-wiring with," he said. He had no idea if it were true.

"Maybe there's some in the glove compartment."

"What if somebody sees us and calls the cops? The cops are always climbing up your back, remember?" He couldn't tell, himself, whether he was qualmish or just teasing. There didn't seem to be a functional difference between the two.

152

She propped her elbow on the canvas roof of the car. She leaned her head into her hand and scrutinized him again.

"Easy," she said quietly. "We'll just tell them we needed a nice, quiet place for me to go down on you."

He took her ear lobe between his thumb and forefinger, a bit of absent-minded fondling. Suddenly she seemed much smaller than he.

"Something about impending felonies that turns you on?" he said.

She blushed.

He reached out to bring her to him and kiss her, but she was way ahead of him, she was gone, nothing but air in front of him as she subsided to one knee. Her face was lit with the most benign and cheerful of curiosities. She popped the top button of his fly with her thumb and forefinger.

"Don't kneel," he whispered. He looked wildly around him. He fumbled for the door latch and opened it. He worked his way backward into the car and drew her after him by the hand. She was all catlike patience.

She closed the door behind her.

She put her forearm behind his neck and pulled him to her for a long, hard kiss, a clumsy kiss full of mutual insistence, a trust-me kiss. They sank into old maroon leather seats, they thumped against the wooden dashboard and the steering wheel. Gordon felt a grained seizure of wanting, as if all the particles of his flesh had been polarized like iron filings by a magnet, pure obedience. He sucked her tongue. She pressed her hand down the inside of his thigh. He edged back against the door on the driver's side and she followed, kissing him while she opened his fly and found him. Then she stopped.

She sat up. Crossing her arms, she worked her T-shirt over her head.

"Now you see them," she said. Then she slid back and bent to him.

He was astonished, and it was all so real, everything

153

around him: the aroma of the leather, the milky light on her back, the canvas top across the struts, the old smells of spilled champagne, lost compacts under the seats, and ashtrays all full, a closeness like a memory while she coaxed and gathered him.

There was lots of technique. She touched him only with her mouth; she stared up at him with sad eyes when she went deep—she was a gallery of X-rated reflexes. But he belonged to her. She'd made him totally powerful and totally helpless at the same time. It was like what he yearned for in his mad nostalgias for Vietnam, except it was here, now. He touched her hair. He realized he was thinking too much, and for a terrible moment it threatened to become ridiculous, the deliberate, industrious grotesquerie of it.

Later, he would guess that the noise he heard outside the car was just a rumble of thunder or a bird flying up to a nest in the rafters, or maybe nothing at all. But it startled him and he looked. When he looked back at Ellen he saw that her eyes had slid calflike toward the windshield too, to look. In just that instant of surprise his sensoria opened and not only the grotesque and the banal but all of Ellen and everything else was beautiful. He saw it, and it was everything to him.

He came and came.

She watched his face from under her slow blinking. He held his hand against her cheek. This was the way the world was supposed to be, as if he were hearing a song that took him back to a place, a feeling, a season, except that there was no song except for planes thundering up the Potomac River from National Airport, and for all its heat and madness, this was the season.

After a while, she sat up and looked away. She ran her fingers through her hair. Gordon held out his hands. She didn't see them, or she ignored them. She picked up her T-shirt and reached inside to find the sleeves with her hands.

"Wait," Gordon said. His voice sounded strange and new to him. He caught her breast in his palm. She looked at his hand, then his face. She smiled a puzzled smile. He shivered. It was a wave of psychic vertigo—there was no end of possessing her.

She shook the T-shirt over her head. He removed his hand. He felt oddly dissatisfied. Dissatisfaction merged with desire. He began to want her again.

She was looking through the windshield at the cellar door.

"Did you check to see if they left it open?" she said.

Gordon shook his head. He didn't want to talk.

"Neither did I."

He watched her. She slid out of the car. She strode around the front. He watched her move: wrists, ribs, her jaw clenching. He loved her quickness.

When the cellar door opened she turned, before she looked inside, to flash him a smile that was eerie with triumph.

## Chapter 14

DANA WAS KNEELING by the bathtub with a Tuffy pad and a can of Comet, scrubbing it down till it glowed, even taking a Q-tip and reaming out the little holes in the drain screen, and working on the chrome till it shone with little stars of light, like the cartoon glints they added to the cleanser commercials.

"I said beat it," she said to the cat. It was a white angora, a puff of light slinking between her legs. Actually, since she was naked, the cat felt nice, rubbing against her. But she knew she was going to throw, smash, pulp, shatter, or otherwise demolish something before the night was out; she was that mad; she'd done it before, and she didn't want to do it this time to the cat. Once, after she'd failed to seduce someone—the St. Elizabeths psychiatrist Gordon always referred to as "the beautiful Mordecai"—she had detonated an antique goose-down pillow against a windowsill and she'd picked feathers off her tongue for hours afterward.

She never felt better afterward, either.

She lifted the cat—named Dandelion—with a hand that

was wet enough to collapse the white fur. The cat draped itself over the hand. It was arrogantly limp. It purred, a phony bitch of a cat, a gangster of a cat, a spoiled brat of a cat. She admitted to herself that she wanted to heave it against the wall.

Ellen Cane, she thought, lowering the cat to the floor: bitch, gangster, brat, cat.

And thief.

That's why Dana was scrubbing the bathroom: because Ellen had stolen her fawn-colored Bloomingdale's panties out of it. Dana had searched through everything: the jumble of throwaway razors she hadn't thrown away; hair conditioner/shampoo/creme rinse bottles standing in a plastic choir; her jellaba/nightgown; the little blocks of Parfum Muguet; the Maroc Powder she'd bought solely for the drawing of the vexed baby cooling its bottom with a fan; a piece of fossilized slate she'd found one weekend with Gordon in the Adirondacks; the hair dryer Ellen had left on the sink.

No fawn-colored Bloomingdale's panties.

When she had become satisfied that Ellen Cane had in fact stolen the panties, she had felt disgusted, and the bathroom seemed unclean. She had taken off her clothes and spent the last hour in a clatter of water and the gritty whistling of cleanser, cleaning the Ellen out of here.

She felt the cat touch her thigh with its nose, a chilly punctuation mark.

"I'm warning you," she said.

She worked the Tuffy pad into the soap dish. The rind of old Ivory inside rose up with a pleasant foam.

Downstairs, at the offices of the Friends of the Environment, the summer interns were having their Friday night party. They played Jimmy Buffett records about the glamour of self-destruction in Key West, accompanied by a giddy clatter of marimbas.

It made her think of Gordon, which made her even angrier.

Not because he'd been a rotten, heedless pig, and not even because she'd urged him on all summer, by treating him like a child—worrying about him, pitying him, trying to make him clean up his act by getting him to worry about how much she worried about him, all those old Jewish-mother moves.

No. She'd been stupid and perverse, she admitted it. She'd hassled him endlessly—about living in Stuckey, having no ambition, or getting stoned to watch the mental patients roller-skate. She'd even tried hassling him about how horny he was, but he'd laughed a big WASP horselaugh and called her the Orgasm Queen and she blushed now to remember how she'd blushed then.

So she could have been angry at herself. She could have wrung herself dry by wondering why she'd been such a fool. But last night, in that nightmare with Eddie Conchis, she'd learned that self-blame is a luxury you can't afford sometimes. So the hell with it. Why not accept the fact that it was him she was mad at—and for letting her behave like that all summer. She knew it was a cop-out, and a particularly bad one, to blame a man for letting you behave badly, but that's the way things worked, sometimes. She was pissed off.

Why didn't he stand up to her? Why did he just lie there on the couch last night with his hurt foot and that little smile? Why did the men who needed good women the most always go for the bad ones?

She drove her fingernail into the corners of the soap dish to extirpate the last ninety-nine-and-forty-four-one-hundredths-percent-pure residue.

She remembered those first weekends together in May, making love all afternoon and then she'd lain on the bed and watched the spring clouds over the trees and everything was fine.

158

"Shit," she said. Best not think about that again. Best to expect a normal grief reaction and a bit of separation anxiety, watch for denial...

"Shit," she whispered again. The pain was really extraordinary.

It was such a waste, a man of Gordon's intelligence running around like some kind of outlaw. But the thing was that if he lived through it, he'd be way ahead of the beautiful Mordecais of this world—the bureaucrats of manhood, J. Alfred Prufrocks in sports cars. They were what she was supposed to have married: open, gentle, life-affirming men. But Gordon was a whole lot more laughs.

She dialed her Water Pik Shower Massage nozzle head to "fast massage" and blasted the last of the cleanser off the sides of the bathtub.

She heard footsteps on the stairs.

She was careful not to hope it was Gordon, although she noted that it would be typical for him not to call, just to show up expecting her to be here, alone.

She was pulling on a pair of jogging shorts and a sweat shirt when she heard the knock on the door.

"We've got a small emergency downstairs," a young man's voice said.

She opened the door. She looked with fond disappointment on a Friends of the Environment intern, a gangling kid with his glasses taped together in the middle and a huge Adam's apple bobbing over a Hawaiian shirt.

Dana said, "Yeah." She said it as if she were answering a question that hadn't been asked yet.

"I mean, not life and death," he said.

"No."

"Yeah." He sucked his teeth and frowned. "We were wondering, we're drinking margaritas and we ran out of lime juice, and we were wondering..."

"Close the door, you'll let the cat out."

The kid shambled backward.

"Try closing it with you inside," Dana said. "We'll see what I've got under the sink."

"Sure. Sorry. Yes."

"Somebody left a bunch of mixers under the sink, once."

"I'm sorry to put you to all this trouble," the kid said.

She could feel him looking at her ass as she strolled to the sink. It felt nicely radioactive, like when you're carrying about five hundred dollars in cash in your pocket.

"Lime juice," she said.

"Like Rose's. It doesn't have to be Rose's, I mean, it can be any kind of lime juice. Or lemon juice, one of those plastic squeeze bottles. Or real lemons, or real limes, too, for that matter..."

Dana hunkered by the doors under the sink. The light shone on her calves. She noted for perhaps the millionth time that she had terrific calves. She also noted, sadly, that the kid had taken off his taped glasses: sprucing up, coming on a little. It was nice to have someone think you were sexy, but it made her feel sad, too.

She marshaled a formation of odd-sized bottles on the kitchen floor: Angostura bitters, sweet vermouth, crème de menthe, Southern Comfort, Old Mr. Boston sloe gin, arak, ouzo, Kahlua, Tia Maria, the Akadama plum wine which, in the manner of his Marine Corps days in Okinawa, Gordon had always referred to as "Akadoo." They were all Gordon's, souvenirs from an exotic-drink binge early in the summer: piña coladas, Navy grog, Singapore slings, velvet hammers, sidecars, Manhattans, grasshoppers, brandy Alexanders, old-fashioneds.

"Triple Sec? Coconut milk?" Dana said with wistful pride, holding up the bottles for inspection.

"Thanks, but..."

She tossed both bottles into the garbage.

"Hey, don't waste it," the kid said.

Dana stood with a bottle of grenadine. "Don't you use this in margaritas?"

"Sunrises."

"Then what's a mimosa?" she asked. She lifted the grenadine as high as she could over the garbage.

"Champagne and orange juice?" the kid said.

"Bombs away."

A crash emanated from the garbage can.

"Listen..." the kid said.

"Bitters? You need any bitters?" She cocked her arm and flung the bitters straight down into the garbage. She studied the result with scientific detachment. "Ouzo? Cream sherry?" Both exploded with such a backblast of spray she flinched. "Mogen David 20/20? Southern Comfort?" They shattered and splashed on the wall.

"Listen," the kid said. "Some other time."

"Curaçao? Blackberry brandy? *The Mixologist's Encyclopedia*?" The encyclopedia fluttered through the air like a spastic bird.

"Listen," the kid said, backing through the door, nodding with wild politeness. "Sorry."

"If I find any lime juice," she called after him. "Or lemon juice..."

After a moment of pride at stampeding him out of the apartment, she was seized with loneliness. Way in the back of the cabinet she saw the paper bag of corks Gordon had said they should save to char and blacken their faces at Halloween. It was a poignant find that reminded her of a happy side of Gordon it would have been easier to forget.

She sponged off the wall behind the garbage can.

She didn't feel any better.

She felt so bad she couldn't even tell if she felt worse.

She loved him. She hated him. Why hadn't she kept after the beautiful Mordecai and settled down to a life of free-floating, as opposed to specific, anxiety?

She sank into the bentwood rocker and wished she had a cigarette. She wished she could cry. The cat sat just beyond arm's reach.

Downstairs, Jimmy Buffett sang the song about "wasting away again in Margaritaville."

She heard more footsteps on the stairs. But this time there were two of them walking up.

Maybe the Friends of the Environment feared for her sanity and were coming up to check. This possibility embarrassed her. She hurried to the door and opened it before they knocked. She wanted to show them she was all right.

Standing on the landing, atop the stairwell filled with marimba music, were two men she'd never seen. One of them was fat with a waist that puddled over a white plastic belt. The other was hard, with a mustache, and with a smile he seemed to accomplish consciously, at great effort, lifting his upper lip till the gum showed.

They looked Latin or Middle Eastern, it was hard to tell.

"We're looking for Gordon Sault," said the fat one, who wore a Band-Aid on the left side of his nose.

She was shaking her head before she answered, "He isn't here."

"Ahhh," said the one with the smile. "He said you could tell us where he is."

"He isn't here." Something about the smiler alarmed her—the way he stared into the middle of her head as if he'd spotted a horsefly there and planned to swat it for her, as a favor.

"We're friends of Gordon," he said.

"I know, but he isn't here."

"He left a number where we are supposed to call him if he isn't here, and he said we should ask if we could use your telephone."

She kicked left but it was too late: the cat had run past her into the hall. Smiler scooped it up. The cat purred.

"Animals love me," he said. "May we use your phone?" The cat lay on his forearm—he held it with level-eyed grace, like a swagger stick. His gums showed around his teeth. The fat one stood with his feet apart and his hands flared from his fat hips, watching her. There was a relentless chaos about them—not the disorder of mental patients, but something inexorable and biological, like decay. They may have been friends of Gordon's, and the cat, in fact, seemed to love Carlos, but Dana felt alarm crawl across her flesh. They were all wrong. They were death, and she knew it.

In an instant—a blur of two steps and a pirouette—she had dashed between them and she was standing on the stairs.

Smiler frowned at her. He was bewildered. The cat licked his hand.

"Make yourselves right at home," she said. She pointed to her open door, and then she was at the bottom of the stairs, running faster than she could have fallen. Her hip bumped the door to the offices of the Friends of the Environment as she turned the knob. She slammed the door behind her without looking back.

Smiler patted the cat, pursing his lips in little kisses. There was a smell of bitters, chocolate, and alcohol, and the sound of marimba music. After a while the kid with the Hawaiian shirt and the huge Adam's apple opened the door to look up at the landing, but all he saw was the cat, alone, preening.

## Chapter 15

*I*T TOOK TWENTY-FIVE MINUTES of hailing to get
a cab, down on M Street.

Ellen was coolly, relentlessly hysterical. Not screaming or
laughing or attacking him, but every time Gordon looked
away from hailing cabs, she'd be drifting away through the
Friday evening crowd, wandering into doorways he'd have
to lead her out of again, hoping nobody would notice that
look of desperate whimsy on her face.

Twenty-five minutes: it was a bad sign. It showed Gordon
that they looked nothing but wrong. Next thing, the police
would be rousting them.

"We're going to a motel out New York Avenue but I can't
remember the name of it," Gordon said when a cab finally
stopped. "I'll just tell you when we get there."

"You got to peh me in ahd-vahnce den, mon," the driver
said. He was an African. His face was filigreed with tribal
marks, bumpy extrusions that looked like they'd been
hammered into his skin from the inside.

"I don't have anything smaller than a twenty," Gordon
said.

164

The driver studied him in the rearview mirror. The whites of his eyes were yellowed.

"You gimme de twenty and I get change when we get deh."

Gordon gave it to him.

"I haven't got one red cent," Ellen said, it wasn't clear to whom, as the cab wedged into traffic. After a while, some tears came into her eyes but it wasn't full crying. It was more of a fight between her eyes to cry and her throat to choke it off. Sometimes she shook.

They drove insanely fast out through the twilight on New York Avenue, past souvenir stores and closed gas stations.

"It was my fault," Ellen said.

"Stop saying that. It isn't true."

"It's true. It's the only way it makes sense."

She was hysterical.

Back in the cellar, Gordon had walked her away from the two bodies and held her still till she could tell him where the gun was stashed. It was in the box frame in back of a gigantic photograph of Gerald. It was a little .25-caliber Browning, the kind ARVN lieutenants liked to carry in their pockets, a ladies' gun. Gordon had it in his jeans pocket, now. The hardest part had been getting Ellen out of the house. She'd wanted to bring the Irish setter with them. Her wrists were still red from Gordon holding them as he pulled her toward the door, saying no.

Now, sitting over the grind of the taxicab's drive train, bucketing out past railroad tracks and stoploads of people, Gordon saw that everything was possible. There were no rules. Everything in the world had equal weight: the driver's scars; Ellen's tears and shaking; a black man in a velvet slouch hat jaywalking across six lanes of traffic in slow, too-long steps; the Irish setter, the pistol; a Scot gas station; a Black Muslim woman looking strangely cool in white robes as she sat under a tree in a packed-dirt yard; the farmhouse fire, the lovemaking; an old man in a sailor hat shuffling

165

under a streetlight that had come on early and was wan in the last flames of sunset; Gerald's blood in the light from the empty refrigerator; a sense of endless summer, the feeling that it could go on indefinitely, ever more rampant and tropical; Gaia's open eyes; the halt and slide and mysterious crowds of a black neighborhood coming on toward night— bright faces, cars cutting around corners going where?

If the world had to end by either fire or ice, fire had a definite edge this evening.

He had gotten out of the Mercedes and followed her into the cellar. It was like a wall you walk into in the dark—no matter how warily you're walking it hits you with incredible force.

Stunned, Gordon had gotten very cool. Ellen had gotten hysterical. She was still hysterical. She was talking about finding a phone.

"I have to call him," she said. Her eyes were lidless— constant and frantic as a snake's.

"Don't call him till you know exactly why you're calling him."

"I'm calling him because it's the only way to make all of it stop is why."

Gordon took her hand. It was damp and bony.

"Just wait. Your daddy isn't going anywhere."

He was jealous not of Cane as much as of something adamant inside Ellen. It was something—whatever it was— she protected with her bravura knack for surrender, so you couldn't seize it by attacking, the way you could with Dana. With Dana you could put an end to things by arguing or coming or getting stoned. But with Ellen you only got in deeper.

"Take another Valium," he said.

"You keep telling me to take another Valium."

"I want you to feel better."

"I don't want to feel better."

166

He peered out New York Avenue. He was looking for a particular no-tell motel he remembered from his Capitol Hill days. One of his duties as an assistant to Senator Moakley had been to rescue the senator from motels like the ones out New York Avenue after hookers boosted his wallet and left him passed-out drunk and fully clothed with the shower running on him.

All the motels looked the same to him now. They glowered through the twilight with a black-light dinginess. No one swam in the swimming pools. No light shone through the rubberized curtains on the picture windows. It was the neon void.

"You don' know whah you go?" the driver said. The keloid bumps on his face stood out in swirls.

"I'll tell you which one."

"Ahsk de girl, mon. De girl always know."

"It isn't like that," Gordon said. He watched the driver check Ellen out in the mirror, and see that she looked too bedraggled for a hooker. Too crazed and tired. She wore the same cutoffs a lot of them were sporting that summer, but there was the F. Scott Fitzgerald T-shirt, and that terrific arrogance of naiveté that signaled a rich girl in a great deal of trouble. Or maybe all American women looked like hookers to the driver.

"That one," Gordon said. "With the blinking sign."

The driver pared down their speed with a thin, dry scream of worn brakes.

The motel was a glum horseshoe of balconies closed in by metal panels the colors of old pastel telephones. It looked like they were seeing it at the wrong time of day or season, like Coney Island in the winter, except that it also looked like it would look like that any time.

The driver got out of the cab and walked to a bulletproof window with a bulletproof carousel on which he placed the twenty-dollar bill and sent it circling inside. The room clerk made change and sent it spinning back. He was a fat young black man in a ruffled mariachi shirt. He looked preposterously serene.

They got out of the cab. Gordon paid off the driver, overtipping him. The room clerk buzzed the door open.

Gordon registered them in the name of Mr. and Mrs. Seton Modnar, which was Random Notes spelled backward, a fact he'd acquired one night from a particularly intense reading of that section of *Rolling Stone.*

On the way to the room he wrung a Coke out of a battered machine. Carbonation stung his mouth, hot and cold at the same time.

"You?" he said, offering it.

"No," Ellen said. "No, thank you."

They could see the Washington Monument from the balcony. It was dark now and two little red lights winked at the top, so close together they made it look cross-eyed.

The room had the dank, dead, linty smell of old air conditioning. Over the bed hung a cityscape painting made with paint rollers, one stripe for each skyscraper. There was a mirror across from the bed, and no light bulb in the lamp on the night table.

Ellen went into the bathroom, small-mouthed and resolute. She closed the door.

Gordon turned on the television. He reclined against the headboard of the bed with his boots hanging off the edge, Marine Corps style: no boots on the rack. He did not watch the television. *The Rockford Files* was on. It was the only light in the room.

He lifted his hand in the television light to see if it was shaking. The light twitched from color to color, but the hand floated still. The only tremor came from his pulse. He would have guessed he was shaking all over. This was a phenomenon he'd noticed years ago with marijuana. When he got stoned enough, which was very stoned, he'd feel himself trembling inside, as if his whole body were a set of jaws that clenched to keep from chattering. Lately, he'd noticed that these shakes would seize him not only when he smoked but when he drank, talked, hiked in the Shenandoah, or made love, all of it with a craving that had come to feed only on itself, getting hungrier and hungrier while the world around him brimmed on the verge of some amazing discovery when everything would be so obvious that it couldn't be explained.

He lay on the bed and tried to calm himself.

After a while he noticed that he was staring at himself in the mirror across the room. He saw himself slouched inside a cave of dead, cold, mirrored television light. He looked impatient. He looked resigned to desperation. He looked like a man who might laugh to himself at a lunch counter and then turn out to be unfriendly.

On the television James Garner said, "I just want you to run a couple of tag numbers for me, Dennis."

Gordon opened the drawer of the night table. He saw a paperback Bible with a cover illustration showing a family standing on a lawn, chatting with the radiant Christ, as if He'd stopped by to borrow a ladder on Saturday morning, and hung around to gossip. The family—Mom, Dad, Junior, and Sis—grinned as if they knew something Christ didn't. The message was that it was a fine thing to be part of that family. Ever since Sunday school Gordon had resisted that message, preferring instead to aspire to be Jesus Himself, especially in His more furious moments, blasting the fig tree or driving the Gadarene swine over the cliff. It was a desire Gordon found embarrassing to recall.

He closed the drawer. He thought about the shakes, and about craving.

He had craved everything. He'd tried everything. Like Mohammed, Gordon was willing to go to the mountain, but even when he was standing at the summit, the mountain would never quite come to him. Everything, as it happened, left him with a small cognitive itch, as if he'd forgotten something, as if he doubted something but couldn't think what it was.

He knew that Ellen had seen this from the moment she floated up to that screen door at the farmhouse; that she'd played on it, lingering just out of reach, giving him everything and nothing. She was unthought gesture, quick and amoral as a baby. She'd never had a second thought in her life. She had the wide pout of the rich, she had that thick hair she'd flung behind her neck to let him watch her go down on him. She had nipples pale as petals and a cunt he wanted his tongue to grovel in. She was so alive, and Gordon felt himself dying.

In a day and a half, he'd gotten mixed up in arson, auto theft, and three murders. Now he was in the cross hairs. The strange thing was that it felt good, the despair burning in him like a dark star. It felt good the way a hangover or getting fired can feel good. He felt free and ashamed at the same time. He'd found a feast of reality, but he was like a dog eating himself sick. He had no control. He'd become everything Dana accused him of being. Then again, he knew who he was. He could lounge on a motel bed and savor the taste of his own existence. He was a desperado. He was doomed, which is to say that his death would not be an accident, which in turn was to say that his life had meaning. It was a roundabout way to get to that conclusion, but he'd gotten there. He shook his shoulders like a man spoiling for a fight or a man who's just found out he's been right all these years after all. He felt lean and solid, the way he'd felt when he talked to Ellen the first time. He made the noise "Nnnnn" through his nose. He felt like he was smiling, but when he checked it in the mirror, he noticed with a pungent satisfaction that his face looked very, very tired.

He felt evil and liked it as only a good man can.

He retrieved his Coke from the floor, finished it, and crumpled the can.

He stared at the bathroom door. Ellen had been in there long enough to slash her wrists or eat all her Valium and be halfway dead by now. Then again, he'd never heard of anybody committing suicide out of fear. People who were afraid killed other people instead of themselves.

He heard water running, and the sound of teeth being brushed.

A bright baritone on the television sang: "When you're talking Ford you're talking Koons."

Ellen opened the bathroom door. She braced her hand on the jamb.

"I threw up," she said.

Gordon went to her, kissed her forehead, and led her back to the bed. Her skin was cool with sweat.

"After you took another Valium or before?"

"After," she said.

He sat cross-legged behind her on the bed and kneaded her shoulders.

"I already took enough Valium," she said. "I feel like my flesh is going to fall right off my bones."

She arched her spine, then sagged into a head-hanging slouch. She curled farther and farther away from him, until he couldn't reach her shoulders anymore. She turned her head, not to look at him, but to let him see her face while she spoke.

"I feel like I'm responsible, is what it is. I feel so guilty. I keep feeling I should've been there; like if I got the chance again I'd stay with Gerald and Gaia. Is that crazy?"

"It's crazy as hell," he said.

"Why do I feel so guilty?"

"Because you lived and they died."

"I keep seeing them, the way they looked when we walked in the cellar. I keep seeing them, and it's crazy, but I keep thinking I should've been there with them."

He gathered her against him. She was tense and skewed. She shook her head in a sad frenzy.

"When am I going to stop feeling like this?"

"When you get tired of it."

"I'm already tired of it."

Some things you never stopped feeling, no matter how tired of them you got. He'd lived a third of his life since he left Vietnam, and sometimes the longing to be back there would grab him like an old dog shaking a rat. It made no sense. Vietnam, for Gordon, had been a place where it was always either stark noon or the dark night of the soul, a dead planet, a grimy mosaic that could skid across his mind in an instant—the flies lifting and settling on the body bags down by the airfield; the ragged bang of grenades going off; the pointlessness and filth; the tiny mark on Sergeant Gomez's forehead, one piece of shrapnel the size of a fingernail paring, and he was dead; tracers drifting out and out and out through the night till they hit something and twitched skyward; the neon void of Tu Do Street in Saigon—the nightclubs packed with a panic of eye whites and bar-girls and slack GI faces crazed with all the astonishment they didn't have time for in the field; the dirty chalk taste of your mouth when the dysentery leached all the water out of it, or of the smoke when they burned out the shitters...and yet sometimes the nostalgia for Vietnam could seize him till he sucked his teeth and swore with the desire of it.

Death was the only absolution, if you kept thinking this way.

Insanity.

Ellen was saying: "It's just that I'm so scared."

"I'm scared too. It's nothing to worry about."

"I shouldn't have to feel like this."

"It keeps you careful."

"I shouldn't have to be careful."

"I didn't make the rules."

"What," she said, her voice grating with accusation. "What, do you like this?"

172

She lifted her T-shirt and dried her face. She took long, slow breaths.

"I'm sorry," she said. "You've been very kind."

Gordon said to himself: kind? He waited for her to turn so he could say it to her face:

"I'm your *lover*."

"Lovers don't have to be kind," she said. "They usually aren't."

"Let's be kind and let's be careful."

The corners of her mouth stretched grimly sideways till dimples appeared like parentheses around whatever it was she was thinking and not saying. She sat by him. He took her shoulders and kissed her hair, the thick, sweet smell of it.

"I have to call him," she said. "I'm going to tell him that it's all crazy and I want him to make it stop."

"Can you trust him?"

"I don't have any choice."

"Sure you do. You don't have to call him."

"But I want to call him," she said. "Why do you and I keep getting in these arguments?"

"I don't know," he said, but she wasn't listening. She was walking to the phone, as resolute as if it were ringing and she were going to answer it.

On the television, a rough, shiny terrain appeared. The announcer asked: "What happens when you freeze a pizza?"

Ellen dialed once and waited. "I'm trying to call out," she said into the receiver. She hung up. She said: "He says we have to use the pay phone down by the office."

Outside, on the balcony, the air and the darkness closed on them. They walked past a chambermaid who waited by a canvas bin of dirty sheets.

Gordon told her: "We're coming back."

Through a broken slat in a Venetian blind he glimpsed a family huddled around a TV set, sitting close enough that they touched each other. Further on, a huge, red-faced man

173

swaggered away from the vending machine bearing two cans of Sprite as if they were the heads of The Enemy.

The moon had lofted over the city. It was a rose-colored smear.

"Wolf moon," Gordon said.

"Don't," Ellen said.

The pay phone was mounted on the wall outside the office, where the room clerk perused a copy of the *National Enquirer*. Gordon mined coins from his pocket. They were warm and sticky. Ellen took them without speaking. Her lips flexed their way through a subliminal litany. Rehearsal? Prayer? Her face was sad, crucial, and distant. The dropping of money into the phone seemed an afterthought. Gordon wanted to tell her: don't tell him where we are, don't make any deals. . .but she was going away from him, as if in a few minutes' time she might dematerialize totally and he'd be left alone with the phone dangling and the moths banging around the red neon VACANCY sign.

She dialed. She appeared to read all the instructions posted on the coin box.

Then a tiny dynamo of a smile tightened her face—a fierce, glassy-eyed modesty. The intimacy of it made him feel squeamish. He heard her speak as he touched the handle to the office door. She sounded as casually apologetic as if she'd forgotten what her father had asked her to buy him at the drugstore, and she'd called back to find out what it was.

"Daddy," she said. "It's me."

Without looking up from the *Enquirer*, the room clerk buzzed Gordon inside.

He had a coffee-colored face full of irony and a sly sweetness. He said nothing, and he said it very conspicuously, wielding silence.

"I'm waiting for her to finish her call," Gordon said.

The room clerk leaned on the counter and mulled his

reading. There was a display case under the counter, but there was nothing in it but dusty glass shelves—no souvenir Washington Monument thermometers, no dishes featuring pictures of the president. The office had four walls but there was nothing on them either, except for a placard showing a cartooned man extending a hand in greeting over the motto: "Credit Makes Enemies—Let's Be Friends." On the window next to the phone, neon gas trembled candy-scarlet inside the glass tubes of the VACANCY sign.

Gordon studied the sign, the molecular jitter of the neon, and through it, Ellen's face leaning against the telephone. He saw her say the words "farmhouse burned down," and after a while, his name. When she said his name she looked at him through the window and the sign. Her face was bitter with bewilderment.

Gordon waited for the room clerk to say something. He began to wonder if he didn't have some wisdom to impart, some lowdown or handy hint. Instead, and without looking up, the room clerk flared a pale palm and caught a moth in midflight.

He carried the moth to the bulletproof carousel, released it, and spun it outside to freedom. It fluttered past Ellen's face, heading for the VACANCY sign. She was doing a lot of listening now. When she talked, she'd only get a few words out before her mouth would freeze in midphrase and she'd sag back into listening again. She frowned at Gordon through the plate glass.

"Seton Modnar."

Gordon looked at the clerk.

"Se-ton Mod-nar. We don't get that many Seton Modnars in here."

"I don't come in that often."

The room clerk's eyelids plummeted in cogitation. There was jail written all over him—the truncated wisdom, the coiled ease.

Outside, Ellen hung up the phone. She seemed to be listening for something very far away. She moved quickly toward the stairs to their balcony. Gordon darted outside.

The metal treads made a dull bell sound as they climbed, her metronome steps and him sprinting around her trying to make her stop and talk to him, tell him what had happened.

In the darkness, at the top, she pivoted and said: "He's going to kill me."

"He didn't tell you he was going to kill you, on the phone."

"He didn't have to tell me, I just know it."

"It's the kind of thing you don't want to guess wrong about."

"I'm not guessing, I know," she hissed. "He'll kill you too."

"Is he the one who killed Gerald and Gaia?"

"He says no. He says he didn't know anything about it."

She sighed and bore off for their room again. The slap of their footsteps clattered off the concrete.

"Why do you think he's going to kill you?"

"He killed my mother, didn't he?" she asked. "If he'd kill my mother he'd kill anybody." She stopped walking. He saw she wouldn't go one step further if she even suspected he doubted her. Her soul was a-writhe with some dogmatism he couldn't imagine, much less share. So he lied.

"I believe you."

"I don't think you believe me." She was clearly crazy with it.

"I believe that you believe what you're saying, but there's something you ought to think about, when you start saying your father is trying to kill us."

"What."

"What the next logical step is, if I know that somebody is trying to kill me, and he can do it, and I can't go to the police."

Behind her head, like an aura, was a swirl of city lights, tired in the summer night. It was a city of the plain out there, a chaos of empty streets, a bummer, a mirror of the certainty that he had deliberately put himself into a position where he could do nothing but evil. Wasn't that an unforgivable sin?

"You don't know what the fuck I'm talking about," he said.

"No."

"What I'm saying is, you make believe somebody's trying to kill me, and I know who it is, you better believe I'll try to kill him first."

"Are you saying we should try to kill my father?"

"Are you saying he's trying to kill us?" Halfway through the question, he knew he'd blown it: he'd dared her. She cocked her head back on her shoulders and looked at him as if he, not her father, were the hunter.

"Don't expect me to change my mind," she said.

"For once, don't be stubborn."

"*He killed my mother,*" she whispered.

It pleased him to believe that Cane might have people hunting them. It organized his life into tactics. It set a clock ticking. It gave him something to live—or die—for. It roused daydreams of himself holed up in the Shenandoah, say, leaping chamoislike from boulder to boulder, lowering the sights on some CIA hirelings Cane had sent after them. But he recognized the pleasure for the simple-minded temptation that it was.

He opened the door to their room. He felt like he'd come back to it after years of absence: *the bathroom door's still open,* he thought. *Rockford's on the TV.*

"Try and get some sleep," he said. "Take another Valium, you'll sleep like a baby."

"Where're you going?" She was scared.

"I've got to call Eddie Conchis," he said. "It's worth a call."

"Can I come with you?"

"Sure. I haven't got any secrets."

"Will you come back if I don't?"

"Where else am I going to go?"

"Come back," she said. "And be careful."

He kissed her frail flair of lips, like a little girl's.

He closed the door with infinite gentleness. He pocketed the key. He strolled down the balcony. He slapped the top of his right fist into his left palm to make a series of hollow cracking noises. Just as she was sure she'd won her father's murderous affections away from her mother, he knew he had finally brought his war home: the whole thing, like a souvenir.

He touched the Browning inside his pocket; a piss-ant little weapon but it would have to do.

## Chapter 16

*T*HE SHAFT. Up the old wazoo. Hang up your jock. Take your little red wagon and go home. A day late and a dollar short. Shot full of holes and shit out of luck. All that was left was to keep on keeping on, and Eddie was good at that, he'd been doing it all his life. Taking care of business, the details.

He humped another two bags of ice back from the freezer and heaved them up on the counter. The 7-Eleven was a cold island of fluorescent light. He snapped a brand-new ten-dollar bill from his wallet. Carrying brand-new money was one of Eddie's conceits, like driving a Cadillac and always having his shoes shined.

"Four bags of ice," the kid behind the register said.

"Right," Eddie said. Beneath the stubble, wrinkles and broken capillaries, his face jumped around like a forest when you look at the leaves to see if it's raining and it is.

He swung two of the bags off the counter, backed through the door, and carried them down the sidewalk to the Cadillac. He'd been doing this all day, ever since he dragged

Lally back out of Gerald and Gaia's cellar in the same Navajo rug they'd used to carry him inside.

It had been a very long day. Now, at the end of it, he sprang the broken lock with a screwdriver, glanced over each shoulder, then opened the trunk just wide enough to toss the ice inside. Water dripped under the car.

Belly up; high and dry; a beached whale: maybe he could get it past Cane, maybe Cane didn't know everything that had happened—Gerald and Gaia, the farmhouse burning down. What the fuck? Who the fuck? Why the fuck? It could have been anybody: Cuban right-wingers or Colonel Qaddafi's hit men or even rogue CIA. Or were they Mafia or crazy paranoid oilmen? Or had Gordon and Ellen done some kind of desperado flip-out, some kind of Bonnie and Clyde number? Or was it Cane's people? He'd find out if it was Cane's people soon enough.

He held his watch up to the last light. He knew what time it was within three minutes, but he wanted to get to Cane's precisely on the hour. It was the way he liked to do things, no mix-ups, nothing to argue about, either you're on time or you're not. The last two weeks, the world hadn't been like that. Eddie liked a clean, hard world and it had gone soft and dirty on him.

He walked back to the store. The light had faded, the night spreading out of the shadows under the parked cars, the crape myrtle bushes, the Goodwill Industries clothing bin, and the Coke machine glowing by the gas station. Three black kids on bikes twitched down the sidewalk in front of the stores. Eddie heard the tires hiss behind him as he went into the store.

"Don't forget your change," the clerk said.

After he stowed the last of the ice in the trunk, he stood with his face tilted toward a starless sky, looking as if he were trying to remember something that would make him cry or rage if it came to him. He took long breaths through his nose. He kept thinking he could smell the body in the trunk—bloated now till the neck shelved over the collar and the arms jammed the sleeves of the suit coat. Eddie wondered if he was only imagining the smell. He disliked that kind of wondering—thinking about thinking. It gave him a skidding, plunging, crazy feeling. In his life until today Eddie had never worried he'd go crazy, but then, he'd always dealt with reasonable people: gunrunners, dope dealers, junkies, informants—people who knew how to play cops and robbers, people who knew the odds and the price of things. Now he was the only one who knew, because he was the only person in it for the money, now that Gerald and Gaia were dead. Everybody else was in it for some kind of principle, and that, in Eddie's experience, was when lots of people started getting killed. Such as Gerald and Gaia.

Eddie had taken that very badly.

He had stopped in the middle of the cellar floor, and turned away and crossed himself. He had hauled Lally outside and thought he was going to have a heart attack getting him into the trunk. Then he'd realized he had no place to go, nothing to do, so on a hunch he'd driven back out to the farmhouse and that made it worse when he saw the chimney and a couple of charred beams standing in the pasture with the butterflies hovering over a black hole. He'd kept driving and buying ice for Lally. He'd driven back to Stuckey, then back past Cane's house, back past Gerald and Gaia's. His only chance was to find Ellen.

He'd seen miles of Maryland and Washington unreel in his rearview mirror, while he looked for whoever might be looking for him, or for Ellen. Whoever: it could have been anybody. If he'd found Ellen it would have changed everything, but he hadn't, and every hour when he'd called home Janet had said no, Gordon Sault hadn't called, nobody had called, nobody but him. By now, Janet was drunk and he didn't like to call anymore, and it was too late anyway, he was driving the Cadillac up Foxhall Road to Cane's house.

Streetlights bulged with glare in the humidity. Trees hung

tired and old. There was no shine or edge to anything, it was all clogged with dust and dampness. Everybody was good guys, everybody was bad guys. It wasn't Eddie's kind of world. But maybe he could finesse it through.

His heart pounded and his breath came short by the time he eased the Cadillac into Cane's driveway. It felt like he was having his blood pressure taken all over his body.

It was a big stone house with a slate roof and all the windows blazing with light.

Cane, Eddie thought to himself: I treated the guy like a fucking hero all these years and now look at me, squeezing him for money. No: I took a fucking all these years. I was a stand-up guy for John Cane, I covered up him killing his wife and didn't even ask for anything and now look: I have to crawl to get what's mine.

Either way, and for the first time in his life, Eddie felt deeply ashamed of himself.

When he saw the guy waiting inside the front door he should have been scared, but in fact the first thing that crossed Eddie's mind was that the car in Cane's garage was an Audi station wagon, a little foreign economy job. No wonder this country was going downhill, guys like Cane driving a roller skate like that. They all did now. Rich guys.

The next thing he noticed was that the guy in the door was a guy he knew from The Company, ex-FBI and Intertel, named Ted Dahl. Dahl was okay, you could talk to him. He was professional—the way he turned out the porch light before he stepped outside into a field of fire, and the way he kept the windshield between him and Eddie as he came across the lawn.

The Cadillac pulsed with the idle of the engine, a rough idle, have to get that fixed. Moths flew through the headlight beams. Dahl wiped the cobwebs off his face. It was that season when the spiders go crazy and the air is full of cobwebs at night.

He strolled to the car, braced a hand on the vinyl roof, leaned down and said: "Eddie Conchis."

"Ted."

So Cane knew about Gerald and Gaia and the farmhouse. Why else would he have hired Dahl for protection?

Dahl straightened up. He propped his hands at the small of his back.

"Cane's going to be coming out to talk to you. He wanted me to pat you down."

"That's bad faith on his part, you can tell him that."

"I can tell him, but it's the way it is, Eddie. You're fucking with the fucker, on this one."

"Cane," Eddie said.

"You know how it is."

"I should know. I should know, all right."

"I can just reach inside and pat you down."

"Tell me one time I shot anybody. Tell me one time I *hurt* anybody bad, you can't do it. Tell me one time I *bullshitted* somebody when I wasn't working under cover, name me the lie I lied and I'll go home. You can't do it."

"I can't do it," Dahl said. "I wouldn't argue."

"I'm an old man, I been going at this too long to make an asshole out of myself."

"So, fine. You let me pat you down, I bring Cane out here, we all do our business and go home."

"You tell him I might get pissed off. Tell him that. No, tell him, he doesn't get his ass out here in one minute, I'm leaving, I don't need this."

"You know what they say, Eddie. If you can't take the heat..."

"I know, stay out of Nagasaki. I heard it about a hundred times already."

Dahl pondered the situation with sad frustration.

"This is going nowhere," he said.

Cars hissed down Foxhall Road. Each one was a dying

breath of a noise. Crickets and locusts roared in the lawn and the trees.

"Tell him he's got one minute."

"I can't guarantee anything," Dahl said. He walked through the garage past the Audi and opened a door into the house.

Eddie looked at his watch but it was just ceremony. He couldn't see the sweep second hand without his glasses. He waited. Eddie shut off his engine and killed the lights. The dark and silence rushed in, and put the crickets, locusts, and the blazing house lights at a distance.

He knew he could twist the key, back down the driveway, dump Lally and the pistol in the river, go home and get some sleep. Find a dog show someplace out in the country and take Janet. Feed her up at the kind of restaurant where they have a stream running over a mill wheel outside. Forget about Florida, one last run, and getting old. That was all bullshit. You had to live one day at a time. He could do it. It was that easy. He saw it all.

It was too late. Dahl was leading Cane into the garage from a door in the back. Cane picked his way past the Audi. He looked like somebody had just taken off his blindfold and his eyes hadn't adjusted to the light. He looked intense and distracted. He followed Dahl up the driveway, no coat, no tie, a rumpled white shirt and his black toe-cap shoes.

Dahl led him up to Eddie and patted the Cadillac on the vinyl roof the way you pat a horse you're putting somebody up on. Then he backed away and folded his arms.

Cane glared down at Eddie.

He had long rectangular teeth, nine rectangular fingernails that showed no cuticle at all, and a rectangular stump of a right pinky. He had a long rectangle of a jaw, and a little rectangle of reflected light in his left eye. Eddie looked at him—all rectangles. That was Cane all over.

He said: "For the love of God, Eddie."

184

Eddie said: "What."

Cane looked at Dahl, then showed Eddie his rectangular teeth again. Sweat bloomed like mold in the shadow of his whiskers.

"What," Eddie said.

"You killed them."

"Not me."

"Eddie, you killed those two friends of hers, the witnesses."

"Not me, pal."

"I never told you to kill them when we talked this morning."

"That's good, John, because, you want to be frank, I drove up here thinking maybe you killed them."

"Ellen called me. She told me about them, and the farmhouse burning. She sounded terrified."

"Sure she did. She's mixed up with three murders and arson, and she thinks her father is trying to kill her."

"She didn't say anything about me, when she called. In fact, I got a powerful impression that she'd much prefer to be home and safe."

"She told you that."

"Not in so many words. But I'm her father, I can hear what she's trying to say."

"You think maybe she killed those two and burned down the house herself?"

"It wouldn't make any difference."

Eddie didn't understand this, but he let it slide.

Cane squinted. He rocked back on his heels. He tapped the soles of his black toe-cap shoes on the driveway. Eddie didn't like it. It was falling apart: the moment, the plan, his life, the world, everything.

"The money, John."

"That's why you're here," Cane said. "But I think you can also appreciate that as long as I even suspect you killed those two, it would be suicidal of me to give you that money. I'd virtually be asking to be indicted along with you, for hiring you to get rid of them."

"Nobody's indicting Eddie Conchis, John."

"Assuming it wasn't you, then..."

"You can assume that."

"...you came to me today offering to solve a problem that was already solved—the witnesses and evidence. You told me I needed a service I didn't need, and charged me an extraordinary price for it—I think even you would grant me that much."

"Fucking amazing." He looked up at Cane and for the first time he saw a face that was now and always had been pinched and stricken—the face of a man who prays that whatever capital he has—financial, moral, political, or personal—won't run out before he dies. For all his charm, Cane was a desperate man.

"I'll be willing to pay you a fee for the last two weeks and call it even."

"Call it even? John, I don't owe you, you owe me."

"You've been blackmailing me for nothing, Eddie."

"Take a look at nothing." Eddie opened the door so fast he caught Cane in the knees. He uncoiled from the car. He spat. "You tell Dahl to wait in the house, we got some private business here, we're gonna look at nothing, John." He strode to the rear of the Cadillac. He crouched over the trunk like a quarterback over a center. He popped open the broken lock. He caught the trunk lid before it rose.

Cane looked back at Dahl.

Dahl shrugged. It was the official hard-guy's shrug, the shrug that said if Cane wanted to get himself into a jam like this, he could get himself out, he was beyond advice. "Judgment call," he said.

"Take a break," Cane said.

Dahl withdrew into the garage.

Eddie let the trunk rise. He reached inside, grabbed

Lally's hair, and hoisted the head up through the ice cubes, which made a crushing noise. He twisted Lally's head around so Cane could see the back. The back was a big, wet, crimson hole with hair stuck in it.

"You're nobody in this town anymore," Eddie said, "and you're trying to fuck over me like you're somebody. Your people are dead and gone. Jack Kennedy, Bobby. . .Maybe you could get Arthur Schlesinger out here in his bow tie and have him talk about what it all means to history."

"You've made your point."

"John, you got a daughter who thinks it's going to happen one of three ways: she goes to jail for blowing the back of this guy's head off, here. Or you kill her because to stay out of jail she'd have to burn you for perjury, maybe burn both of us for attempted kidnaping. Or you come through with enough money that she can stay gone for a long time."

"She knows I won't let her blackmail me."

"She thinks you killed her mother, so she figures you'll kill her. She wants to live, and she doesn't want to go to jail, so she has to get that money."

"I won't let her blackmail me."

"Then you got me, with a stack of tapes you had me make of your wife doing Jack Kennedy. And then the night we put her under the bridge together."

"Nobody's going to believe those tapes," Cane said, in a petulant bark. "Nobody's going to believe you either. The FBI would look at Eddie Conchis and see just another broken-down ex-spook trying to shake somebody down."

"Fine. But put it together with the plutonium scam, a phony kidnaping, perjury, arson, and three people dead, four including Carol, and it's a hell of a package."

"It's a package if you get Ellen to cooperate with you. But you already tried it, and she wasn't that venal or easily scared. It didn't work. She ran away from you."

"That's because she thought I was working *for* you, John, not against you."

"I don't think she'll go along with you," Cane said.

"I think she'll jump at the chance."

"You don't even know where she is."

"I think I'll find her. I think Gordon Sault has enough brains he's going to get hold of me, and then him, me and Ellen are going to put together a package that'll make John Cane the biggest thing since Watergate."

Cane creased his brow. He folded the furrows between his eyes. Then he worked out the long horizontal lines that ran from temple to temple. It was like a calisthenic.

"When you find some witnesses who aren't dead and you can put it all together, Eddie, then give me a call."

"You don't understand, John—she thinks you're going to kill her."

"No, she doesn't. Not really. Her problem is that she thinks I'm God. She's too old for that, but she does. It's her biggest problem." Cane tossed a bouquet of long, rectangular fingers at Lally's body rotting amid the ice, the knifed spare tire, and a bag of golf clubs. He turned to walk away.

"Here's the gun she shot him with, John." Eddie pulled it from his belt. He jacked a shell into the chamber. The slide slapped forward and left the hammer back, a little piece of bare metal that shone in the lights from all over the house, a thousand windows, it seemed like.

He stood behind the trunk so that Dahl couldn't see him.

"Are you going to shoot me?" Cane braced his shoulders and set his face into a ghastly pleasantness, as if he were about to have his picture taken. "Shoot me," he said.

"You want to say that again?" Eddie asked. It was all he could think of to say.

Cane walked away from him, across the lawn. The only thing that surprised Eddie was the fact that he'd stop and turn around to say it: he said it with the kind of face you remember as a smile, but it wasn't a smile at all.

"No."

# Chapter 17

$I$T FELT TO GORDON the way American cities feel the first time you drive through them in the middle of the night—a deserted sprawl of parks and streets, a boarded-up shoeshine stand, a bus wallowing past with its empty windows—the stoplights blink yellow for miles and the city is whatever you want it to be: snug or crazy, home for everybody, a repose, Detroit, New York, Albuquerque...

"Those blue lights," Eddie said. The Cadillac slid downtown on New York Avenue. Gordon looked from his window, over a guardrail at the mercury arc lamps at the bottom of a slope.

"They look like they're holding a ball game down there, but then I realized what time it is," Eddie said. "You get so you forget other people keep normal hours."

"It's a parking lot full of trucks," Gordon said.

"What they spend on lights, they could give half of it to the people gonna sneak in and rip off the trucks and they'd all come out ahead."

They rolled over a railroad bridge, past a Scot gas station

with bargain cigarettes, past the twilight inside a closed McDonald's, and then past a cop car with its flashers hacking away at the night. Its doors stood open but there was nobody to be seen, no cops, no robbers; and quiet everywhere, except for thunder grumbling in the Virginia darkness across the river a few miles away. The Cadillac's headlights floated down the avenue. On doorsteps, cigarette ends swelled red.

"You got anyplace in particular you want to go while we talk about this thing?" Eddie said.

"I don't care, as long as there's people around."

"I could care less, my man."

Gordon felt comfortably alienated, a sensation of possessing a very long perspective indeed: he was both hunter and hunted now. It reminded him of the feeling he had when he got off boats onto islands. He felt so comfortable with it that Eddie, his blocky fingers darting around the steering wheel, looked foolish in his intensity. Gordon observed him for a while—his old, tired, scarred snapping turtle's face. He said: "Are you the one who killed Gerald and Gaia?"

"You the one who broke into my trunk last night?"

"No."

"There you go. Somebody punched my trunk and somebody killed Gerald and Gaia."

"When the farmhouse burned a couple of guys drove up in an old Chevy. They looked Spanish, or Middle Eastern."

"Sure, it could be anybody. It could be Cane, Fidel Castro, the Mafia. But it could be burglars killed Gerald and Gaia, and the salad boy out at the restaurant punched my trunk. Anybody."

"Anybody."

"Present company excepted."

"Sure," Gordon said.

"It's not my style. It doesn't seem like your style either."

"No."

"I gotta think, though—Ellen, there's a woman could do something cold, she thought she had to."

"Anybody could, if they thought they had to."

"The female of the species, push comes to shove, they can get cold, they'll surprise the hell out of you."

They waited at a stoplight. Gordon smelled the stale breath of downtown, like a combination of basements and short-order cooking. Across the sidewalk, in the window of a sporting-goods store, a million gleams rested on a mob of trophies. Over the store, the sky was pink.

The light changed. They rolled across the intersection.

"You hit me quick enough for a guy who it isn't his style," Gordon said. "You did a nice job of trashing my car, and scaring the hell out of Dana."

"I wanted to make sure you took this thing seriously."

"It worked."

"If it would've worked, you wouldn't be here right now. A guy like you, your background, wading around in this shit."

"A nice boy like me," Gordon said.

"Let me take a guess. It's Ellen, right? Am I right? Hell, yes. You come walking down that road like a kid who just saw the cheerleaders' panties for the first time. You don't have to tell me why you're still around. I'd be around, too. I've been seeing her since she was so high and she was always like that, that thing about her, so near and so far. Am I right? You know what I'm talking about?"

"I know what you're talking about."

"What interests me is how you got into it to start with. They tell me you were married to a girl stood to inherit half of southern California. You were Senator Moakley's L.A. And next thing, you're mixed up in a thing like this. What were you, bored? Broke?"

"Both. You could say both."

"How's a guy like you get bored? I'm serious. I'm curious to know. I can see it, the kind of job I do, the surveillance, the waiting around..."

"I'll put it this way: I'm not bored anymore."

Eddie thought about it. "Good."

"It was like a fog," Gordon said. "You ever get to that point in your life when you can't taste anything, you can't feel anything? It's like being in a fog, and you want to get out. So you get drunk, say, and that doesn't do it. Or drugs. Even fucking doesn't do it, feeling good doesn't do it."

"The fog," Eddie said, mulling it, pure indulgence.

"I wanted to feel real. Nothing like a little adrenalin to make you feel real. Clear the fog out of the air."

"It work?"

"Clear as a bell."

"Sure," Eddie said. He drove with his head tilted back a little, as if he were shorter than he was and had a hard time seeing over the wheel. "When I was a kid in Pennsylvania, you'd wait all year to go deer hunting. Freeze your buns off and get maybe a two-second look at a deer, but your heart's pounding, you smell everything, you hear everything, and you'd remember it all year, those two seconds."

"You got it," Gordon said.

"Except I couldn't imagine living my life like that. I get the feeling you'd like to live your whole life like that, those two seconds."

"We'll see."

"You want to keep the adrenalin coming, getting on Cane's shit list is the best way I know how. And now we're all on it. You, Ellen, and me."

"Strange bedfellows."

"Talk about it," Eddie said. "You talk about cold, you're talking about Cane. I've known John Cane ever since he was right out of Princeton with the OSS. He'll charm you out of your fucking boots, but you get to know him, you realize he's so cold you got no idea how cold he is, you can't imagine it in a million years, the way he thinks. I could tell you shit, I'm serious: him and John Kennedy. They were birds of a feather. Rich guys who wanted to be tough guys. Play gangster. They don't give a fuck about you and me, we're just the price they have to pay for whatever it is. It's a game to them. That's why you didn't see me shed one tear when Jack Kennedy got killed. Bobby, that was different. He was a prick, but he had a heart, too. Don't let these rich guys fool you. They get their hands dirty, just like you and me, except they do it for fun. That's what's bad about them. You know?"

"I know," Gordon said. He heard the grudge in Eddie's voice, and saw his face muscles shift in ghostly focus, telling a story he'd told himself a hundred times in the mirror.

They rode around Dupont Circle. A conga drum tickled through the darkness. Three black kids sat on the rim of the fountain, staring down Major L'Enfant's broad boulevards at the anticrime lights, the cold burn of justice through the trees.

"You know what I mean by charm you—how he makes you think you're the only person on earth can do this job or that job? The Mission Impossible routine. Did he give you that?"

"Sure." Gordon wondered how long it had been since Eddie talked to someone who listened.

"You love him and then he fucks you—it's what they call charisma. I've known him since 1943, I taught him radio. I was a dumb kid from the mining country. I'd been in submarines since 1940. Then I got the shit shot out of me in the Pacific, and I end up in the OSS teaching radio to Cane and half the Ivy League."

They drove up Connecticut Avenue past the old masonry façades and chanceries and shrouding trees that reminded Gordon of Paris. It was quiet. He heard the stoplights click when they changed. They drove out onto the long, empty stretch of bridge over Rock Creek Park. Gordon felt dwarfed and exposed, as if he and Eddie were the only humans left alive in the city. At the other end of the bridge were restaurants, closed now. A neon cactus burned green in the window of the Tucson Cantina.

"I ran into him again in 1951. We're both at the embassy in Athens for this thing; we were going to overthrow Albania—send these Albanian exiles crawling across the border at night and that's the last we'd ever hear of them. Real college-boy shit, pranking around, except a lot of people got killed. I was still in the navy, Office of Naval Intelligence, and Cane was CIA. They had him as third secretary at the embassy. I'd be on radio watch at night, and he'd come in to shoot the shit. He'd get me telling stories about growing up on the other side of the tracks, bar fighting and that. The rules of the game."

"Like what?"

"Like never hook your feet behind the rung on a barstool. Like never hit a guy with your hand unless you have to. Cane loved that shit. I showed him how to fight with a knife. They taught them all this fancy commando shit, but the real world, a knife fight is just one guy getting his knife out faster than the other guy, and he cuts him once and the guy runs."

"I didn't know that myself," Gordon said, out of the notion that a little confessing of naiveté might go a long way with Eddie Conchis.

"Oh, yeah," Eddie said. He leaned back and sprawled his knees. "But how's a guy like Cane going to know shit like that? So I'd tell him and he'd tell me shit about the system— Wall Street, the government, how you got ahead. Nights, we'd shoot the shit like that. That's how come I got out of the navy. He talked me into quitting. He says, 'Eddie, you're too smart.' And sure enough, after we folded the Albanian thing, we both end up in Washington, and he helps me get a job tapping phones for Bureau of Alcohol, Tobacco and Firearms. Pretty soon, I'm out in the field, New York, three years up there when I hear from Cane again. He says there's this job working for the junior senator from Massachusetts, doing security. I didn't even know who he was. Jack Kennedy. My instinct was no. We had a place out in Sheepshead Bay, my wife is raising Scotties, but the way I felt about it, I owed Cane one. And I'm a man who pays his debts. Always. The thing was, I didn't owe him one, I realize that now, because let me tell you, in case you wondered, if you felt like you were into him, you don't owe Cane jack shit. He'll make you think you do, but you don't. Nobody does."

"It hadn't crossed my mind."

"So what happened, the reason you and I are sitting here talking about it, the reason Ellen Cane blew that kidnap scam all to hell, maybe the reason for all of this, is what happened next. Okay, it's early in the campaign, February or March 1960 now, and Cane gets hold of me one afternoon. He has me over to this office in the State Department. We talk about this and that, and then he says, 'My wife is having an affair with the candidate. I need something on tape to protect myself.' I said, 'Okay,' and I'm thinking, he's the boss, right? It's his ass, not mine. And besides, I owe him one."

"Carol Cane was found under the bridge..."

"October 1963."

"Okay," Gordon said, thinking: just let him tell his story.

"He tells me she's going up to New York the next week while Kennedy's up there talking to Alex Rose and the Liberals. I'm going along anyway, for security. This was before they all got Secret Service when they ran for president, you remember. Okay, I put microphones in both their hotel rooms. His, it's easy. I'm supposed to be doing a sweep to make sure nobody else put a microphone in the room. About one A.M., I'm sitting there with the earphones on, half asleep, and in she comes, tippy-toe time."

He skittered his fingers through the air.

"I got tape on them three times after that, twice in New York and once up in Cape Cod I'll never forget, he keeps a *Life* magazine reporter waiting an hour while he gets his roll in the hay. I had to laugh. And then I'd run into Carol Cane here and there, and she'd look at me like she knew I knew, but I could never tell—maybe that's the way she always looked at men."

They drove past darkened flower shops, outdoor cafés with the chairs stacked on the tables, and the Uptown Theater with its sign flashing in red, U,P,T,O,W,N...UPTOWN. Gordon felt as though there'd been rain—a feeling of sheltered resignation. But there hadn't. The only visible moisture swarmed around the streetlights like bees.

"Anyhow," Gordon said.

"Anyhow, that's the last I hear about it for three years. Kennedy gets elected, Cane goes to the White House as special assistant, and I go to the Democratic National Committee, on staff. Everybody's happy. I don't ask questions. Then one Sunday night in October, three years later, Cane calls me at home, asks me can I get over to his house, right away, and not tell anybody. Okay, fine. I go over. He opens the door, calm as you or me sitting here. He's got a drink in his hand. He walks me over to the middle of the hall, where the staircase curves around. He points down at her like she's a new puppy he's showing off. He says, 'She fell.' She's lying there, all crumpled up. She's dead. He says: 'She fell.' I said: 'Fine, call the police.' He says no, he can't explain it all to me, but the White House is involved, and he can't let the police find her there.

"Okay, we're talking possible homicide, we're talking an accessory beef, misprision of a felony, I'm shitting bricks. I want out of there. But back then, you got to understand, a man like Cane said 'the White House,' it meant something. A man in my position, they said jump, you said how high. Besides the fact I trusted Cane. I don't say this for an excuse, but it was a whole different town back then. A different country. Back then they get Walter Jenkins for smoking bone in the men's room at the Y, it's a national scandal. Nowadays he'd get what, a parade. Anyhow ...we're standing there in the hallway and Cane says, 'I can't let them find her here.' I said, 'Okay, you better move her someplace else, then.' He thinks about that for a while, then he starts coming up with this James Bond bit, how he should leave her in the middle of the Ellipse in a cross shape, like it was some kind of voodoo deal. I said, 'John, she fell off something, so you got to make it look like she fell off something where you put her, right?

"I tell you what I remember thinking. I said to myself: 'He doesn't need me. If he wants to get rid of a body, he doesn't need me to help him.' But I figured, Cane's Cane, and John Kennedy's going to be president for another six years. I thought: Here's a chance to let them owe me something, for a change."

"Something for nothing," Gordon said.

"Exactly. I look back and say: 'How could I have been so stupid?' Trying to make John Cane feel like he was into me...I might as well have tried it on a cat. For one thing, a lot of rich guys are like this, he's the cheapest bastard you ever met, the original dime tipper. He wouldn't give you stink if he was made out of shit."

He had turned right on Porter Street and they headed back down Rock Creek Parkway, past deserted side roads and bridges and picnic tables. Sometimes the headlights caught the creek, which was low and still. The air smelled bitter, August in Washington. They went through a tunnel. The shiny walls clouted in on them, tore at their peripheral vision, and then they were released into the slow darkness again.

"So, sure, we load her in the trunk and we drive all over Washington. Key Bridge, Chain Bridge, everyplace there's something wrong: too many lights, too much traffic, or how the fuck would she have gotten herself all the way out there. We even checked out the stairs they used when they shot that movie over at Georgetown University, the priest fell down them."

"*The Exorcist,*" Gordon said.

"All the time she's getting stiffer. I think, Jesus, we drop her any distance she'll break like glass. Maybe we better lay her under a bridge, not drop her. But you got to find one you can drive under. I don't want to be humping a corpse through the boondocks. By this time Cane, unbelievable, he's hurrying me. Like, 'Let's get this over with, I haven't got all night.' I said, 'Fine, I'll drive you back to the house and you can figure it out yourself.' He says no, I don't realize how tough he's got it: the police to deal with, the newspapers the next day, Carol's family, Ellen...And I got to give him credit, the fucker had some feelings, at least. I look over at him..." Eddie looked over at Gordon to illustrate. His face was sharp and still in the flutter of light through the windshield. "And he was crying. Fucker just sat there and cried and cried, the tears dripping off his chin. Didn't embarrass him one minute. Finally I think of this place off Cathedral Avenue under the Calvert Street Bridge. I'm going to show you, right up here."

They paused at a stop sign. Eddie wallowed the Cadillac around a hairpin turn onto Cathedral. The bridge swelled overhead. Just beyond it, on the left, was an apartment house. The windows were dark, or bore the frangible glow of fish tanks or bathroom lights left on. It was very late. Between the apartment house and the bridge was a patch of ivy and some trees.

"In there," Eddie said. He flicked his forefinger, as if he were shaking a drop of water off it. He didn't look where he pointed. Gordon looked. He twisted in his seat to see it, but there was nothing there. It was conspicuously recovered from the tragedy: empty, absurd, null set.

198

"Perfect," Gordon said.

"Sure. She could have jumped, she could have been mugged and dumped in there. Somebody could have thrown her off the top of the apartment building. You name it. The police didn't know whether to shit or go blind."

"Okay," Gordon said. "What does that have to do with the tapes?"

"Tell you the truth, I didn't even think about it at the time. But then afterward, after Johnson came in and I got fired at the committee, and I couldn't get a job anyplace else, I started asking questions. Finally somebody down at this bar I go, The Company, says, hey Eddie, nobody's gonna hire you. Everybody says you're the guy who bugged John Kennedy and her when you were his security guy and that's why she killed herself."

"Killed herself," Gordon said.

"That was the story going around."

"But who started it?"

"Who else? Had to be Cane."

"But why would Cane want to tell people about the tapes?"

"He wanted somebody to take the blame for her killing herself."

"Why?" Gordon said. He waited with an unblinking predator's calm. He liked cornering Eddie. He liked lying back at terrific distance and sniping.

"How should I know? It was just a cover story, just more John Cane bullshit."

"It doesn't make sense. He'd be afraid you'd tell the truth, once he opened up a Pandora's box like that."

"What can I tell you?" Eddie said. "Who can figure Cane? Besides, what good would it do me, badmouthing John Cane?"

They drifted up Cathedral Avenue. The park fell away to the right.

"How about this?" Gordon said. "The real reason Cane

wanted to blame you for the tapes was because somebody was blaming *him* for them."

"Who would be blaming him?"

"Kennedy, before he died, who else?"

"But how would Kennedy have known?"

"Cane had something on Kennedy with those tapes, right? They gave him something to threaten Kennedy with."

"Why should he threaten Kennedy?"

Gordon glanced upward. His hand rolled slowly while he thought about it. His lips moved while he tried to nail down a piece of reality in his mind.

"What's he going to ask for?" Eddie continued. "A better job? Hey, Mr. President, I got these tapes of you putting it to my wife—make me Secretary of State."

"You've got a point," Gordon said. He rummaged around for yet more logic to lead him to some single, overwhelming truth. "But listen to this—what if he was trying not to get something out of Kennedy, but to get himself out of trouble? Like he'd actually pulled the plutonium stunt, and got caught, and Carol went to Kennedy..."

"Fine," Eddie said. "You can talk about this all night and still not know anything."

Gordon was excited. "She goes to Kennedy and says, 'My husband is in trouble, I want you to back off or I'll go to the media and ruin your chances for re-election. What's more, it's all on tape.' But it backfires. Kennedy calls Cane in and says: 'Your wife is trying to blackmail me.' So now Cane's only hope is to prove his loyalty to Kennedy..."

"Sure," Eddie said. "Why not? Why not have him killing Kennedy too? He likes that kind of setup—get some bozo ex-Marine like Lee Harvey Oswald to do the shooting; all these Cubans and Mafia and New Orleans faggots...Cane loves that seamy shit."

"Are you serious?"

"Fuck, no, I'm not serious."

"Why not?" Gordon was reeling with the wine of epiphany.

"Guys like you always want to explain everything," Eddie said.

"I don't understand."

"What," Eddie said.

"This doesn't really seem to interest you."

"You're right."

"It's like you never wondered what the truth behind all this is."

"The truth," Eddie said.

"Seriously."

"Sure. The truth is what you got when you're a poker player, and the other guy beats you five times in a row filling an inside straight. You say: 'The odds against that are a million to one.' He says: 'That's the truth,' and then he goes home with all your money."

"So why did you tell me all this, then?"

"I just wanted to show you what I got on Cane. I already know I got him on trying to scam out of the Senate hearings with a phony kidnap, and then perjury. I got his daughter on murder..."

"But if you want to prove contempt of Congress and perjury, you'll need Ellen to help."

Eddie's head changed position with a peculiar tracking motion as he turned to face Gordon.

"We're talking two hundred fifty thousand—split, half for you and Ellen, half for me."

"Big bucks."

"I know for a fact he's got it. All it's going to take is one shove by all three of us, and he'll cave in."

Thoughts rocketed through Gordon's synapses—whims and imagery—buying tramp-steamer tickets to Sri Lanka, with the money...or shooting Cane, fuck him, don't deal with him...or heading out to the mountains, or driving to

Las Vegas, or—and this was the moistest, murkiest temptation of them all, the one which had tracked him like a bad conscience ever since he'd lain in the tree line studying the farmhouse through Cane's binoculars—the hell with it, go home, forget any of it ever happened, and why not?

"What happens if Ellen and I say fuck it—we're not going to do anything?"

"Then you leave me in the lurch. I have to protect myself. I go to the cops, I cut a deal, and Ellen goes up for murder."

"But it wasn't murder," Gordon said.

"Shit, yes, it was murder. She's going along with the whole plan for five days, and then we have one argument about it and she shoots a guy."

"He threatened her."

"Prove it. He didn't even knock her around. You see any bruises on her?"

Gordon was frightened and relaxed at the same time. A light, cool sweat evaporated in the wind off the river, to the right of them. The river was a plain of black gleams with the dark woods of Roosevelt Island behind it. They curved past the balconied convolutions of the Watergate. Gordon's head lolled. He sagged into his leather seat.

The problem, he realized, was to act without being violent. He was a profoundly nonviolent man, at heart. He saw this now This was why he'd never fired his rifle in Vietnam. It wasn't his style. Once he'd watched a prisoner try to run, and he hadn't even thought to reach for his rifle when a communicator with an AK-47 fired a burst into the prisoner's back that blew the guts right out the front like an apron. The prisoner fell down and tried to stuff his guts back in with little, dirty fingers. You could hear the fingers working in the guts.

Afterward, Gordon told people he wanted to paint a picture of the VC grabbing at his gut, and title it *And in the End, the World Will Break Your Heart,* this being the sort of irony that got you through the day in Vietnam, that explained things. Gordon knew he'd been lucky that way: out of thirteen months in Vietnam there were only forty-five seconds or so that he couldn't explain.

The Cadillac drove under Memorial Bridge, a quick sigh against the concrete, and Gordon told himself the story of those forty-five seconds for the millionth time. Told: there was no explaining, how you were walking down a jungle trail north of Chu Lai at night, you had your eyes twitching back and forth, you're smelling that dirt-green air, you're listening to the footsteps and breathing and the equipment creaking... and you're thinking *what the fuck time is it, how far is this fucker taking us*? Then it's like the air explodes, the darkness explodes, it's like the air is screaming at you and people run and shout, everything happens so slow and so fast at the same time, it takes you hours to get to the ground, people falling in this weird light, muzzle flashes jumping around when they shoot back and then just as fast it's quiet again. And people are dying.

Gordon told himself the story the way people keep looking in empty pockets for the money they lost, hoping that some inexorable and universal law might be suspended, a miracle, and it would come out differently. It didn't happen. It was all too simple: in that forty-five seconds, he had seen no one to shoot at, it had happened too fast, it was over too soon, he might have killed one of his own people, but still...he felt guilty for not firing his rifle that night. He had grieved his own survival, worse and worse as the years wore on. And now he realized, for what it was worth in the dank, small-hours sprawl of summer Washington, that it hadn't been his style. He wasn't meant to hurt people, even the ones shooting at him, and in the world as he'd known it ever since Vietnam, that made him a fool. Fine, be a fool, strewing mercy around like a madman burning money. It was his nature, his karma. That was easy enough to take.

What came harder was admitting that most people were no less kind than he'd just found himself to be; that he could climb on their bus whenever he got up the courage to accept that. He understood that now. He wondered if it might not be the greatest discovery of his life.

Behind some trees on their left, Abraham Lincoln brooded over a predawn marble emptiness, and there was the sweet oracular dome of the Jefferson Memorial, and the flags hanging slack against the poles surrounding the Washington Monument. Gordon recalled sighting the monument from the motel balcony, and he stared off across the Mall, trying to spot the motel's pastel desolation in return. He wondered if Ellen was sleeping.

"I'm not sure Ellen sees it this way," he said.

"You got a job ahead of you, all right," Eddie said.

"All I can do is try and talk to her."

"If you fuck up, I'd get out of town," Eddie said. "There won't be anything left here for you."

"I'll ride it to the end of the line," Gordon said. "I don't have anyplace else to go."

"One thing," Eddie said. "About those guys in the Chevy you saw, that looked Spanish or Middle Eastern."

Gordon told him everything he knew, which was hardly anything—the car stalling, the one blocky guy with the mustache, pissing in the light of the fiery farmhouse.

After that, there was nothing more to say. They drove out New York Avenue. Gordon found himself feeling sorry for Eddie. He didn't know why. He had Eddie drop him off two motels up the avenue from his own. He walked back. He watched Eddie's taillights dwindle until they were nothing, just thoughts.

# Chapter 18

---

*E*LLEN FELL ASLEEP with her clothes on. She lay curled across the bedspread, a frozen moment of a pose, as if she were a fallen chrysalis. When she awoke, hours or minutes later—she couldn't tell—the television was still on. She opened her eyes and found herself staring at the screen. It was smeared by fingerprints. Behind the fingerprints, a black-and-white Lauren Bacall sidled after Humphrey Bogart, who was carrying a woman's body through a doorway. Lauren Bacall said: "What are you trying to do, guess her weight?" Ellen wondered what time it was, wondered if Gordon had deserted her, was long gone back to Dana, the two of them heading off for the emerald trout pools of the Shenandoah while she waited for nothing, here with the whores and huddled tourists, a fool. The thought had a bittersweet taste. She uncurled with a flutter of anxiety and sat up to look for a rim of grey dawn motel light around the curtain. She walked across the room and stood by the rush of cold from the air conditioner. She peeked outside. It was still dark, a bower of dark with a sprinkle of city lights beyond the balcony. She felt comforted by it. Gordon would be back, she decided—though she noted that if she thought of him too specifically a small glow of resentment would appear in her gut. Best not to analyze it, she knew. Best to think about being in love, rather than Gordon himself. She was skilled at falling in love, and she knew how to nurture it along, to avoid the morning-light judgments that made you pity or hate people you'd much prefer to love.

Through the batting of the air-conditioned silence she heard a trailer truck whine down New York Avenue. The sound tapered to nothing. It was late. It was dark. She touched the security chain on the door and hefted its tiny weight. Things weren't so bad, she thought. If she could feel like this the rest of her life, it wouldn't be so bad. It was the hint of a respite that she felt. It felt like the room belonged to her now, like the farmhouse before she burned it. She savored the feeling. It took only the tiniest permanences to heighten it: in the bathroom was the towel she'd dried herself with and dropped on the floor a couple of hours ago; in the wastebasket was Gordon's crumpled Coke can. Souvenirs. Tradition. A household. You had to start somewhere. Even a crumpled Coke can and a soggy towel in a motel room on New York Avenue would do.

The thought took her so deep that she was surprised to note, coming out of it, how loud the television was playing. Just now it showed a Scottish piper playing "My Bonnie Lassie" as he strolled among rolls of wall-to-wall carpeting.

She decided that if she'd slept so well in all that racket, she might as well get some serious rest. No sense waiting up for Gordon, for appearances' sake. She turned off the television. She unbuttoned her cutoffs and let them plummet to the floor. She stepped out of Dana's panties, but decided to leave on the F. Scott Fitzgerald T-shirt. Being half-naked, the bottom half, made her feel lascivious. But taking off the T-shirt too would make her feel exposed and helpless.

Feeling lascivious added to her sensation of ownership of this room. Feeling exposed and helpless would dispossess her. She went into the bathroom and took another Valium. The air was cool on her belly. She walked back in and pulled the bedspread down to reveal a blanket made from some spongy, sparkly material she didn't like. She climbed between the sheets. She marshaled two pillows, one for hugging, the other for her head. When she was sure she had it right, she turned out the lights. The tailings of distant neon sifted in around the curtain, hardly any light at all.

She was so tired. Her eyes swiveled under dry lids, out of some useless reflex she couldn't turn off. Her joints ached, her scalp itched. She sucked air through her teeth to make her mouth feel cool and clean. It was as if some membrane separated her from sleep until the Valium took hold and she felt herself sliding through it, gaining speed, plunging. Her stomach turned. She opened her eyes and darted them around the room until they found purchase in the light around the window. Reality gathered back around her like a consoling family. She closed her eyes again. This time the plunge was slower, more oblique. Along the way she saw a phantasmagoria from the last week, accidental as the half-pictures at the ends of rolls of film: the heel-blackened risers of the farmhouse stairs, Gordon floating under the spatter of streetlight through the honeysuckle on his porch, the farmhouse garden with the zucchini creaking in the sun, the lights shining down on acres of empty asphalt at the Stuckey Shopping Mall, the crosshatchings of lines on Eddie Conchis's face. When the visions eased, she dwindled toward sleep. At the last moment before she let go, one image came to her, as if it were merely offering her one last choice of sleep or waking, but of course there was no choice. The image was Gaia, dead in the cellar, and suddenly Ellen was awake and choking in the darkness to think of her. She kept going back to it like a tongue to a sore tooth, testing. When it palled, her mind's eye could not resist Gerald, the blood hanging from his mouth. She gagged until her ribs hurt. It only stopped when she realized that she was teasing herself with monstrosity, and it was wrong to do it.

After a while she tried to make herself cry. It didn't work. The world swayed inside her head. Her feelings shifted like qualities of light or season—changes that meant everything to Ellen: the way she felt about something was the way it was. She thought, for instance, of her father's shoes lined up in his closet, and the dry air of his bureau drawers, and the shine of his cheeks in the morning after he shaved— images that provoked a cool fever of wariness. She liked that feeling. It made her feel like herself. She breathed out and out, a final, definitive breath. Her ribs gathered. She decided her father had killed Gerald and Gaia. She said to herself that he would kill whoever he had to: Eddie, Gordon, her, whoever. It was a natural law. She'd railed against it, on the balcony, but now she felt comforted by it: it narrowed the choices, even to none. What had shocked her was Gordon spoiling for a fight, proposing to kill her father. It was coarse. Her shock hardened now to a refusal. She wouldn't be able to explain this bridling to Gordon. He didn't understand. He was bright, he'd rescued her and she loved him a lot, but he didn't understand. She thought of him the way she'd been taught as a girl to regard people who weren't in her class—befriending them would be wrong, because it would embarrass them. Except that Gordon's disadvantage was more dangerous: he failed to understand that she'd invoked an inevitability. She'd be trapped before long, with no choices. This thought made Gordon seem even more helplessly alien. Her consciousness teetered on the edge of pity for him, a sorrow, just the thing to ease off to sleep with.

She slept for a moment, she slept for an hour, it made no difference: she woke in terror to a pounding on the door, great fisty clouts of noise that made her fear, when she got up and peeked around the curtain and saw Gordon outside, that she'd fallen way deeper asleep than she ever liked to think was possible.

Her eyes burned. Her cheeks felt stiff. She opened the door and her mouth fumbled with his kiss. She smelled him, the sunlit-canvas smell she had first smelled at the farmhouse. He looked proud and shy.

"We've got a plan," he announced. "It's not much of a plan but it's a plan."

Watching him, she retreated to the bed. She gathered the covers around her.

He sat in the chair next to her and unlaced his boots without looking at them. He seemed intense and offhanded, almost unaware of her.

"We got a plan," he said. "It gets us out of Washington, nobody gets hurt, maybe it gets us a lot of money. The worst thing that happens is if your father stonewalls, he could get busted for contempt of Congress or perjury, but I'll tell you, when I left here tonight I was worried the only way out was to kill him. Eddie has this plan, and if your father goes along, maybe we'll end up in Ireland riding horses after all— wasn't that your fantasy?"

"That was Gaia's fantasy."

"Whatever," he said. On his way into the bathroom he wrestled his shoulders out of his shirt, which he tossed on the bureau. "If it works, you can take your pick of fantasies." She heard him brush his teeth with her toothbrush. He reappeared in the door, licking his teeth. He winked at her. He leaned against the jamb. She noted how small his nipples were, and the way a line of stomach muscle traced down from his hipbone, under the waistband of his Levi's.

"It's a package," he said. "If we can keep it together and make your father know we're not bullshitting for one second, it'll be the best thing for everybody. I believe that."

She listened while he explained it all, from the tapes to the death of her mother to the kidnap scam to the murder

209

charge hanging over her for shooting Lally. "And there's always an arson charge. Plus Gerald and Gaia."

"I can't stop thinking about them," she said. It was all so pointless. She couldn't think of anything else to say.

He said: "This is for real. Live bullets. Real money."

She listened to him in the shower: he sang. . . *for I am just a monkey man, I hope you are a monkey, too* . . . His feet thumped. He grunted with pleasure. He had her by six or eight years, but she thought of herself as older. He was the fire maker, the problem solver, the battle joiner; but she was tougher. He'd worked all night but she was tireder.

When the shower stopped running she lit a cigarette. He came out of the bathroom in his pants, with his hair combed wet against his neck.

She raised her hands next to her ears. Cigarette smoke rose absolutely straight from her fingers for the moment before she spoke. "Eddie Conchis. . . you know who Eddie Conchis is? Eddie Conchis is just some washed-up wiretap man my father helped a long time ago and ever since then he's been calling him every three months looking for a handout. Eddie Conchis is a loser. He's a bum."

She wanted to anger Gordon, but he remained profoundly pleased with himself. He lay down by her on the bed. He spread his elbows like wings and massaged his eyelids with his middle fingers.

"What if we simply refuse, flatly refuse to go along with him?" she said.

"The answer is, he goes to the police with Lally's body and the pistol and he says you murdered him."

"Why not kill Eddie Conchis, then?"

"Why kill anybody?"

Ellen wished he'd open his eyes and look at her while he talked.

"You were the one who proposed that we assassinate my father, I might point out."

210

"I said I was worried we'd have to, if it looked like he'd kill us."

"He'll kill us if he thinks he has to. That's what I think. He told me on the phone, Eddie was going to try pulling this, try to get us to help him, but he said: 'It's not going to happen that way.' And what he meant, I know that tone of voice, was, we'll end up like Gerald and Gaia, if we're not smart."

"There's only one way to find out."

"I already know."

"But why would he put himself in danger of spending the rest of his life in jail for murder just to avoid a minor scandal?"

"You sound like all my old shrinks: *why, why, why*. I'd say, what difference does it make? And they'd say, so you make better choices in the future. And I finally said to one, once you make a choice, you don't have it anymore, so what difference does it make, answer me that? And she couldn't."

His eyes were open now, but aimed at the ceiling as if it were the back of a cereal box he was reading at the breakfast table.

"Let's say I'm just curious as to why he'd go to all this trouble."

"He doesn't have the money," she said. "He never had any money."

"He has that house, he has the boat..."

"Right. Sure. That's why he doesn't have any money, he spends it all. You don't understand. Believe me, the people everybody thinks are rich, half of them don't *have* anything, they just spend a lot. That's why they're so nervous all the time. Kiting checks, and Daddy is always firing his broker, and hoping somebody will die and leave us something. That's what I remember when I think about my parents— them screaming at each other about money. It never stops. It's sick."

She toured her eyes around the room, through the chaos of a civilization as small as two people with no luggage: cigarette butts, a wet towel, a dirty T-shirt on the bureau; boots sprawled by the chair, water on the bathroom floor. It had the strewn intensity of her whole life. Lately, she craved order in the worst way.

She tightened her fists against the sloppy feeling the Valium invoked. She'd been right: he didn't understand anything. There was no telling him the truth about herself, her father, any of it. He didn't want to hear it. The inertia of ignorance was too strong. She thought of him with the sort of satanic compassion that comes from knowing that there's no need to buy souls—the godly are pounding down the doors to hell. Her smile bloomed bleak. She heard her voice mocking him, her lips dancing around the words as she spoke. "You should go away, you should go home and forget all of this, you should leave me and never come back, Gordon."

"Where's all this coming from?"

"It's true," she said. "You should forget me, forget sweet young Ellen Cane. Forget the farmhouse, the money, making love, all of it. You should go back to Dana. You may think she's boring, but she's a good woman for you, Gordon. She might be the ideal woman for you."

"You're tired."

"I'm not tired in the least."

"Back around noon you were asking me to marry you, as I recall."

"Sure, that too. There's no end to my corruption." She shuttled her jaw from side to side. "I'm a bad girl, is what I am, and you have no respect for me. You have no respect for how bad I am."

Gordon puckered his face with annoyance. "You feel guilty that Gerald and Gaia died."

"I feel guilty for everything, all the time."

"I thought you were a bad girl. Bad girls don't feel guilty."

"Bad girls *always* feel guilty. That's why they're bad."

"What if I say yes, I want to marry you?"

"Don't," she pleaded.

"What if I told you I loved you?"

"Don't."

"Do you want me to prove it to you? Is that what this is all about?"

"No."

"I think you do."

"You're wrong. Please listen to me."

"You're lying."

"I'm not lying. Go back to Dana. You deserve Dana."

"You're like a cornered little animal," he said.

She flung her cigarette hand outward in extravagant fatigue. "Maybe you're right. Maybe I'm tired."

He rolled over and circled her waist, blanket and all, with his arm. He kissed the small of her back. It was an audible and ceremonial kiss. It meant that he wasn't going to try to make love to her. She was glad.

"We're both tired," he said.

"I stayed awake in case you wanted to make love," she lied.

He squeezed her thigh with fatherly heartiness. "We're both tired," he said.

In a moment he had stood, shucked his pants, and climbed naked into the bed. He folded his pillow in half with a gesture so crisp it was clearly part of every night's bedtime ritual. He braced the nape of his neck on the pillow.

"Wait. What are we going to do?" she said.

"Nothing. It's your ass, not mine. If you don't like my plan, we can use yours."

"I don't have a plan."

"I know."

"Don't be smug. Don't be a prick, Gordon. Please."

"We'll go out to my house tomorrow, pick up my gear, and head down to the mountains."

"The trout pools," she said. "Water the color of an emerald."

"And the sunlight through the trees."

"Making love on the warm pine needles. The first time I ever made love was on pine needles. I masturbated a boy named Freddie Phipps out in back of the clinic in Massachusetts. He ended up with pine needles pasted all over him. I was thirteen," she said.

"What ever happened to Freddie Phipps?"

"I think he killed himself. Everybody at that place killed themselves, sooner or later. It was like getting your graduate degree."

"Suicide."

"Suicide."

"Kiss good-night."

She kissed him. A kiss seemed hideously inadequate to show either the love or the hate she was feeling, an exaltation of confusion Gordon couldn't understand.

As quickly as he'd undressed, which is to say in moments, he fell asleep. His lips parted. She could see teeth glinting. She felt abandoned and crowded at the same time. Somehow he had taken all her dares, and he had let her spite herself, besides. Anger flashed through her, then a rush of desire to wake him up and make love. But there was nothing left but to turn off the light and try to go back to sleep. She turned it off. The glow around the edges of the curtain had brightened. Was it dawn already?

She slept a sleep from which she kept waking convinced she hadn't slept at all. She'd open her eyes and find herself contorted and choked, with her hand crushed beneath her. She sweated. She hovered in a state of consciousness that had a dirty, silvery transparency to it. Images and words repeated and repeated: Gaia... *kiss good-night*...the cold prod of her father's voice from the telephone mouthpiece, all the words and silences meaning *no*...And then she'd

214

wake to the shuddering of the air conditioner, and Gordon snoring. She remembered a line from somewhere about it being a fearful thing to fall into "the hands of the living God." She woke again to see a sunlit morning diffusing around the edges of the curtain. The light reduced the room to a shabby, temporary scatter of material objects, the neon void. She was seized by a vision of the world turning like a machine. The sensation was disillusionment, as if she'd spent her whole life pretending that the machine didn't turn, or that she could stop it, freeze the world into perfections: trout pools or the shine on her father's cheeks after he shaved...

This was hell, now, everything disintegrating. She looked to Gordon and was taken by a fit of pity so painful that she began to blame him for it.

This was madness. The only thing to do was to turn and face the dogs, let them tear her apart. She had to. It was inevitable, and this knowledge was the only rock she could hang on to. She got out of bed in the grey light. No choice. She dressed. She brushed her hair without looking in the mirror. She squatted by Gordon's side of the bed and went through his pockets, looking for phone change. When she found it, she touched his hair on the pillow. For a moment, looking at him, she might have been a mother finding the child she'd abandoned years ago.

*

Outside, it was a bright, clear, hot Saturday morning in August. A thunderstorm mustered downriver from Washington so that against it the temples of government, as seen from the motel, glowed an intense, almost imaginary white. Three kites flew tiny over the Mall. The green of the capital's trees glittered. A truck jostled down New York Avenue with a joyful, fleeing sound. In the parking lot the sun sprayed off chrome and windshields. A little pool behind a chain link fence was deserted. Inside the motel office the fat, coffee-colored effeminate room clerk slept in an armchair. The elastic top of his Jockey shorts showed over his belt.

Having breakfasted on Diet Pepsi and a cigarette; having smoked a second while she paced the arcade; having rehearsed what she would say not so much out of insecurity as out of joy and relief at saying it, Ellen stood at the pay phone, dialing with a hand that held a third cigarette. She turned to wrap herself in the chrome-sheathed cord and scan the view: the thunderhead, the Capitol dome with its plastic shine, the kites and trees.

She listened. She waited. She lifted her hand and settled it on top of her head with the cigarette pointed skyward. She blinked. A cigarette ash tumbled onto her fingers, which she lowered again. Her face thickened with disappointment as the ringing went on. Then it leapt to life, fastened, focused.

"It's me again," she said. The first tear rolled down her cheek. "Everything has gone crazy."

Standing tiny and alone under the morning sky, Ellen nodded, sighed, wept, and told her father everything. Sometimes she jerked her hand back and forth, fingers spread, to show she did not want to be misunderstood. She scarcely noticed anything he said. His voice was just a medium for her to work in: a constant, a given. She didn't bother to picture him on the other end of the line. She might as well have been talking to the telephone receiver itself. She knew she had waited half her life to say what she said now. He could listen.

"I argued with Gordon till dawn," she said. "I said to him: 'The only way Daddy will give us that money is if he wants to.' But he said Eddie would have me arrested for murder...Eddie is crazy with this thing, Gordon just thinks it's a good idea. Except that I think I talked him out of it."

"Fine," Cane's voice said.

"Daddy, don't ask me *why* I talked him out of it..." She

held her hand next to her ear as if to shield it from some uproar, even though the parking lot was quiet. "He's trying to get me out of this the best he can. And he loves me. I truly think he loves me. It's Eddie we have to worry about. He's gone crazy with it. I said to Gordon: 'Why does Eddie think I'll go along with it?' And Eddie told Gordon I knew you were responsible when Mummy died. He said I hated you for it and I was scared of you. And that's why I'd go along. But that's why I'm calling you, too. That's all part of it. Do you understand?"

"You don't have to explain anything," her father's voice told her.

"No," Ellen said. She cupped her hand over her mouth. Tears tattered down her cheeks. She waited to be able to talk. Inside the motel office the clerk had roused and was looking at her from his armchair.

"No, please listen. What I had to tell you was: I'm sorry. I'm sorry for the way I treated you when she died. And I'm sorry because what you never knew was I was glad she died. I was glad, but I was so scared it was something I did that made her die. And I was so scared you'd find out that I was glad, or I'd killed her somehow and then you wouldn't love me anymore. Because you loved me and she hated me, I knew that. But you had no idea—I was so young and it was all so crazy, how could I tell you? I was so scared you'd hate me after she died that I wanted to die. I wanted to waste away from hunger and have you beg me to love you on my deathbed. I wanted to be as hateful as I could so that you couldn't disappoint me by not loving me."

She stood in the sunshine in the helpless solitude of people crying. Her shoulders shook. Her mouth ached. She tried to corral her face into some kind of public order. She lit another cigarette. Her fingers were wet with tears and they kept soaking the matches. Finally a flame popped pale in the brightness. She spit smoke.

"I can't tell you," she said. "Last night, you don't know

the hell I went through. But then I knew what I had to do. I realized I had to take responsibility for myself for the first time in my life. I'm the one who got us into this mess and now I have to get us out."

"Yes," Cane said.

"You and me, we're the ones who could go to jail or get tortured or murdered or any of it. Not anybody else. Anybody else is in it because they want to be. We don't have a choice. Eddie is like a vulture. He's my fault, too, I never should have let Gerald and Gaia talk to him, but what could I do? Gerald and Gaia..." Her voice melted into weeping again. "And Gordon. I feel so sorry for Gordon now."

"Yes."

"But it's okay, I may be crying but it's okay."

"I know," Cane said.

"Don't worry, Daddy, I love you."

"I love you too, Ellen."

"I'm helping you, but that doesn't mean I don't love Gordon."

"I'm sure you're loyal to him."

"I'll do everything I can to get us out of this. I could come home right now, I could walk out on New York Avenue and stick out my thumb, but then Eddie would ruin our lives and Gordon would go crazy. I'm the only one who can get us out of this now. And I will. You watch."

"I'm glad."

"You can trust me."

When she hung up, she knew her father didn't believe her, but her faith in herself was unshaken. The sky, the air, the wind wrinkles in the empty swimming pool all shone with certainty. The world was ranked, filed, numbered, and readied: she had no idea for what, specifically, but she knew she would act when the time came. She had taken responsibility for herself. She would carry her load. She smiled with relief. She ignored an urge to finger the change slot on the telephone. She put her hands on her hips and wandered across the parking lot in a free-form goose step, her weight shivering from leg to leg. When she got to the asphalt curb at the edge of the lot, she surveyed the billion trees of Washington, the tin roofs and brick, the kites twitching and diving over the Mall. She listened for the band organ playing on the carousel in front of the Smithsonian, but all she heard was the murmur of the terrific August hush over the city.

She was sad, of course, about Gordon. She felt as though she had cuckolded him with her father and sold him out, she wouldn't deny it. She felt guilty, but she felt free. She didn't fear his kindness or coarseness or madness anymore. If she felt guilty and obliged, now she could make it up to him.

Desire: it made her feel like a universe in herself, moving with endless, gliding, circular grace through the morning with her puffy eyes, flying hair, and day-old underwear. Desire was the universal solvent. She dodged the glints of light off the cars in the parking lot. She aimed for the shade of the arcade that ran past all the motel-room doors. She guessed that she felt just now the way Gordon wanted to feel all the time. She wondered if he ever had. If not, maybe she could show him what it was like, when he woke up. It was the least she could do, given the way things were shaping up.

# Chapter 19

GORDON AWOKE with one eye gazing over the berm of his pillow. Ellen sat in the Danish-modern armchair. She looked startled, happy, scared, pranksome, and wary. She sat so primly as to be ridiculous: ankles crossed, knees touching, both hands gripping a supermarket tabloid newspaper. A headline on the newspaper read: BIZARRE DISEASE CAUSES VICTIMS TO WAVE CONSTANTLY. Next to her feet rested a cantaloupe that had been halved and reassembled—it bore a sliced equator.

"For me?" he said.

She nodded, still staring at him with her cyanide eyes.

"Thanks," he said.

Instantly she blushed—a great mottled roar of color into her face, a revelation like the blossoming of some way-too-beautiful flower, wicked in its simplicity. Her cheeks burned, he could even see the scarlet creep around the rims of her ears. It filled him with wonder, then triumph, then compassion. He had no idea why she was blushing.

"Don't," she said.

"Don't what?"

She couldn't answer. The blush climbed past her temples and into her hair. She touched her fingers to her forehead and flared them away in a salute of apology.

"I don't understand," he said.

"It isn't anything."

The blush ebbed. Gordon gave up trying to understand. He contemplated the cantaloupe. He snaked his arm out from the bed and retrieved the northern hemisphere. The flesh inside was damp and pink. It shone in the tarnished silver light of the room.

Ellen handed him a plastic spoon.

"Good morning," she said.

"Is it still morning?"

"Actually, it's afternoon."

"Seriously."

"But it's okay. That room clerk said we could check out whenever we want. I asked him and he said: 'It don't make me no never-mind.' " Her voice made cuddly balls of sound in imitation of the room clerk's accent.

"The world's greatest fat-black-homosexual-no-tell-motel room clerk," Gordon said.

"I think he lives in that office. He gave me the cantaloupe. He said somebody left it in a room and the Costa Rican maid thought they meant it as a tip and she got insulted that they'd tip her with produce. So if you don't want it we have to throw it away."

"No, no," he said. Lying on his stomach, with his weight braced on his elbow, he carved at the cantaloupe with the spoon.

"He says he can get us a car, too. He'll lend us his brother's car for ten dollars, he says."

"Scaud-wenting," Gordon said. He experienced the collapse of cantaloupe flesh between his molars. He swallowed, and said again: "It's called renting."

"His name is Damian St. Croix. Isn't that wonderful? That isn't his real name, though. He says he changes his name all the time. He used to be an interior decorator named Zenith Pocus before he got this job. He went to jail once for trying to rob a Christian Science reading room, too. He said that before that his life's ambition was to be in the water-skiing show at Cypress Gardens, but he says they don't hire convicted felons so his life is ruined. Isn't that sad? I think that's so sad."

"It don't make me no never-mind."

"And he gave me the cantaloupe and the newspaper and he says he can get us a car, too."

"Great." He sat up and mopped cantaloupe juice off his chin with the sheet.

"Piggy-wiggy," she said.

Holding the cantaloupe aloft, Gordon rolled to the far side of the bed. He lodged his feet firmly against the floor, sighed, and when he felt certain that gravity still worked on a principle of verticals, he stood and moved slow-hipped into the bathroom.

With an insouciance bordering on the barbaric, he got into the shower and let the water scald his back numb while he labored at the eating of the cantaloupe right down to the rind. The steam tickled his nostrils and hung in clouds over his tongue when he opened his mouth. His back itched with prickly heat. When he finished the melon he dropped the rind on the shower-stall floor. He liked kicking it out of the way; garbage; wallowing. He faced the nozzle blast until his heart pounded from the heat. Then he turned off all the hot water and turned on all the cold. His body seemed to gather into a single, solid center. He remembered how his body had looked in his football days, his pectoral muscles standing out in cords, and a vein riding over each bicep. He braced his hands against the corners of the shower stall and shoved until his back muscles rose and his stomach muscles were tight and trembling. Flex. Flux. By now the water didn't feel cold anymore. In fact, it was lukewarm. August. Washington. He stepped out of the stall, leaving the cantaloupe rind half-full of water.

He dried himself.

He belched.

He tied a towel around his waist. He felt pagan, brash, cavalier, notorious. He had just slept a deep and dreamless sleep, and whatever doubts he'd awakened with had evaporated in the noon of Ellen's blush. Even better, he had the pleasure of observing himself: I am arching my back, I am inhaling so deeply the ribs press through the skin...He felt better than he'd felt in a year.

He returned to the peculiar light of the room, which was supplied by brightness prying from either side of the curtain.

"Good cantaloupe," he said.

He liked parading in front of Ellen in a towel. The tropical lankness of a hard-on began to manifest, a state a friend in the Marines had always called a "mini-grizzler."

He peeked out the window and saw a leached-out, colorless glare.

"It looks hot out there," he said.

"The room clerk says it's supposed to rain. What do we do if it rains while we're in the mountains?"

"We'll get wet. You try to keep dry but you always get wet."

"I won't mind. You'll see."

He sat on the bed, in front of her. He beckoned with both hands.

"Come here."

She stood in front of him. She was obedient. She was amused.

He leaned his brow against the old denim of her cutoffs. He pressed against her belly. It was cool and warm at the same time, soft and hard, sad and eager, hello, good-bye.

She wandered a mulling hand over his head. He slid his palms under the back of her ragged cuffs and up over the cleft, passive heft of her.

"No panties," he said.

"You don't like it?"

"It don't make me no never-mind," he said. He knew she'd taken them off because they were Dana's, which meant that for all his swagger, she'd been planning this since before he woke.

"You'll make me blush again," she said.

He tugged her zipper down to a hypotenuse of ginger hair. She pivoted away. "I'm bashful," she said with an urgency that angered him: what right did she have to be bashful?

He caught her arm. He pulled her down to him. Before they had even landed on the sheets, she kissed him with remorseful ferocity, then filled his mouth with her tongue. Everything moved so fast, everything moved so slowly, like a fight in a dream, or under water. It seemed to be a question of emotional engineering that Gordon couldn't resolve. She broke off the kiss at last and looked away with numb lips, a look of bleak frenzy. She writhed out from under him. He chased her across the bed. What did she want? She kissed him, she pushed him away, she sighed, she whimpered. She seemed to be trying to turn him into a rapist, and it wasn't his style.

He sat back on his heels. His skin was grainy with sweat in the metallic light. He said: "Do you want me to fuck you or not?"

"Yes."

He eased her T-shirt up to her shoulders. She draped her arms in back of her head. Her wrists touched with martyred languor while he undressed her. She lay like that, watching him as if everything he did were beside the point, like foreplay with a whore. Her breasts had stretched nearly flat against her ribs. He kissed them. He thumbed the damp points of hair beneath her arms. He nuzzled at her skin as if he were performing some microcircuitry repairs that could only be done with the gentlest of tongue and teeth. Clean and dirty. Hot and cool. He trailed kisses down her belly. She had skin rich and fresh as iced butter, skin that fell away under the ginger hair—he could smell the breath of her now—and she said:

"Don't."

He looked up, astonished.

"Don't," she said again. It was the same *don't* she'd said before when she blushed.

He stared across her foreshortened bodyscape to her face. He'd never known a woman to resist this. Groans of virtue forsaken, yes; or warnings of force-ten passion; but not *don't.* He was alarmed, he didn't know why. He felt as if he were missing some point, the signal, the chance...

The hell with her, then.

He rose, caught her behind the knees with his hands, and shoved her legs back like heavy furniture.

Bemused. The happy victim, straight out of a cold-cream-and-Kleenex fantasy at fourteen. Except the fantasy was *hers,* he realized, as they worked, watching her watch him until all of it started to evanesce into pure thought the way it had yesterday afternoon in the Mercedes...something he didn't understand...while her lips swelled and she lifted heavy eyelids to promise him that if he didn't understand it this time, he'd get it the next. There was no end to her giving, a very cool mercy from which he was rescued, as it happened, by the smell of her rising to sparkle in his nostrils rank and brassy. He came so suddenly it startled him. He closed his eyes with the strange, fierce business of it. When he opened them she seemed pleased, even relieved for him.

He moved away from her, into the cool solitude of rumpled sheets and the grey air of the motel room. His only satisfaction was in seeing that he was still so hard he arched.

It was more satisfaction than coming had been, a fact he decided was wicked. Did she know what she was doing, leaving him shiny and huge, spooky as a goat?

He gazed upward. A rainbow, like oil in a mud puddle, trembled on the ceiling, having reflected off some piece of hardware by the window.

Ellen laid her hand on his chest.

He blushed. Why? Then again, why had *she* blushed?

"That wasn't my ordinary style," he said. "Ordinarily I'm Mr. Was-It-Good-For-You. Mr. Gentle. Mr. Sweet."

"You were very sweet."

"Ordinarily I don't come on that rank."

She reached down with a quick coarse, measuring hand. "You're such a horny devil, aren't you?"

He sat up next to her in the pose of Narcissus looking down into the spring. She didn't let go.

"And what are you?" he said.

"I'm just the girl next door."

"What would your pal Pammy say about that?"

"What made you think of Pammy?"

"You told me about her. The one who used to get beaten up by the Moroccan fisherman."

"Were you thinking of beating me?"

"Not me."

"You'd better not."

"I wouldn't think of it."

"It would probably hurt—Pammy was so brave, that's the thing."

"Even worse," he said, "I'd feel silly."

"It's an aphrodisiac. You don't need an aphrodisiac."

With a comfortable snuggle of a move, she was going down on him. Her lips stretched until they shone.

Fast and slow, sad and eager, hello, good-bye.

It took the afternoon, but she fitted him out as the gentleman pirate, the wenching duke, the rogue in her life, a sadist. It wasn't his style but he got the hang of it. Wasn't

226

this what every man wanted? Not that he had any choice. He tried telling her he loved her, needed her, even liked her, but she wouldn't hear it. She wouldn't even let him compliment her.

"No," she said, looking down at her breasts. "They're too small."

"They're beautiful."

"If only they were bigger."

All afternoon she immolated herself. And he thanked her. He didn't know what else to do.

"I'm crazy about you," he said. "I am."

The strange thing was, he felt so helpless, and he didn't know why.

They skidded in each other's sweat. The rainbow reflection crept across the ceiling. Sometimes he walked to the bathroom through cool air to bring back cool water.

"Don't you ever come?" he said.

"I don't know."

"You don't know if you come or not?"

"Either I'm coming all the time, or I'm not coming at all."

"You never lose control."

"I never felt like I had it, not once in my life."

"I'd like to drive you out of your mind."

She cried, and he held the slow jumping of her ribs. At first he pitied her, then found a contentment that he'd eked a little chaos out of her. Contentment became sadistic fascination, which became anger with her, which became disgust. What was she doing to him to make him feel like this?

He had come and come, but he got more ease from the sweat standing out all over him. She was working him. In a moment of exhaustion he'd survey the world from this dark-lit bed and it would be a soft-edged place of infinite promise where everything was permitted and everything was real; where he came to understand that this, in fact, is the Other Shore; Dixie; Oz. Then he'd lose it, and even though he'd realized by now that her capacity for surrender alone was

227

more than he'd ever conquer, he'd go at it, and she'd be there: the girl next door.

She knelt, she splayed herself, she pressed her cheek to the sheet and seemed to be waiting for something, proving something. The soles of her feet glowed white in the gloom. Once she scared him: her skin rose all over in goose bumps. The blonde down along her spine stood on end. Her teeth chattered. In that instant, she was The Beast, and then that vision vanished too.

When they lay back again, the ceiling rainbow was gone. They heard luggage thumping on the concrete walkway outside. Doors slammed. Televisions came on and made a cheery barking noise through the cinder-brick walls. Ellen dressed herself in a sheet and shuffled into the bathroom. She closed the door.

Water pattered pristine in the sink. He listened from the bed and pictured her face, the corners of her mouth turned down with the rich girl's cold certainty she'd show sometimes when she forgot he was looking at her. He guessed that she had dedicated the afternoon to making him feel not that he owed her something—that was easy, Dana could do that without even trying—but that she owed him nothing.

He'd been had.

# Chapter 20

$W$HEN CARLOS GOT OFF the pay phone with the Fatah case officer in New York, he saw that Farhad had gone berserk here in McDonald's and bought everything but a balloon.

What he did, Carlos saw, was to arrange it very neatly to make it look like less food than it was: sheaves of French fries hidden behind a milk shake; a Quarter Pounder and a Big Mac, both in their plastic cartons, precisely stacked, a package bearing a picture of cherry pie, plus a box of McDonaldland cookies.

"We stay one more day," Carlos said, sitting down.

"That's what they say in New York?"

"That's what I say."

"What do they say in New York?"

Carlos didn't answer. He watched Farhad insert a drinking straw into a grainy mass of strawberry milk shake. It was so thick the straw stood upright. It was like everything American: too thick, too big, too rich. An illusion of abundance. They boasted of their excess. They put too many

French-fried potatoes in a too-small bag, so it would overflow. They talked about "giving it one hundred ten percent." All illusions: the wooden plaque of the American flag, made to look antique; the costumes denoting pride and happiness on the Negroes behind the counter.

"Why? Why do they say we stay?" said Farhad. He talked around the hamburger he didn't seem to be eating as much as fitting into his mouth.

"I didn't ask."

"But why do you think?"

"I don't think. I work. That's why the revolution sends us away to be educated: so we won't waste time thinking."

"I think that the police are going to find out what happened in the cellar yesterday. I think about that a lot. Does New York know what happened?"

"I told them."

"What did they say.?"

"They were very angry. They said we were fools."

"You," Farhad. "Not me."

"You. If you had kept the gun with you, the woman wouldn't have panicked and none of it would have happened. You were the fool."

"Why did you give me the gun in the first place, then?"

"Because it scares you," Carlos said. He bared small wet teeth the color of fluorescent lights. "I like to see you scared. The revolution turned you into a man and then you came to America and fell in love with this pornography they call a culture and you lost your courage. Life here for you is one big masturbation."

"Masturbation," Farhad said. He didn't know the word.

Carlos made a loose fist and waggled it on his wrist. "You do it too much."

"Why are you insulting me? I don't insult you."

Carlos worked his fist. "Too much. The next time I have to carry a gun, too."

230

"Take your medicine. You hate me because I sit here and eat like a man while all you have is that medicine you drink for your stomach."

"Too much. This whole country—too much."

It was true, Carlos thought. It was more than a way to tease Farhad. Everything here was just dreams. You could see it destroying them, see it in their faces while they drove cars, watched television, or sat in McDonald's on New York Avenue in Washington, D.C., fat and sad, full of dreams, a strange, hypnotized, milling atmosphere like people in a theater lobby before the movie starts.

It made Carlos happy to think how well he understood this country.

"Stop being a philosopher and tell me what they said in New York," Farhad said.

"They say: is Farhad still eating like a pig? Does Farhad have gonorrhea? Does Farhad keep asking about things he has no need to know about?"

Farhad wiped each greasy, tapering finger with a napkin. Then he held out his palms in surrender. "Lie to me," he said.

"They say Farhad..." Carlos waggled his fist. "Too much."

"You feel happy, huh? You must be happy. That's why you insult me. Otherwise you don't pay any attention to me at all. If you felt any better you'd probably shoot me."

"I should shoot you. I should shoot you as a deviate and a betrayer of the revolution. I should rid history of a degenerate."

"Why not?" Farhad said. Pink milk shake lingered at the corners of his mouth. "You don't need me. Feel free to shoot me. Make me a martyr. Just let me finish my lunch first."

It was true, too, that Carlos was happy. He was so exhilarated that he hadn't slept or eaten for days, except for the Maalox he drank for his ulcer. The ulcer stabbed and burned like the spear he remembered seeing in Christ's side in an old engraving in one of the thousand attics and back rooms he'd lived in as a boy. But even the pain felt good, like an ancient and terrible itch being scratched. Lately, Carlos had suspected that everything was coming to a climax for him. In airports he heard his name being called over and over on the loudspeakers. In cities, all the traffic seemed to be proceeding toward him—intentional and slow, like funeral caravans. Where ordinarily he would have feared that an FBI agent was watching them, he found the idea acceptable now, even pleasing.

"They say that Cane has gotten rich," he said. "They say the South Africans hired him to be a consultant, they say the Israelis are putting money into a Swiss bank for him, they say the Libyans offered him asylum and a billion dollars."

"And you agree."

"Of course."

"Of course."

Carlos watched Farhad tuck the cherry pie into his mouth lengthwise until it vanished and his eyes scuttled through the litter of paper and plastic for more food.

"There's nothing else for us to do," Farhad said.

"They say we should go back out to Gordon Sault's house, keep driving past, see if he comes back with Cane's daughter."

"So you can shoot them too."

"We tell them we're West Bank journalists and we want to pay them for their stories. We tell them we want to do a television interview but we have to go to New York to do it."

"If they agree?"

"There's a place we take them to be interviewed, to see if they are sympathetic."

"How could they be sympathetic?"

232

"Don't forget Patty Hearst."

"But..."

"She's a degenerate heiress, very impressionable." Carlos pressed his hands along the table, like someone smoothing wrinkles out of a tablecloth.

"Gerald was lying. He was trying to give you a reason for letting him live."

"The woman made it impossible," Carlos said.

"What if they don't agree? What if only one agrees? What if..."

"We make them agree."

"Like you made the last two agree. That's how you make people agree."

"Why should we do that? Then they can't tell us anything."

"The man can't tell us anything at all."

"He could be a problem, he could be very difficult."

"We don't know where he is," Farhad said in the nasal, retreating cadence of a losing argument.

"We have the address Gerald gave us."

"What if he's not there? We break in and search? Like yesterday?"

"It will be good for your courage."

"No."

"If he comes home you get a chance to redeem yourself. Then I won't have to shoot you for the good of the revolution."

"You love death. That's why you don't eat, you don't drink, you don't fuck. You hate life and love death."

Carlos's face worked with the delight of a man hearing people struggle to define him. It was like watching children stagger around in blindfolds at birthday parties.

"My mother used to tell me about death the way other mothers tell fairy tales," he said. Farhad watched him. He'd never heard Carlos talk about his past before. All he knew was the blurry newspaper photographs and stories about the Lod airport massacre, the kidnapings in Milan, four policemen killed with five shots in Amsterdam the year before.

"My mother was French, a party member and a doctor, a Russian-trained doctor. She used to tell me that in Spain, in the field hospitals, they would walk down rows and rows of the wounded and decide which ones they'd save and which ones they'd let die. She said they'd operate on the ones they'd chosen to live. Then those would die too. She told me this when we were living in Algiers, during the revolution. Then one day the French police came and took her away. I was still very small. I thought it meant that they were going to save her and let me die. Later the police told me she had died of a heart attack. Always after that someone who was taking care of me would take me aside and tell me that I should be proud and happy—that the French police were lying, that she hadn't died of a heart attack at all, she'd been tortured to death because she wouldn't betray the revolution."

Farhad gazed at the windows, which blazed with the heat of late afternoon. Everything outside—cars, flags, New York Avenue—looked like a scene painted on the plate glass.

"This weather makes me feel crazy," he said, after a while. He had vacuumed the bottom of his milk shake dry. He was pressing all the paper trash flat in search of last, stray French fries.

"No," Carlos said. "It's merely an interesting optical effect. In extreme brightness, your pupils narrow so that you have great depth of field in your vision. Everything is in focus, even the foreground. It's all the same. Meanwhile, in the humidity, the background looks blurred. This reverses the usual experience of blurred foreground and clear background. This is why you feel crazy. Do you understand?"

"No," Farhad said.

234

"It's true."

"I don't care. It's too hard to think about. All I know is that I feel crazy."

"You refuse to look at objective fact. You are turning into a dream, just like all these Americans."

"That's why you love death. Because it's an objective fact."

"Death is a tool," Carlos said. "Death is a means to an end."

With the cringing delight of the oppressed, Farhad said: "I thought death *was* the end." He smiled his huge wet smile around the last French fries he stoked into his mouth. He grinned and laughed and ate, a great wet, spitty, joyful, triumphant gnashing.

Sometimes, even with Carlos, Farhad could be right.

## Chapter 21

"*I* THINK IT'S STOLEN," Ellen said.

"Who'd steal a car like this?" Gordon said.

"Why else did Damian have to hot-wire it?"

Ellen had loved the hot-wiring. She'd made Gordon watch Damian-the-room-clerk's fat brown fingers vanish into the gloom under the hood, touching alligator clips to terminals.

"You don't steal cars like this one—you find them," Gordon said. "People throw them away. It's too old even to strip for parts."

It was a 1964 Dodge with a bullet hole in a side window, two different license plates, and a collection of decals that had admitted it to parking lots at every army base, hospital, and trailer park within fifty miles. It lowered them down a long hill to the Stuckey Shopping Mall, and into a windless heat, and the poignance of an endless summer twilight, an August evening that implied that the seasons had surrendered, that it was going to be August for the rest of time. Lawn sprinklers would twitch forever on the lawns of traffic-blasted little houses Gordon couldn't imagine living in, with their Venetian blinds in front closed day and night against the noise. Kids would keep passing them in the backs of pickup trucks, holding bathing suits in the wind like flags, and jolting away into the dirty-rose haze. Forever. And ever. Hallelujah.

"Well, we've got the pistol, we can sell that at least," Ellen said.

"And your daddy's binoculars." The pistol was in the side pouch pocket of his jungle utility jacket, a tiny .25, a ladies' gun. He'd hidden the binoculars under a couch cushion on his porch.

They drove down the potholed eternity of Patapsco Avenue. It was quiet. A lawn glistened light and dark where it had been mowed that afternoon. There were bicycles sprawled on front walks like things fallen from the sky. There were boats and trailers missing from the driveways and side yards they'd stood in all summer. The boats were hauling families around Chesapeake Bay and the camper-trailers were lined up in state parks somewhere, each with its own fire permit and raccoon-proof garbage can. People were having fun, people were perfectly happy, that was the feeling. America the beautiful.

In his driveway, Gordon shut off the Dodge and listened to a silence made audible by the out-breath of air conditioners. In his own house the air moved through torn screens, when it moved at all. For all that it had been less than two days since he'd left it, the house looked long abandoned, as if its windows should be smashed, with rainwater on the floors. The grass lay a foot long in the front yard. It had been his pride that he'd never cut it; now he felt sad that he never would. Honeysuckle hung in the heat. It all shone with a light that appeared to rise out of it, rather than shine down from the sky.

"Home," he said. His car door grunted open. "We grab my stuff and go. If Eddie shows up, you break straight for that swamp out back. There's a drive-in theater on the other side, and then you're back on Stuckey Highway."

"Don't you hate him? Don't you hate that we have to be scared of him like this?"

"No," Gordon said. "I don't hate anybody."

Except, possibly, Ellen Cane, just now. And himself for hating her. Because what he hated was not her as much as his own helplessness. His whole life, he'd wanted her—that thick, blond hair, that voice aching with regret, her petal nipples, her chronic preoccupation, her passivity, her class and money. He'd wanted to be her demon lover but instead she was his. All afternoon she'd made him the conquistador he'd always wanted to be. He saw that now. And he was much obliged. Truly. He felt as if he'd sold his soul to her— that being the price of attaining his heart's desire.

He would take her to the Shenandoah.

He would be her man, whatever she wanted.

He had never felt this trapped even when he was married and enduring rainy Santa Barbara afternoons listening to his father-in-law discuss the Eastern establishment and the Trilateral conspiracy.

His boots boomed on the porch. He reached deep into the ball-fringed sofa and pulled out John Cane's binoculars, with the brass showing through the black. He left the door open and strode through the house to his bedroom. It was like a summer house that doesn't get opened for four or five years after some family catastrophe, and then you come back and it's shabby, old, and small. In only two days things had lost the charm of the familiar and had reverted to being merely a coffee-stained card table, a bent shoe, and an aluminum chaise bought at a drugstore.

He went into his bedroom. He changed his jeans and underwear. He threw his dirty clothes in a corner. He hauled his backpack out of a closet and carried it to a window for an inventory: a poncho, a Primus stove, maps from the

Potomac Appalachian Trail Club, a knotted plastic bag of rice, thirty feet of nylon line with the ends melted to black knobs. He tried to remember if the poncho had holes, if the rice might have mildewed, if the stove had any fuel. Everything seemed so long ago.

He looked out into the living room. Ellen was fingering through his records. Some of them had his name written on the covers in Magic Marker, relics of college.

"Put one on," he said.

"Would it be all right? I have this feeling we're supposed to be sneaking about very quietly."

"Put one on," he said. But she didn't.

He squatted and unscrewed an electric-plug cover from the wall. He retrieved a rolled hundred-dollar bill. He left the cover and the screws lying on the floor.

Love, adventure, freedom: he had everything he wanted, now. It was pure disappointment. He was heavy with it. He was sodden with certainty. He heard Ellen walk through the kitchen—the snapping of the bubbled tile. The house shivered as she tugged open the back door, which was swollen with the humidity. He resented her presence. She was an invader. He thought of Dana for a moment. He summoned up the visceral sensation her name or face always caused in him, infinitely focused and forgiving. He had never understood why Dana loved him. He guessed now that it was because she was convinced he loved her.

Ellen ambled around the house, the back yard, and everything they represented to Gordon, and she was no doubt finding them quaint.

He saw her kick through the high grass. He wondered if he just feared the electric chaos of the liberty in front of him; or did he feel guilty for having sold out the first bit of personal history—his life here in this little house in Stuckey, and with Dana—that he'd ever felt belonged to him? It had been failure, but it was *his* failure. Ellen was nothing but success, wandering around out there in the weeds that had begun the summer as his garden. She glowed with success, like a big pile of money, or a cocked pistol, or a secret somebody won't let you in on.

Gordon had a small pile of money, no secrets, and a pistol with no round in the chamber.

He gathered his toilet gear off the old oval sink with the drip stains under each faucet. He saw himself in the mirror. The gloom of late afternoon light pushed through a paint-covered window and heightened the darkness of his whiskers...a werewolf in the works, a monkey man...he'd wanted to be that, too, he recalled. The house shuddered again, and from the back came the sound of Ellen swatting the swollen door against the jamb.

He stepped out of the bathroom. He said: "I'll have to close it from the outside." He was so agonized that he was surprised that she didn't notice it. She moved on to the sink, where she conducted an inspection of drinking glasses. She rinsed one, a glass that had once held a drink called a Hurricane at a New Orleans bar named Pat O'Brien's.

"The water's warm. You finish drinking it as thirsty as you started," she said.

"There should be some ice," Gordon said.

She looked in the refrigerator. The condenser pounded in the dead air.

"Better let me do it." He found a screwdriver in a Tropicana orange juice bottle. He opened the freezer door and attacked the frost. He freed an ice tray and slapped it against the sink. Cubes scattered, riding up the rounded porcelain. She watched, Gordon noted through his anger, with an attitude designed to advertise a quality of pride and mercy that lights up women sometimes when they decide they no longer have to baby men along with seductiveness.

*Who the hell is she to be taking me for granted?* he said to himself, going out the back door into the storm of stillness that an August day becomes when the cicadas and crickets have been rasping so long that you don't hear them anymore. He walked through the henbit, and cowlicks of grass. A cluster of tiger lilies was dying by a dry birdbath. Weeds gone to seed snapped against his boots: *niggerheads,* he thought, and couldn't think of what they called them since civil rights.

*But who am I to be hating her?*

At the back of the yard, behind a trellis bearing grape leaves, half a dozen marijuana plants huddled shoulder-high. Gordon tore them out of the ground, carried them back to where the ground got hummocky and damp, and threw them into a thicket.

No sense leaving yourself open for a harassment bust, on top of everything else. *I am in trouble,* he said to himself in so many words. Being in trouble...*in trouble...*He wasn't complaining. He was admitting. *I am in trouble.* He said it like an alcoholic confessing to an AA meeting. Hearing that tone with his mind's ear he realized that this trouble was a high to which he'd finally become addicted, after a lifetime of trying.

Being in trouble meant that the world made no demands on you for bravery, goodness, justice, or love. Survival was the sole ethic and virtue; a sense of humor the only prerequisite. *Sorry about that...it don't mean nothing...better him than me...*all those Vietnam punch lines.

Not that he could blame it on Vietnam—that was a cop-out, like blaming your troubles on women.

He re-emerged into the naked silence of his back yard. Then out front he heard the moan of an untuned muscle car slouching down the street—a sound that might have been the Stuckey town song, just as the town color would be primer and the town bird was Kentucky Fried Chicken.

*No, I've been looking for trouble all my life,* he thought. But the world had always backed down, because they knew he had to know better: football coaches, professors, commanding officers, bosses, Dana. They'd all been wrong. But so had he. What he hadn't realized was that there was never any need to look for trouble: he'd always been in it. He'd been running on nothing but his own luck and everybody else's mercy. And now he'd met a woman who was even better at it than he was.

*You should have known better,* he said to himself.

The car stopped. The cicadas scraped and screamed at a sky that was moving toward a surly afterthought of a sunset.

And answered: *You did. That's why you're a fool.*

He leaned inside the back door and caught the knob. He braced his feet and heaved. The door didn't quite make it inside the dropsied jamb. He nudged it back open with his shoulder, then humped it shut with an effort that left his heart pounding. He walked around the outside of the house. He thought about his afternoon spent as the rogue in her life, Mr. Macho. She'd wanted him to want that, and he had nothing to show for it but mat-burned knees. He had left the motel room finished, but not satisfied. And now, he thought, she ambled around in that cool state of preoccupation, owing him nothing.

*What difference does it make?*

He spotted the dirty blue Malibu, then, parked in front of the house on the other side of the old wire fence that sagged and rusted under the vines. His heart stammered. He remembered a car like this one from the night they lay on the hill and watched the farmhouse burn. He remembered two men.

He faced into a holly bush by the corner of the house and huddled over the little Browning. First he popped out the clip, then he pulled back the slide and cocked it. He tested the safety on an empty chamber. A little lever, to be kept parallel to the barrel. Until ready to fire. He inserted a clip: puny .25 caliber cartridges. *Ladies' gun. Vietnamese officers liked them.* He sent the slide home again, lifting a round into the chamber. He checked the safety twice.

Then he paced at speed around the corner of the porch, prowling. His feet moved through the grass and then up the porch steps as if they were darting from toehold to toehold on a familiar rock face. He noticed this sensation, and noticing it, worried that he was just looking for more trouble.

Two men stood in the living room with Ellen. He debated pulling the pistol, but that would be crazy. They were just two men who'd arrived in an ordinary car, and they watched him calmly, the two of them and Ellen, waiting for him. The thought came to him that they might be Mormon missionaries, or Jehovah's Witnesses handing out copies of *The Watchtower.* You couldn't go pulling a pistol on missionaries—this country was already too full of people crazy enough to do something like that. Gordon wanted things to be clear, sane, and true.

He filled the doorway. He looked at Ellen. He said: "What."

They looked Spanish, maybe Middle Eastern, both in safari jackets, one of them fat and hangdog, the other one with a mustache, and eyes he held tightened, even in the gloom of the light dying through the honeysuckle.

"They're journalists," she said. Gordon couldn't tell if she remembered them. She flashed her eyes at him to signal the existence of some main chance, a dodge, a con. She looked like she'd looked when she talked him into burning the farmhouse.

"Terrific," he said to them. He raised a clenched fist of brotherhood. "But we haven't got the time, that's the thing, we're in this very big hurry."

Clearly, in the few minutes before he arrived, they had won Ellen over so thoroughly that they waited for her to press their case with him.

"They're from Jordanian National Television," she said.

"Right on," Gordon said. "Peace."

"It's like your Public Broadcasting System," said the one with the mustache in a voice higher than Gordon expected, a voice adolescent enough to clash alarmingly with the chronic slow-eyed fatigue of his face. "My friend and I were here on holiday when we were called from New York to see if we could contact you."

"And here you are. Ace reporters, right? You can tell New York you scored a real coup. But like I say, we're out of time. Why don't you ask us a couple of questions while we're packing up here, then we'll take your phone number and get hold of you first thing."

"Ah, but we're journalists, and we need everything now," Carlos said. "And our closest studio is in New York. We're here to invite you to come to New York with us."

"What you should have is one of those minicams," Gordon said. "Tell New York they should have given you a minicam. Little tiny things, set up right here, shoot in natural light. Because the way it is, you're out of luck."

"They've been authorized to pay us five thousand apiece," Ellen told him. She moved her lips as if she were mouthing a whisper.

"Perhaps you don't understand," said Carlos, "that in our part of the world people are very eager to learn everything about this story because they are frightened that irresponsible people may have obtained nuclear devices."

"Where does Jordanian National Television get ten thousand dollars to pay for interviews?"

"We are Arabs. We have friends who have oil wells." It was meant to be a little joke.

"Hell, let's make it a hundred thousand, then."

"Now you're making fun of us."

"How did you know where to find us?"

"We only got our message from New York, that we

should try to find you, am I right, Farhad? And then we saw your name in the phone book."

Farhad nodded. Farhad had a soft face with shiny, anxious eyes, and a scab down the side of his nose.

"Sure. But why my name?"

"You were an employee of Mr. John Cane, am I right?" Carlos furnished the modest shrug of a man who knows he has a lock on truth, sanity, and brotherly love. Gordon didn't believe any of it. For one thing, this pair had been tracking them for days, journalists or no.

"Gordon, it's all we need," Ellen said.

"Sure. Take the money and run."

"That's what you wanted to do with Eddie, so why not go to New York and do it?" she said.

"Because."

"Because why?" She sounded so plaintive.

Because his heart kept stammering; because they seemed to hang there in the living-room gloom like some kind of daylight foxfire, negative phosphorescence...*the neon void...*

"We don't have the time. They've got the money, honey, but we don't have the time."

She tightened her face. "I am so tired of being paranoid. I am so tired of being scared all the time. We've got to behave like human beings once in a while."

"Nobody said anything about being paranoid or scared."

"So can't we just talk about it? This could be our chance to be free."

Gordon saw that once again, as she'd been doing since the instant he met her, she had swelled a scene to an ultimatum: save me, fuck me, marry me, leave me, conquer me. She made things so drastic. She made them so simple. But wasn't that what he'd always wanted from a woman? Wasn't it what he'd divined in a moment, a twinkling of an eye behind that screen door at the farmhouse? Now the choice was sitting

245

down and bargaining, or pulling the pistol—a charade either way, since both agreeing with them and shooting them were out of the question.

The light and air hardened around them in a smoggy gel. Carlos and Farhad studied the floor, which was painted brown with the wood showing through. The wood was worn down far enough that rectangular nailheads glowed silver here and there.

"Were you two driving around in the country a couple of nights ago? Were you out in Maryland watching a farmhouse burn?" Ellen's face awakened as her mind reeled back to the Chevy walloping through the potholes, and the mustached one pissing in the firelight.

Carlos lifted his arms, Mr. Nothing-In-Either-Hand, all humility. He said, with some sadness: "Ah. You know more about us than you're telling."

He was like a stalking cat, Gordon saw, closing distance no matter which way the prey moved. They weren't journalists, they were the people Gordon had figured would shoot him from the farmhouse windows, they were the people he'd warned Ellen about, while worrying that it was just paranoia talking. Now here they were, and there was nothing to be done, without getting way crazier, pulling the pistol and blowing them away on mere suspicion.

Gordon hung his hands on his hipbones. He was priming for a shoot-out, but his only confirmed enemies, as yet, were Ellen's snap redemptions of reality and his own fear.

He wanted to be sure. He needed more time.

"How about you show us some ID," he said. "Press passes, passports..."

"Our passports are at the hotel."

"How about we sit down at the table, you talk your talk, you leave, then we get hold of you tomorrow?"

He moved to a card table flanked by two folding chairs, an old red-white-and-blue plastic hassock, and a picnic bench.

246

Gordon chose the folding chair farthest back in the room, facing the door. Now, with his hands hidden by the table, he had a chance of getting the little Browning out of his pocket, even if they drew first.

"First, I'll tell you what we can offer, then afterward we talk about schedules, okay?" Carlos said, sitting down.

"Not okay. We don't have the time."

"Do we need a parliamentary discussion about how we're going to talk about these things? Is this really necessary?" Carlos said to Ellen. She sat stiff-elbowed with the heels of both hands braced on the picnic bench.

"I don't know," she said. "I don't know what's going on here anymore. It can't hurt to talk about it, can it?"

Carlos turned back to Gordon. "Can it?"

"Talk," he said.

Carlos leaned forward with his short, wide fingernails glowing dark pink on the stained tabletop. He explained again the anxieties of the peace-loving peoples of the Palestinian nation. He proposed that they all drive together to New York, where the studio and the money waited. He lied with such listlessness that it was clear he didn't care whether Gordon believed him or not. Hard way or easy way, Carlos seemed to say: take your pick. After all, he had reason and power on his side. Gordon had only madness and presumption. The light and heat hung in the air with a scorched tang. Silence kneaded them, pressing on every word. Everything was impossible.

So it wasn't that Gordon saw the burgundy Cadillac park behind the Malibu as much as he felt it had been there all along and he'd overlooked it, like an obvious truth. Eddie not only existed, he was necessary. He unfolded from the Cadillac like a muscle-bound forearm in the haze of the porch screen, the honeysuckle, the heat trapped in the lawn.

Carlos's voice pattered on. He made a strange metallic noise with the consonants.

*At least it'll be interesting,* Gordon thought. *And now . . .*

Eddie swelled across the grass with an even, grinding pace, like a tank; when he changed direction, he'd do it all at once, like a tank twitching on its treads. He was pure decision, no bullshit.

*. . . is as good a time as any.*

Gordon waved at the front door.

He pronounced the word: "Eddie."

Ellen came off the picnic bench in one wafting reflex of a motion that carried her the length of the living room.

"Bring her back," Carlos said. There was already a pistol in his hand, pointing at Gordon as casually as a gas-gauge needle might point at empty. Carlos glided to the front porch. He kept the gun on Gordon while he watched Eddie coming across the lawn.

There was no question of going for the Browning: *I'm afraid to kill, I'm afraid to die.* They were good and reasonable fears, but just now Gordon couldn't afford either one, much less both. They were luxuries. Just as Ellen's frail back was a luxury she couldn't afford—she heaved against the damp-swollen back door until her whole body was convulsing in futile shudders. Farhad caught up to her in his fat man's skitter of a run. He had his pistol out, too. He held it with both hands, military style. He was nervous. His forefinger floated inside the trigger guard. Ellen's frenzy evaporated. Her face wizened back against the bones. Her hands tumbled from the doorknob.

"Go in there with him," Farhad said. He rocked the pistol between them, painting the air with it.

She walked back inside. She looked at Gordon with eyes that were hard, dry, vengeful, bitter, desperate, and ancient.

She lined up by him, facing Farhad, who had followed her back from the kitchen. She tapped Gordon's jacket pocket with the back of her hand. It was a bellows pocket with the flap unbuttoned. They could both see the pistol. It shone

248

blue-black and oily, like a starling. It would be suicide to go for it.

On the porch, Carlos had tucked his pistol back inside his safari jacket. He reached in his right pants pocket and palmed what looked like the butt of a huge clasp knife. He walked down the wooden steps to the grass. His weight jolted from side to side, a casual strut designed to inform Eddie that he took a friendly, though puzzled, interest in his presence.

Gordon heard the first exchange and knew Carlos wasn't ready for Eddie, for a truly angry man.

Carlos said: "May I help you?"

Eddie said: "Who the fuck are you?"

Carlos hesitated. "This is my house. I'm the landlord. I rent this to Gordon Sault."

"The hell you say," Eddie grunted. He cut around him so fast that Carlos had to spin to chase him.

Eddie's square shoulders and his square face came up the steps. The tangle of lines on his face blazed like a brush fire, the fire of wrath.

"This is private property," Carlos said. He reached for Eddie's elbow.

Eddie tore it away. "You can have the whole place when I'm through, pal."

He stormed across the porch and through the door to the living room. Then his pupils dilated in the darkness, or seemed to catch it like parachutes and brake him. He coasted forward. He saw Ellen, Gordon, and Farhad's pistol. He turned to see Carlos slam the door behind him.

"Now," Carlos said. "So now." That was all he said. His face sectioned through the twilight. It was all vexed diagonals. He waved his hand at Eddie, signaling him to stand by Gordon and Ellen. Farhad held his Walther on all three of them.

"Hands behind heads," Carlos said.

Ellen rapped Gordon's pocket again, as she lifted her hand.

"This is crazy," Gordon said. He knit his fingers at the nape of his neck. "We don't know anything."

"That's right, you don't know anything, you don't know anything at all," Carlos said. He panted and flared his teeth, apparently unused to whatever emotion had seized him.

"He's right," Ellen said. "Gordon and I are just people who hang out, is all. We don't have anything to do with politics or anything else—we just got caught in this thing." Her T-shirt hung from her raised shoulders. The hem rocked with her talking.

"These are your boys," Eddie said to Gordon. "The ones you saw out at the farmhouse."

"Shuttup," Carlos said.

"That's right, don't listen to him," Ellen said to Carlos. "Eddie's our enemy. He's your enemy too."

"Shuttup."

"They want to kill us and keep her," Eddie said to Gordon. "Except they're afraid to start shooting with all the windows open."

"Shuttup."

"There'd be cops all over here..." Eddie was saying; a warning lecture, actually, to Farhad, when Carlos flung his hands out from his chest like a man throwing confetti. A knife flashed. Carlos sailed at Eddie with utmost simplicity and speed. Eddie's forearms hadn't quite crossed when Carlos was on him and the blade flicked down to spring loose a tangent of Eddie's nostril, then slash both his lips. Eddie staggered. He cupped his palms over his mouth.

He crouched, he shuffled backward, grey-faced. He blew a shower of blood on the floor.

"Now," Carlos said. "Now you shut up. Now you know something." He braced his hands on his hips. He shouted at Ellen: "Now you look at him and you know something, you know the truth, you know the first lesson."

250

Eddie shook blood from his hands, he spat it onto the floor.

"You are all crazy," Carlos shouted at Ellen. "All Americans are crazy, you think life is some kind of idea you get from television or your country club. Your father tries to fool the whole world with this plutonium business, he tries to fool the whole world! Think about that. You want to know the truth? I'll show you the truth right here, this is history, now!" He went to Eddie, who had braced his hands on his knees.

"Stand up! Show suffering to the woman! Stand up!"

Eddie shook his head just slowly enough to hollow a pause in the chaos. It was a moment long enough that Ellen could get her hand down into Gordon's side pocket and grab the Browning. At that point, in that blood-dripping twilight, Gordon knew he was dead, Ellen was dead, Eddie was dead. He knew it even before she'd gotten the gun out of his pocket, and so when she darted backward and squeezed the trigger with her left hand, and the gun didn't fire, Gordon watched with the terrible complacency of the damned. It didn't fire. She moved it to her right hand and squeezed again. Her face writhed and whined. She couldn't work the safety, Gordon realized. She hadn't even thought of it. Everything moved in Gordon's mind with terrific slow clarity. *We're all dead.* He could even admire the ease with which Carlos perceived that Ellen wouldn't be able to fire the pistol.

A triumph of contempt blossomed on Carlos's face. He strode at Ellen bearing the knife aloft.

"The safety," Gordon yelled, but it was pointless.

Her hand pulsed around the pistol like a snake trying to swallow something big. *All dead, even Ellen, and it's her fault now...but I've got him by one step, I can beat him there...* And so the instant was transformed again, all of this happening in a vacuum of time, as if everything were simultaneous. Gordon and Carlos were rushing her. Ellen aimed the pistol at them both. Her fingers scrambled around the blued steel. Sooner or later she'd hit the safety by accident. She squeezed the trigger. She was aiming at Gordon, as it happened, but it didn't matter. She would kill them all if she could, it would solve everything, and she was free to do it by right of panic, a right she'd been invoking for three days now, for maybe her whole life.

Gordon had one step on Carlos, but Carlos had the knife. Gordon had even grabbed Ellen's gun arm when Carlos bulked in the corner of his eye. Gordon made the mistake of turning to face him. Carlos cut him from ear to nose. Gordon felt the blade crack against cheekbone. The dingy glare of shock filmed his vision. He curled. He hid behind his own arms. He rolled and fell. He knew then with perfect clarity that the next cut would kill him, unless Farhad shot him first, or Ellen shot him. He was dead, that was the point. He surrendered.

In that moment he was freed. He had no fear. Death was easy, he saw that. Life was the hard part—pain and all the million betrayals of reality. Death was the perfect emptiness. The Void. Death was where Nothing Made Any Difference. Death was beautiful.

His knees banged against the floor. Death was home. His hands skidded in blood. Death was peace.

*But what the hell . . .* This was a new voice. It spoke in words inside his head: *What the hell? Why not?* He sprawled on his hands and knees while the voice uncoiled in his back brain sly and slitty-eyed as any temptation he'd ever known; as any spite or mulishness. *What the hell—why not live?* He was cut to the skull, his flesh was doughy with the cold of shock setting in, zero at the bone; and death was perfect. *But what the hell, why not live . . .*

And so for no reason whatsoever, out of nothing but perversity, with a room full of both friends and enemies shooting and cutting at him, with love lost, his face torn apart and all his future behind him, he decided to fight. He drew himself into a blind crouch. He stumbled forward, ridiculous. He milled his arms like a man who grabs for something, anything, as he falls. He swung his arms. He hit cloth over rigid flesh. He grabbed. He drove forward in a crazy scramble that had Carlos either lifting or falling suddenly, Gordon was too wasted to know which until the floor pounded against both of them. Their whiskery faces ground together. Gordon lunged to pin the knife arm. The first two times he heard the pistol go off—a high, sharp sound like something cracking through paper—he felt Carlos's head jolt against him. It felt quick and intentional, as though Carlos were trying to give him some signal. The third shot tore at Gordon's sleeve. He rolled away. Carlos was dead, head-shot. She was shooting at everyone else. She cowered behind the gun and pointed it like an accusing finger that jerked higher and higher. Bullets walked down the floor and up the wall. She fired the last one into the ceiling. She stood with her hand pointed at heaven but her eyes veering from Gordon over to Eddie and Farhad, who were by the porch door.

Eddie was gaining speed toward Farhad. He shouted. Blood blasted away from his lips. Farhad backed toward the porch door. Eddie kept shouting. Farhad stumbled over the sill. Eddie reached out to grab him. Farhad turned, stampeded over an aluminum chair, and, gun and all, slammed through the screen door of the porch and was gone.

Through the numbness and the ringing the pistol had left in their ears they listened to the hiss and roar of the Malibu starting. Tires spun in the dirt in front of Gordon's fence. The Malibu stalled, started again, and drove away with its tires yelping like a terrorized dog.

Then it was quiet.

It was almost dark now. Windows the drear color of television light appeared in the view outside Gordon's windows. They glowed through the darkness—the rectangular moons of the machine age. Air conditioners sighed. Insects screamed. There were no sirens. In its preoccupation with beating the heat, be it mental or meteorological, Stuckey, Maryland, hadn't heard a thing. The strobe light blinked blind and dead down at the intersection with Stuckey Highway, but there were no trucks whining through tonight. It was Saturday night, and summertime. It was time betrayed and infinite. Gordon, Ellen, and Eddie stood in the dark. After a while, they all realized that they were simply listening to each other breathe.

## Chapter 22

*I* N THE BARE-BULB BLEAKNESS of Gordon's bathroom, with the blood tearing down the drain in pinkening
streamers, and the sound of Ellen crying on the porch, and
the great American Saturday night careering along somewhere beyond the crickets and streetlights of Patapsco
Avenue, Gordon and Eddie patched each other back
together.

Their hands shook. They leaned against walls. They
mopped each other with cold wet wads of toilet paper. There
was a strange, harrowed joy about them.

"Bed sheets, fucking Scotch tape, anything. I don't care,
just stop the bleeding, get the fuck out of here," Eddie said.
His cut lips blurred the consonants.

"Got some little Band-Aids," Gordon said. He upended a
white metal can and tiny Band-Aids, the kind that are
always left in the bottom of the can, flurried into his palm.
He jerked at the protective paper with hands so greasy with
blood and sweat the adhesive wouldn't stick. He pressed
them into Eddie's whiskery lips. He taped the flap of his
nostril wing back against the body of his nose.

"Fucking Jesus, you'll bleed to death yourself before you finish," Eddie said.

They fussed at each other like an old couple who can't decide whether to fight or fuck.

The blood sagged from Gordon's cheekbone. The pain was like air on a broken tooth.

"I can see the bone," Eddie said, when it was his turn to be a nurse. "You need something bigger to hold it together. You need a doctor, is what you need."

Gordon reached in a closet. He knocked shelfloads of junk to the floor—Listerine bottles, half-empty tins of Cepacol lozenges, hotel towels, dried-out sponges, metal film canisters, mink oil for his boots—until he found a squat silver cylinder: "Duct tape. Sticks like a bastard."

Eddie tried his best. He hacked with a pair of nail scissors at the tape, but he couldn't make two cuts line up, his hands were shaking so bad. Gordon took it from him and cut the tape himself.

"We're all fucked up, Eddie." His mouth moved in the shape of a wedge when he talked. Had a nerve been cut? There was a triangle of tingly-numb sensation between his nose, the corner of his mouth and his cheekbone. "But you backed that fucker right out of the house. Barehanded. I saw you do it, backing down a man with a gun."

"You get angry enough, you can back down the devil himself."

Gordon pried the packing cotton out of a vitamin bottle. He tore it into a pile of wisps.

"When I pinch the cut together, you put the cotton up there and I'll cover it with the tape," he said.

Eddie's thick fingers darted around Gordon's face. The two of them, old soldiers, buddies, worked along the cut, pinching and taping. One war too many, but they'd survived it anyhow. Lucked out.

"She sold me out to those spics, Arabs, whatever they

were," Eddie said. "And now she's out there crying because she don't like the sight of blood."

"She was scared. I'll take care of Ellen." He couldn't stand to think about her, just now.

"We got to get out of here before the other one comes back with more. Cane told me the woods are fucking full of them, every weirdo in the world. I don't want to see her get another chance to fuck things up."

"She's scared."

"She's always scared. She was so scared she didn't mind shooting at you. She's good at being scared. It's how she gets along."

"I'll take care of her."

Eddie laid his hand on Gordon's shoulder and turned him so they both faced the mirror. It was blood-spattered. Behind the veil of blood spots, Eddie's mouth and nose were crusted with little Band-Aids, like rectangular plastic boils. Gordon's cut oozed between chunks of silver tape.

"Happy Halloween," Eddie said. "You got you a beauty of a scar. My face, nobody'll ever know the difference."

Beyond Gordon's face in the mirror was the door from the bathroom to the living room. Gordon waited, hoped, for Ellen to appear in it. He couldn't imagine what she could do to salvage him from his astonishment at what he knew now, but she was the only one who could.

The thing was to hang on to your dignity, not grovel with hope. Desperate lovers were the lowest form of human life. They were like people who got so drunk they shit their pants, or picked fights and then cried when they lost them.

Eddie sat on the toilet to rest. Gordon went out into the living room. Carlos lay on his side on the floor. His eyes were open. He was no more or less a presence than when he was alive, except that his shirt had pulled out of his pants and Gordon saw a collection of scars on his gut: surgical ones like punctuation from some other language; and keloid ideographs from shrapnel, bullets, or knives. Carlos had talked about history. Here it all was, a Rosetta stone of political nightmare.

Out on the porch, Ellen sat crying on the sofa where she'd sat two nights ago, the difference being that now she had her hair brushed, and she'd shed her F. Scott Fitzgerald T-shirt for an old white dress shirt of Gordon's. Light shone in from a streetlight. Behind it, and through the trees, there was a thin billow of heat lightning.

When she finally saw Gordon standing in the door, she looked at his face, and gasped. She seemed mournful and hardened, as if her last hope beyond failure had been martyrdom, and she'd been denied that too, and so had no claim on anything or anybody.

"It looks that bad?" Gordon said, thinking: *doesn't she understand what she did*?

"Does it hurt?"

"It hurts a lot."

"I thought he'd cut your face in half. You were very brave."

Gordon said nothing. He didn't like her telling him he was brave. After this afternoon and this evening, it meant nothing.

They were silent for a while. They had no adrenalin left. They were fueled by nothing but intention. They looked as if they'd just been illuminated by a trip flare. It was a sad, surprised animal quality Gordon remembered from V' t-nam. He remembered how they'd find bodies on the wir in the morning, so real in their sunlit dead flesh that the· had nothing to do with those bad flare dreams of the night before.

There was heat lightning but no wind.

Gordon's face hurt. There were different modalities of pain: electrical, hot, pounding, glaring, constant—a chord of pain accompanied by the bourdon tone of thinking about

Ellen now. She had sold out Eddie, she had nearly gotten them all killed grabbing the gun to save only herself, and she'd fired at him, too. The worst of it was not only that he'd lost her, but realizing that he'd never had her to begin with. He hated knowing it was his own illusions that were causing him this anguish.

"I didn't know about the safety," she said.

"I know that."

"I didn't mean to shoot at you. I didn't even mean to hit *him*. I was just panicking when I shot him. But I did it."

"I don't care."

She rose from the couch and touched his face with hands that were amazed and patronizing at the same time. He loathed them. They made him feel helpless.

"I'm trying to take responsibility," she said. 'I've always blamed mistakes on other people and then expected them to take care of me too."

"You take responsibility for everything but your own fear." He had to work his mouth consciously to make the words come out; something was wrong with his facial muscles.

"I just don't want you to feel like you have to take care of me."

"I don't, but I am," he said.

"You shouldn't. You have no reason. Nobody's saying you were the one who killed anybody. Nobody's trying to kidnap you. Nobody's blackmailing your father."

"Now you're telling me everything I did was a waste."

"You don't understand."

"What the hell," he said.

"Please."

"I mean it. What the hell."

"What about the mountains? Are we still going to the mountains?"

"I can't think about it right now."

"You have no reason to believe this," Ellen said, "but I love you and I'll always love you."

"Why shouldn't I believe it?"

"Because you got hurt, you almost got killed on account of me," she pleaded in a voice aimed at making him smile, cry, something: she was losing control.

"What the hell. There's more important things in the world than being in love."

"We can talk about this."

"It's going to have to wait. Right now, we're going to the river."

*

After Eddie drove his Cadillac around the hot-wired Dodge to the back door, and they turned out the lights and horsed Carlos's body into the trunk, Eddie gave Gordon the keys and said: "You drive, kid."

Out on the highway, it was Saturday night, anywhere in America: vans twitched past in lacquered metal blasts of teardrop windows, sunset murals, and whip antennas. Steve McQueen and Ali MacGraw jostled in huge pale silent colors on a drive-in movie screen. Golf clubs carved silver arcs under the lights of a driving range. A pillar of a spotlight teetered over a used-car lot. Carnival rides chopped at clouds of moths. Doors swung open on air-conditioned bars where men in clean T-shirts bent over pool tables. Gordon felt like he was viewing it all like a prisoner being shuttled from one jail to another.

Then they were curling onto the Beltway, heading north and west over endless, hourless concrete, Eddie with his eyes closed in front, Ellen huddled in back, by Gordon's pack. The Beltway was nothing; it was statistics: deaths, duration of traffic jams, number of cars in foggy-morning pile-ups. The only sight to see was the Mormon temple, which was a collection of spires the color of white plastic. Maybe they *were* plastic, Gordon reckoned: God's own fast-food joint. The Angel Moroni sounded the trumpet from atop a spotlit spire apparently intended to appear infinitely high. What it seemed to prove, instead, was that infinity ended about two hundred feet off the ground.

"Take River Road north," Eddie said. Sweat stood heavy on his skin, like the serum when you pop blisters. He looked small-faced and old.

They drove through the pallid quaintness of Potomac, Maryland. A Bentley slipped past in a tremulous hush. Farther on, the land began to roll. Under the heat lightning, wooden fences staggered through pastures. Ordinarily, Gordon would have been roused to scorn everything they passed: the prairie-schooner daydreams of the vans, the bourgeois pastorale of Potomac. But the voice in his back brain said: *What the hell, why not?*

His face hurt. He fought the urge to keep touching it with the gentlest of fingertips.

"I know a place, we put him in, he'll be half a mile downstream in ten minutes," Eddie said. "The problem is, Saturday night, you got to go far enough north to get away from all the colored out catfishing all night. That's all we need, a bunch of spooks seeing a stiff and going crazy."

Gordon found this funny. What the hell. He also found it possible that Eddie was a bit delirious. Even in the air conditioning, he kept sweating.

"You all right, buddy?" Gordon said. He tapped him on the thigh.

"Be fine," Eddie said. And then, as if they'd been discussing it all along: "Cane is paying for it, it don't make any difference to me. He wants this kind of risk, this kind of casualties he's taking, he can pay for it."

"It's not his fault," Ellen said from the back seat.

Eddie's face flattened with contempt. He spoke to Gordon in an angrily parenthetical tone intended to inform Ellen he was ignoring her.

"What we can hope is, those were the same guys that

killed Gerald Ravenel and Gaia Stern, the same ones punched my trunk, the same ones you saw out at the farmhouse that night, because if they aren't, that means there's more of them back there looking for us. On the other hand, let's face it, Cane hired me, he hired you, he hired two other guys I saw, he could've hired them too. Huh? Tell me."

"I don't know."

"They been doing a fuck of a good job for him for free, if he didn't. If they got you and me, like they were supposed to, Cane would be all set. Tell me about that." He hiked himself up in his seat and turned to Ellen, who watched him with fascinated hatred. "It's the God's truth, Ellen. I've known your father since before you were born, I been with him in some tough places, and I want to tell you, you have to love him, he's your father, but the world's a lot more complicated place than you want to think."

Cornstalks loomed in the headlights. Gordon braked while a rabbit crossed in front of them in soft, dreamy bounces.

They turned left onto Dunne's Ferry Road, which became dirt. Pebbles crackled against the undercarriage. Behind them, Gordon saw the dust rising so thick that when they passed a tin-roof matchbox of a house, the late-sitting family on the front porch got up and went inside. The roadside was dead and diffractionless with it, and the headlights poked two simple holes in the dark, no hint of a world beyond heaps of dirty vines.

Gordon saw Ellen's face flicker around something she wanted to say. He hoped she wouldn't say it, but she did, in the same self-conscious upper-class chime of a voice she'd used on the phone when she'd awakened him, two nights ago.

"What happened to Lally?"

"You talking to me?" Eddie said.

"Yes."

"I took care of that. I got him stored away. Don't worry about Lally."

"At your house?" Gordon said.

Eddie didn't answer.

"No, what happened to him?" Ellen said. "I never found out what happened that night."

"My dear lady," Eddie said, "you blew the man's brains out."

"Enough," Gordon said. "No more."

The road opened then to a delta of dried ruts. It was a parking lot. There was a trash can chained to a tree, and surrounded by a slope of beer cans. There was a four-wheel-drive pickup with an empty boat trailer hitched behind. Sycamores receded sulkily when Gordon turned the headlights off.

Beyond them, a piece of the river shone black and white.

"My wife and I used to bring her dogs out here to run, there's a whole park," Eddie said. "There's an island that runs down the shore from here. Nobody fishes there, the banks are too high. We just get him into the woods, there, we'll be okay."

"I'll go look first, make sure there's nobody," Gordon said.

His face gnawed and pounded.

"I'll go," Ellen said.

"You let him take care of this," Eddie said.

Gordon saw she was scared to be left with him.

"We'll both go," he said.

"Be careful," Eddie said, as if he were warning Gordon against Ellen.

He hunched forward to let her out. Under the interior light his face was pale to a fresh-bone blueness. "I'll be ready," he said. They closed the doors on him.

They floated in the darkness, their feet not landing on the ground as much as bumping into it, skidding on stones, snagging on roots. The tiniest slopes wrung their bodies with muscle shifts. There was no difference between big and small, fast and slow—everything was an emergency. The god of this night was neither forgiving nor vengeful, merely awful by virtue of how close it was. Cobwebs tracked across their faces. Cicadas screamed big as birds. Sycamores yawed against the dingy pink of the sky downriver. Lightning trembled and showed the sooty speck of a fisherman's boat against the Virginia shore.

The path cut through the woods toward the island and the channel Eddie had talked about. River noise clicked, a breathy obbligato to some other sound too big, low, and soft to consciously hear, a noise that made them both stop. They listened. They heard mostly their pulses thumping in their ears, but they could tell something huge was out there too, a subliminal booming that didn't stop, the river moving like an old urge. They walked until the sound changed to the water of the island channel moving between the two shores. It chattered, like the sound of people talking. The path launched out into blackness. Gordon saw they were at the bank, which was a ragged, root-haired scallop of caved-in dirt. The water moved six feet below. The glints were so small and pale the water seemed to churn past with terrific speed.

"There's nobody here," he whispered. He turned to go back through the woods.

Ellen held his wrist. "He's crazy, Gordon. This thing is never going to end. He's got this thing about my father, he's a madman, listen to me, you can see it in his face. If Daddy gave him the money he'd be raging about something else. It would be me he'd be after, or you."

"You're worried because he's crazy. He's worried because you're scared."

"Of course I'm scared."

"You make him crazier, he scares you more. You make things worse for each other. Try to hang on for a couple more hours and we'll figure something out."

"I can't think what." She gripped his wrist till it hurt. He laid a hand on her waist. They touched each other to certify their corporeality in the blackness.

"Something simple. Maybe we go to the bus station and we buy tickets for the first long-distance run out of there."

"What if he pulls a gun on us?"

"I don't know."

"What about going to the mountains?"

"I don't know."

"You say that so casually: 'I don't know.' "

"Maybe so. After three days of not knowing anything I'm not as worried about it as I used to be."

She released his wrist. Let go. Gave up. She drifted away from him, back down the path. He could feel her disgust. He wondered what kind of man he'd have to be to keep her. He wondered if that man could be a good man.

The walk back to the car was quick. They could see better now. Rocks and roots rose from the dark with a dingy glow. The mystery had gone.

Eddie was standing by the trunk with a screwdriver in his hand. He panted. His mouth clicked when he opened it to inhale.

"Let's do it," Gordon said.

Eddie inserted the screwdriver blade behind the Cadillac emblem. The trunk lid lifted. Gordon leaned inside and rummaged his hands across Carlos's body—dead hair, dead clothes; old, dirty death—until he found the armpits. He heaved the top half of him over the bumper. He moved away to let the rest of him collapse to the ground. He remembered now how heavy they always were. Eddie shut the trunk and laid the screwdriver on the bumper.

Gordon took the shoulders. Eddie got between Carlos's legs and hooked a hand under each knee. They moved in a quick, heavy shuffle down the path. They made the noise men's feet make in fistfights. They fidgeted for better grips. They stumbled. They leaned and squatted for advantage against gravity, which pulled the body down until it scraped the ground and they had to wait while Eddie sucked at the darkness for breath.

"Too old for this," he said.

Ellen's face and white shirt floated pale a few yards down the path, waiting for them. "I can help."

"That's all right," Eddie said.

Out on the river, Gordon heard laughter fractionate across the water. It made a sound like rocks cracking together. A flashlight chopped at the distant air for a few seconds and was gone. The fishermen were too far away to worry about: getting drunk, catching fish in the middle of the night, laughing.

The path bent and the river vanished. They heard the island channel. They staggered into vines. They sweated and swore.

"Here," Ellen said. She was standing at the edge of the bank. The water glinted beyond her.

"Not yet," Eddie said. They dropped Carlos on the ground. He made a wet, pounding sound. Eddie panted. There was a frantic aspect to his breathing that Gordon didn't like. He waited. It was Eddie's show. Eddie knelt to frisk Carlos before they threw him in.

"The pistols," he said. "We forgot the pistols."

"I'll go back for them," Gordon said. "You get your breath."

"I'll go with you," Ellen said.

"You stay here," Eddie said.

"She's scared."

"I'm not gonna hurt her. I'm an old man, for Christ's sake."

"Why shouldn't I go?" Ellen's voice was full of a querulous misunderstanding that set Gordon's teeth on edge. How could he explain to her that Eddie was afraid they'd run off, steal his car and leave him—a sick old man in the woods in the middle of the night?

266

"Fine," she said. It was an absolution that clattered with irony.

He went back down the path again. He was stale with fear, the pain pounding in his face, and the banality of it all. He hurried, but he was careless and he fell. His hands drove against the ground. He scrambled to his feet and beat the dirt off his palms. Then he heard Ellen and Eddie talking. He couldn't hear the words, just the sounds they made, hissing insistences at each other.

Then Eddie screamed. The water made a deep, walloping noise. Gordon sprinted back up the path. He saw Ellen pointing to the water. Her other hand covered her mouth. She shouted through her fingers:

"It wasn't my fault."

He heard Eddie choke and thrash. He postponed outrage—there were more important things than justice. He sidestepped the corpse of Carlos and leapt. Like everything else in the last three days it was unnecessary—he wouldn't have done it if Eddie had only fallen, instead of being pushed—and there was no reckoning the outcome. But for the first time in Gordon's life freedom had acquired intention, and he could count every moment of it: one step planted his right foot in dirt halfway down the bank; then he flew, flat as he could tighten his back, not a martyr or even a lifeguard but just Gordon Sault. And it wasn't his life that passed in front of him, knowing that in the next instant he might hit a log or gut himself on an old car frame canting out of the August low water. It was the shock of his quiddity; his Gordonness; himself.

He smashed into the water. He tried to kick but his boots had his feet moving with muffled slowness, like in a chase dream. He sank. For an instant it was quiet and peaceful—the current had been tearing at him and now he floated with it. He wasn't sure which way the surface was. He floundered. He jacked his head into the air. The cloth of his fatigue jacket slapped the water. He sank again, collapsing under the water in a lather of failure. He wrestled out of the sleeves, his old jungle fatigue jacket. It wrapped and clung. It was preposterously hard to peel away. Then it spun away from him in the current. It was a sudden, manta-ray hulk of a thing embroidered once by an Okinawan sew-sew girl with the capital letters: SAULT. And gone now. His naked skin felt newborn and slimy. He grabbed a breath and dove to unlace his boots, but then one of them touched bottom. Stones crunched. He kicked. He burst from the water. It was getting shallower. He sank again, this time only to his chin when his other foot hit. He bounded down the rush of channel water with long, dreamy, moon-walk steps. Eddie gasped and splashed in the dark somewhere in front of him.

"You can stand up!" Gordon yelled. The banks tore by. They were black palisades with the sky far above. "You can stand up!" He spread his arms. He watched. He listened. He worried he might have either passed Eddie, or he'd never catch him in this current. When he saw him it was a glimpse of his face—a dirty white, like the last piece of snow rotting away in a spring rain. Eddie was stumbling and floating backward, curled in on himself with his eyes closed. Gordon caught his arm, pulled him close, embraced his huge chest, and ran with him through the heavy water. The weight of both of them pulled at him as the water fell away. He tripped and they both went down on their hands and knees. Eddie rolled. Gordon dragged him onto a mud flat. His boots sucked in the mud; chunks of it boiled around them. Eddie hung on to him with fumbling fingers. He grunted and coughed.

"Bitch got me," Eddie said. "Bitch got me. Can't swim. Bitch finally got me, didn't she? Didn't she?" He clung to his chest with one hand and his gut with the other.

Gordon hovered over him on hands and knees that sank in the mud.

"You're going to be okay," he shouted at him. "You have to lie here while I get help."

Eddie's lips worked dark and silent against his face. He tore at the air for breath. His ribs heaved. "Heart," he said. He patted Gordon's arm. "I wouldn't lie to you." His breath came softer. Gordon heard it diminishing as if each one were a smaller and smaller decision, a last detail Eddie wanted in place, just so.

"Eddie," he said.

Water stuttered down the craze of lines on Eddie's face. His lips flared to show an old man's teeth, brown stained. His breath went away, halving and halving to a last soundless sound. Gordon strained to hear. Dying. Gordon pressed his ear to Eddie's wet shirt. There was no heartbeat. He was gone. He felt Eddie's warmth as something that belonged to him, now, not Eddie. He rocked back on his heels. He braced his hands on his thighs and stared up through the banks and the overhanging trees to a patch of the tinged sky hanging over the city downstream. He listened to the chest once more. He put his ear to Eddie's lips. He was gone.

Gordon shuddered with a rush of God-cursing anger—but it was more a reflex from Vietnam than grief for Eddie. In Vietnam they'd died for nothing, and Eddie had died for something, Gordon told himself. He wasn't sure what it was—honor, money, anger, or the wife or the daughter of Cane—a man Eddie had admired until he feared him, and feared until he hated him. But it was something. Besides, Gordon wasn't in the God-cursing business anymore; he saw that now.

He tipped Eddie into the water, face down. He watched while the body drifted broadside to the current, mingled with the darkness, and vanished. Even in this dry season, and with the banks rising huge over him, the channel seemed swollen. Maybe it was the busy, sanctimonious smacking sound it made, maybe it was the eerie malignancy of the certainty that it didn't give a damn about any of them. It didn't care. If Gordon, Eddie, Ellen, Cane, Gerald, Gaia, Lally, Carlos, or anybody else wanted to live or die, that was their business.

He swam for a fallen log, but the water was moving so fast by the far shore that it sucked him under it, and ripped patches of the duct tape off his face. The cut tore open. When he grabbed his cheekbone he couldn't tell blood from water. He thrashed, cursing at his boots, until he fetched up on the mainland bank. He clambered through kudzu vine.

At the top was a boil of thickets. He shoved it away with bare forearms. Branches scourged at his chest and face till tears jumped from his eyes. It didn't matter, he thought. He just wanted to get it over with, one way or the other, Ellen waiting for him or Ellen gone. *Whatever...sorry about that...* He was a free man now. She owed him nothing—it had been like that since this afternoon at the motel. Now he owed her nothing.

The woods opened into sycamores and grass. He hulked through the trees. He trampled through the dry squeal of charcoal in an old campfire. He ran where he could see the path glow in front of him. His wet jeans sagged on his hips. He skidded inside his boots. Then he saw the darker piece of darkness that was Carlos's body lying where they'd dropped it. He stopped. He listened. Insect noise and the click of the current wattled the silence. The million scratches of the thicket lit his chest and arms with tiny fires. His cheek pounded with bone ache. And Ellen wasn't there. He thought of shouting for her, but then considered that there was a difference between taking a chance and giving it away. He'd go looking for her. It would be like walking down that trail in Vietnam, but what else could he do?

First he had to dump Carlos. Or he didn't, really—getting rid of him was only a courtesy to some anachronism of thought or ambition. It didn't make any difference, but it felt easier to do it than not. He hauled the body to the edge and spilled it down the bank. It slid into the water. It drifted away.

He eased along the path to the parking area. Water chiffed in his boots. It dried on his skin and left it feeling tightened and dirty. He fingered the split flesh on his cheekbone. He touched the numbed corner of his mouth to see if it drooped. He couldn't tell. His pulse slapped in the heel of his left foot and he had to think hard to remember all the way back to three days ago when he'd chafed it raw walking back from the farmhouse.

The path opened onto the lambency of the parking lot. The Cadillac squatted huge. He looked for a silhouette of a head—maybe she was waiting inside for him. He couldn't see her. Maybe she'd started walking for River Road. Maybe she waited in the woods. Or had hidden. Or maybe the reason he couldn't see a silhouette was because the back window was blackened by the trunk lid, which was raised. He could see that now. If she had found Carlos's pistol he'd have to wait in the woods all night, even given the possibility that she wouldn't be able to work the safety on this one either; wait, or walk out with his bare chest shining like a muddy moon for her to shoot at; draw fire; *reconnaissance by fire, their fire*—that had been the line in Vietnam.

So he stopped. He listened.

Lightning quavered. For the first time that night he heard a groan of thunder. And in the suspension between lightning and thunder, he heard the tiny music of metal banging—a jack against a wheel, the clatter of golf clubs. She was ransacking the trunk for the gun. He closed on her, floating from one foot to the other.

She was still crouched under the trunk lid, her hands spread blind and frantic, rooting for the pistol, when she heard him. She wailed. She spun backward. Her white shirt was a smear of light against the trees. She ran in a flurry of motion that was more an idea in Gordon's mind than

271

something he could see. Her sandals cracked against her heels. Gordon thought about waiting to see if she'd turn and stand her ground, which would mean she'd found the pistol. *But what the hell...*

He caught her in one burst of running. He brought her down in a slow, easy ride of a tackle. The wind crunched out of her. He smelled the almond scent of the roots of her hair. Doubt grabbed at him, then guilt. He lifted from her, appalled at himself for attacking her...*he'd been had, she owed him nothing...*except that it wasn't like the afternoon at all: she writhed onto her back. Her face screamed but no noise came out. Fingernails flashed. He flinched. He caught her arms, spread them, and pinioned them against the dirt. His sweat and blood dripped on her face. She was a stranger flashing eyes and teeth at him. She was sure he would kill her now, he could see that. And she was fearless. Transformed. She was as changed as Gordon had been when he saw himself in the mirror back in Stuckey. He didn't know her. Her alien eyes told him nothing, the telegraphy of eyes being illusion anyway, just greasy balls of tissue twitching inside caves of bone; more meat.

With clinical regret and precision, he raised his hand only high enough that she couldn't protect herself before he punched down again with a choppy, slapping stroke like the last stroke of a hammer driving home a nail. He hit her face. He waited until her muscles subsided and her breath came free and she looked at him. She had surrendered, unsullied by any thought whatsoever, except that she hated him.

He swung her onto his shoulders in a fireman's carry, and hauled her back to the Cadillac. He stopped, staggering, to slam the trunk. He nudged open the door on the driver's side and dumped her on the seat. He climbed in after her. In the interior light she touched her hands to her cheek where he'd hit her and she stared at them for a sign of blood. There wasn't any.

He had to stretch his legs stiff against the floorboards to work his hand into his wet pocket and find the car keys.

She waited for the right moment to speak, except there wasn't any right moment. "It wasn't my fault," she said, finally. All he heard was the lie of it.

He started the car and skidded into a ponderous huge-car U-turn past the four-wheel-drive vehicle and the boat trailer. Lightning loomed behind the trees now. Gordon was sorry they'd be driving south, away from the storm. The storm would feel good.

"Why'd you run, then?"

"I saw you coming at me—do you have any idea what you look like right now? Do you?"

Gordon turned on the headlights. The last haze of the dust they'd raised on the drive down here lingered in the beams. He sped up until the car's wheels stuttered over the sinkholes and the corduroyed dirt.

"I was scared, I was terrified," she said.

Gordon tried not to look at her. He tried not to hear the lip-curled squalor of her voice, that insistence on either a lie or a truth, which was actually a kind of whining doubt. Eddie had been right. She was always scared. She liked being scared. She used fear like a weapon.

"I was going to throw the guns in the river like Eddie said."

"No, you weren't."

"I ran because I panicked."

"It doesn't make any difference."

"You don't understand," she pleaded.

"It doesn't matter. I'm not going to hurt you."

Dusty vines bounded past. He was driving very fast. He had a lot to get done. At the house where the late-sitting family had surrendered their porch to the dust, all the lights were out.

"You curious to know what happened to Eddie?"

"He drowned. I don't know."

"He died of a heart attack."

"I'm not going to say I'm sorry to hear it," she said.

Gordon didn't care what she said. Even her honesty was worthless.

"I put the other one in the river," he said. He turned right onto River Road. The car was suddenly silent on the hardtop. He looked in the mirror as they climbed a hill. The lightning was standing in sheets behind them.

"Gordon, we can still do it. We can drive out to the mountains. We can be out at the Shenandoah by dawn."

"No."

"I admit it, I thought you were going to kill me because of Eddie and so I would've used the pistol to defend myself if I had to. But if not, I was going to throw it away."

"Bullshit."

"It wasn't my fault," she hissed, leaning forward in a reflex of exasperation and despair. "He grabbed for me, and I pushed him away, was all."

A white fence purled past, then stone gateposts.

"Why did he grab for you?"

"I changed my mind. I decided to go with you back to the car to get the pistols. I didn't want to stay there with him, alone. I knew something like that would happen."

"Which it did."

"You don't understand. He was crazy."

"I understand that you just tried to kill me, maybe for the second time tonight. That you killed Eddie. That you killed the guy with the mustache. That Gerald and Gaia got killed on account of you. That you killed Lally. That's just the last three days. I didn't know you before that. Your father kills people too. He killed your mother, he killed a lot of people when he was in the CIA."

"You don't know that," she said, but he couldn't be brooked. He leaned forward, bracing the steering wheel

274

between stiff hands, a frozen gesture of insistence. He crooned his words at the road gathering under them.

"People keep dying around you, and you survive. It's like you're a carrier, a hereditary carrier, and the disease is violent death. There isn't a jury that would convict you of anything. The media people would probably make you into some kind of Joan of Arc. I admit it, not a lot of people would agree with me. But I look at these people dying, I see you make a deal with Gerald and Gaia to sell your father out, and then you sell them out, then you sell Eddie out, and shoot at me and bullshit me blind. And I realize it isn't a disease or some psychological trauma about your mother, or the disintegration of society or anything else. It's not even that you're a woman, and you think you have a right to be scared enough to do whatever you want. It's a lot simpler than that. It's so simple I can hardly understand it, but I know it's true: you're evil."

She made a dry, kindling laugh of a noise. She said: "You never cared about me. You never loved me at all."

"You're right. I was wrong. I didn't love you at all. I just loved the way you made me believe that I was somebody I wanted to be. And all the time I wasn't, and I didn't love you, but I was letting you do it anyway."

He wanted to tell her how losing somebody you didn't really want hurt even more than losing somebody you did, because it was all pride at stake, but she was already yelling at him that if she was evil, and some kind of disease, maybe he should pull over and strangle her, help yourself pal; go ahead and kill me if it means that much to you; fuck you, I don't care what you do.

They drove past a prep school; past stoplights shining color at no one but them. Houses clotted around River Road. They crossed the Beltway and headed straight for the city. Radio towers winked red against close, black clouds. They passed closed gas stations with cars inside left up on the hoists. Huge, dead-windowed apartment buildings curved out of the lawns of Bethesda.

"Are you taking me to the police?"

"No."

"You're taking me home."

"Yes."

His face ached. His legs chafed inside the wet denim.

"What if he kills me?"

"You've been asking me that for three days. Is there someplace else you'd rather get out?"

She didn't answer. They turned onto Western Avenue, then Massachusetts. They drove past houses heavy with air-conditioned smugness under all this heat. The city seemed pathetically ordinary and unforgiving, like a place you have to go back to because you forgot something, or you failed.

She sighed: outrage, fear, or boredom, despair—Gordon couldn't tell.

They passed the grey bureaucracy of American University, and the Presbyterian Cathedral, which, floodlit, rose weirdly isolated out of a parched lawn like churches out of cornfields and deserts all over this country. Foxhall Road, on which he turned left, was more reassuring, one platonic perfection of a house after another.

Gordon drove a few feet past Cane's driveway, then backed in, swaying the stern of the Cadillac toward the garage. There were upstairs lights in the huge house, as if they would always be there, as if the house had a sun or moon of its own, a universe under that slate roof.

"Gordon," she said. "It all went wrong. I thought I could make it right, but it went wrong."

"I'm sorry."

"I just wish you understood."

He remembered thinking about her, three nights ago on his porch, while Dana slept: *Sail on, silver girl, sail on by.*

"If I understood, then it wouldn't be all wrong, would it?"

He didn't want to feel bad. He didn't think that he ought to feel bad, that he owed it to her, or deserved it for his sins or even in spite of his virtues, but freedom was something you could only give away, and he'd given it all to her, and it felt awful. And every wish in him raced frantic and trapped looking for the last light of a world he knew wasn't there anymore. Maybe she was right—he was a hard man. Maybe he destroyed worlds as casually as she invented them. But he wondered if she ended up feeling as bad as he did now.

She stood in the driveway. She arched her back in a small stretch. She looked to the house with the smallest of curiosities, like a lost space traveler learning she'd landed on only another deserted planet.

Turning the old Cadillac out of the driveway, Gordon glimpsed the shadow of a man waiting at the front door. Cane? Some bodyguard, the new Eddie Conchis? The shadow became in his mind the patience of true murder, as opposed to the mere squalid selfishness of Ellen. It was a different order of evil. How, in her infinite persuasion that the world was hers to invent, and no one else's, could she understand that? Gordon touched the brake. He wanted to warn her, give her another chance, stop her. *But she already knows,* said a jaw-clenched susurrus of a voice inside his head. *She's had her chance.* And when he swung desperate eyes back across the lawn he saw there was no stopping her because she, the man, the light and shadow in the door were gone. There was nothing there.

## Chapter 23

*H*E PARKED UNDER the ailanthus trees, next to Dana's Toyota. His pulse smashed against his cheekbone. His chest burned with scratches. He took long, tense breaths, mediating between his metabolism and the anguish burning in his throat and behind his eyes. He was hungry. His spit was thick with thirst. He was dirty, half-naked, and sweating.

He swiveled the mirror. His hair was matted and muddy. He saw the wrinkled shine of duct tape over the meat yawn of the cut. It was like a railroad track across a swamp, his skin a topography of crusts and stains of mud and blood. He was a monster. His eyes moved like eyes behind a mask. *What the hell,* he thought. *Sail on, silver girl.*

He stepped out into the stingy brooding of a Georgetown summer night. He climbed the steps, and found Dana's bell inside the stone porch. He rang and rang. There was no sound inside the dusty, paint-layered institutional emptiness of the stairwell. He kept ringing. The city panted behind his back.

Two pairs of legs, men's legs, appeared in the stairwell. The police? Other terrorists? The Israelis, the Japanese Red Army, Cane's people...They marched down behind the banister with deliberate speed. They were coming straight at him. One of them had a huge Adam's apple and glasses taped together in the middle. The other had been the one who parked his Land Rover in Dana's spot the other morning: college kids, Friends of the Environment.

"Who is it?" the one with the Adam's apple said through the glass.

"Tell her it's Gordon," he said. His voice echoed back at him off the stone.

"Gordon who?"

"Gordon. She knows who I am."

The kid thought about it. His Adam's apple moved up and down.

"There's been some trouble," he said. Gordon went blind for an instant with the imagining of it: Farhad, Cane, somebody, one of those people had found Dana. The thought of it was unbearable.

The kid waved to erase Gordon's misunderstanding. "She's okay, nothing happened to her," he called through the glass.

Then he unlocked the door and both kids watched Gordon walk in, a wetlands ghost crusty with blood.

They followed him up the stairs.

Dana met him on the second-floor landing.

"It's okay," she said to them. She looked up and down his body, the way people watch cripples when they're afraid they're going to fall.

"I got all fucked up," Gordon said. "But I'm okay now."

The apartment seemed preternaturally bright and clean, the terrific and busy dormered coziness of it: cushions on the rug, photographs on the walls, the white cat stretching sleepy legs as it walked across a newspaper folded in front of the television. Gordon saw a grove of beer bottles around the newspaper. They'd been drinking beer and watching *Saturday Night Live,* the three of them.

"They said there was some trouble," he said.

"You need a doctor, you need stitches in that," she said, reaching up to float her fingers over his cheekbone.

"I don't have the time, I have to get out of here."

"I'll call Mordecai, he'll come over."

"Don't call fucking Mordecai."

"You need a doctor."

"I need a shower. I need some clothes. Have I still got any clothes in your closet?"

A sad sound hacked out of her throat.

"And a drink of water. You can't believe how thirsty I am."

Cautiously, as though she wondered whether this or anything else in the world was a good idea, Dana rustled ice cubes out of her refrigerator and covered them with water. The sound of it was wonderfully clear to Gordon, and the water lolled with conspicuous and bright perfection in the glass. He sucked it down and left the cubes standing. He poured in more water and drank that too. Dana watched him, still looking him up and down as if he might fall. He wanted to comfort her. He wanted to laugh but he was afraid of insulting her compassion. Everything was so clear and depthless, bright and dark at the same time like the starry sky after the last fireworks fade to earth on the Fourth of July. He wondered if it was his wound, his exhaustion, his anguish over Ellen, his fear that Dana had been hurt...

"They said there was trouble."

"There wasn't any trouble, it was just me being foolish and scared last night. These two men came looking for you, and there was something about them."

"One of them fat, the other one with a mustache."

"Yes."

280

"Bad people. You were right to be scared."

Gordon filled his glass again and sat in the bentwood rocker. He realized he'd never sat in it, during all his months with her.

"The guy with the mustache is in the Potomac River right now. Along with Eddie Conchis. Remember him? There's one more body someplace, I don't know where. Eddie's house, maybe. You can't believe it, what's happened."

He wanted to bring her back into his world with the telling of it, but all it did was make her seem more of an outlander as he recited it all. She seemed uncertain how to respond, a look that puzzled Gordon until he understood the miscreant enormity of what had happened to him. He could hardly expect her to understand it. If she'd understood, she would have been Ellen, and he didn't want Ellen now, he wanted Dana, even a provisional piece of her life, a mere half-hour until he could get out of town.

"I don't know what to say," she said. "Are there people looking for you? Is that one person going to come back? Or the police?"

"No, he won't be back. Yes, there may be people looking for me, yes it could be the police." He laid his hand on his cut and closed his eyes. "It's like an abscessed tooth, like something's eating the bone."

"You need a doctor."

"No doctor. You clean it out, you tape it up. You can do it."

Her throat made the sad noise again.

He finished his water, left an ice cube on his tongue, and went into the bathroom. He tossed a wet collapse of clothes on the floor. He turned on the shower. He revolved under hot water and patted at endless dirt with a bar of soap. He couldn't imagine being clean again. He bent to keep the water off his cut. His hair sagged as he tore at the dirt in it. Filthy water wound around his feet. When he washed his face, pieces of dried blood came away. He pulled off the last of the duct tape. It hurt.

Dana was waiting for him with a towel.

"I can't believe that cut. You're talking out of the side of your mouth. Is your mouth numb?"

"On that corner."

She had decked the sink with a fringe of peeled Band-Aids.

"He may have cut a nerve."

He stood patient, dressed in a towel, while she pulled the cut together with the Band-Aids. She touched each Band-Aid with antibiotic cream. Her lips flexed with wariness. She was a better doctor than Eddie. Gordon wondered if he would have recognized her fingers on him if he hadn't known it was her. She covered the Band-Aids with two strips of white adhesive tape. He considered the certainty that the pain was going to get worse, not better. It felt like some huge metal animal struggling to lift itself, rising very, very slowly.

"Have you got any codeine, Empirin three, Valium, aspirin, anything?"

"Codeine would make you drowsy. You have to drive."

"Only to the bus station."

She walked her fingers through her medicine cabinet. "Some old Percodans and some Valium."

"Do it."

"You should wait till you're on the bus." She went to the kitchen and brought back a strip of aluminum foil to wrap the tablets in, big beige ones and little yellow ones.

"Now we get you dressed."

She found an old pair of his jeans, torn out at both knees, and a T-shirt. He put them on. They felt so clean that they felt warm.

He stepped back into his wet boots.

"You could stay here. I shouldn't invite you, but it's true: you ought to stay here," she said.

"I have to get out of town."

"Where are you going?"

"I haven't decided yet. West."

"Have you got money?"

"Some. Could you lend me some cash?"

She opened a drawer on her antique sewing machine and lifted out a curl of bills. She didn't count it. Neither did he.

"I'll send it back. I don't know how soon, but I will."

"How long will you be gone?"

"I don't know. Maybe a long time. It depends."

"You can write me without sending the money. I'll understand."

There was nothing more to say. He was clumsy reaching for her. She moved to him and he kissed her. He knew then how crippled his mouth was.

On the landing, under the bare light bulb on the paint-flaky ceiling, she tightened her jaw against the small, slow frustration of tears making her eyes shine.

"Maybe I'll find someplace good," he said.

She walked with him to the edge of the stairs. He looked back over her shoulder. Her apartment glowed in the doorway. He wondered if he was getting a fever.

"Thank you for everything," he said. "I'm sorry for everything."

He walked down the stairs.

"If you find someplace good," Dana said, "don't forget to let me know where it is."

*

He considered parking Eddie's Cadillac in the loading zone in front of the Greyhound station, but he didn't want it to be towed by the police. He wanted it to be stolen, to vanish. He would have liked to have given it to the motel clerk in exchange for the 1964 Dodge. Just handed him the keys without a word. But he was too tired.

He parked it on 11th Street, and left the keys in the ignition. He felt a civic pride in knowing that it wouldn't linger there long. He slung his pack over one shoulder and strolled through the grimy heat of late-night bus-station sidewalks, the hustlers and the hustled, the hooked and the crooked. Inside, the air conditioning preserved the eternal grey tunnel smell of cigar smoke and diesel exhaust that is bus stations everywhere: the stale, sweet, sooty urban odor of old sweat and waiting; the starchy heaviness from the cafeteria steam tables.

A nun stood by her suitcase. A six-foot-tall transvestite glided toward the men's-room stairs. Two black men in silver windbreakers and sunglasses studied the waiting room. Gordon heard them say:

"Hey, man, I think we messed up the night."

"I think we did."

Bus Station Nation, Gordon thought. Bus Station Nation was everywhere. It felt like home. He'd spent a lifetime in it, it seemed to him suddenly—as if its time and humanity were gathering now to critical mass inside him—old men in men's rooms shaving with bare razor blades; the people in the restaurants staring at each other's food, then buying post-cards and throwing them away whenever they got where they were going; a big-wristed Appalachian woman he remembered laying her baby on the floor of Port Authority in New York to change its diaper while a rush-hour crowd stampeded past her; grandmothers in their catalog clothes; army-navy-store gangsters with garrison belts buckled on the side, and their sad sideburns; people with Bibles and faces that looked intensely simple, as if the brows and lashes had been removed; failed hitchhikers; winos taking the first bus back from the VA hospital to the Bowery; the butcher, the baker; Mr. and Mrs. Front Porch USA; The Pep Boys (Manny, Moe, and Jack); missing persons and suspects; mental patients with their Thorazine softness; run-aways;

284

hipsters with their failed goatees; John Doe, Uncle Sam; soldiers waking in their shined shoes to hear only the sound of somebody else's bus releasing its air brakes with a hiss, and heading on down the road. Everybody. Always. Suffering.

Gordon looked around the waiting room on this Saturday night in August, and Washington, D.C., and examined humanity rising and sinking, aflutter like lost angels. Suffering. Life is painful. The Buddha had said it, the first of the Four Noble Truths. Gordon had never known what he meant. Now he knew. And he was one of these people. Always had been. He knew that too, now.

He walked with his pack to the Arrival and Departure boards. His face hurt so much and he was so tired that he had a hard time keeping the two categories separate, but it seemed, after a while, that the soonest and farthest west this bus station had to offer was nonstop Pittsburgh, in seven minutes. He carried the pack past the slumped nation in their plastic chairs, and braced it against the ticket counter.

Chicago, Gordon thought. Why not Chicago? Wasn't Chicago in the middle of everything? Gordon wanted to be in the middle of everything from now on. At least he didn't want to make any more decisions till he got there. Bet your bottom dollar you'll lose the blues in Chicago. Life is painful. His face hurt.

The ticket seller on duty was a moon-faced man in bifocals. He wore a huge necktie covered with blazing suns which proved on closer inspection to be merely yellow polka dots.

"I was wondering if all the Chicago buses went through Pittsburgh," Gordon said.

"You want the next bus out of here to Chicago, is that it?"

"If it's the one that goes to Pittsburgh. Otherwise I just want to go to Pittsburgh."

The ticket seller looked at him with what appeared to be a

special, professional sympathy, like something he might have poured from a keg around his neck, had he been a Saint Bernard.

"They all go through Pittsburgh, if they're going to Chicago."

"Fine."

"Which one, Pittsburgh or Chicago?"

"It doesn't make any difference. As long as I get on that Pittsburgh bus."

"That's the bus for Chicago."

"Chicago, then." He loved this ticket seller. He saw him as the patron saint of a world that had no idea where it was going when it stepped up to buy the ticket.

The ticket seller scraped a little machine over a ticket. He made change for Gordon's hundred-dollar bill.

"You've got four minutes," he said.

Gordon spent his change on Cheez-It crackers and a ginger ale to wash down his pills. He watched a little line shuffle through a glass door. He followed it out into the heat. He waited behind them until the driver pitched his pack into the baggage compartment. He heard sirens baying in the city. He saw lightning.

"You can board," the driver said.

He climbed up into the speculative darkness of the bus. He took a seat in the middle, on the right side by the window. In his youth, he recalled, he'd always been a front- or back-seat man, leading or leaving whatever group he happened to be with. Now he wanted to be in the middle.

He opened the ginger ale and sipped it down until it could safely be propped between his legs. He two-fingered the foil packet from the watch pocket of his Levi's. He swallowed a Percodan and a Valium. He thought about it—actually just conjured Dana's face for a moment, loving her—and went for another half a Percodan, which he broke off with his thumbnail.

He took off his boots. The air was cool and dry on his feet. He felt an ethical twinge that he had not called the police on Ellen, or at least Farhad. Not to mention the bodies drifting downriver. What the hell. He decided that all of us—rich man, poor man, the lamed and the blamed—probably depend some time or other for our lives and walking papers on some fool's mercy. And it might as well be his.

Or was this thought the mere pastel pensiveness of the Percodan snuggling up in his synapses? Yes. He was getting a little silly.

His face hurt, but now the pain rode with him more as passenger than driver. *Life is painful.* It was the first truth, and a noble one at that. All his life, he'd tried everything to ignore it, all the best and oldest drugs: hope, fear, desire, war, love, pride, self-perfection, and self-destruction. They had given him a willful ignorance that had proved to be the one suffering he might have avoided. It was all so obvious now. He wondered if it would be so obvious in the cornfield dawn of some Midwest highway. He hoped so.

The bus backed out of its bay and swung into the streets. The driver bent to the wheel, hand over furious hand.

Gordon watched Washington drain away outside the windows. It was an evacuation that seemed to proceed very pleasantly from inside himself. The world began to be a gentle place, soft like a day-old balloon that has lost just enough air to wrinkle a little. The Chicago bus: Gordon couldn't imagine a better place to be. He liked it enough that he wanted to stay awake to see the storm he expected they'd hit on the road north. He got as far as the first pastureland, the huge single oaks and stark farmhouses against the sky. To the north, thunderheads smote the horizon. Off across the fields, cattle stood in lightning light like their own ghosts.

By the time the first raindrops hit the bus, he was long asleep.